WHERE I LOST HER

This Large Print Book carries the
Seal of Approval of N.A.V.H.

WHERE I LOST HER

T. GREENWOOD

THORNDIKE PRESS

A part of Gale, Cengage Learning

GALE
CENGAGE Learning·

Farmington Hills, Mich • San Francisco • New York • Waterville, Maine
Meriden, Conn • Mason, Ohio • Chicago

GALE
CENGAGE Learning

LIBRARY OF CONGRESS CATALOGING-IN-PUBLICATION DATA

Names: Greenwood, T. (Tammy) author.
Title: Where I lost her / by T. Greenwood.
Description: Large print edition. | Waterville, Maine : Thorndike Press, 2016. | © 2016 | Series: Thorndike Press large print peer picks
Identifiers: LCCN 2016007051| ISBN 9781410490391 (hardcover) | ISBN 1410490394 (hardcover)
Subjects: LCSH: Missing children—Fiction. | Large type books. | GSAFD: Suspense fiction.
Classification: LCC PS3557.R3978 W47 2016 | DDC 813/.54—dc23
LC record available at http://lccn.loc.gov/2016007051

Published in 2016 by arrangement with Kensington Books, an imprint of Kensington Publishing Corp.

Printed in Mexico
1 2 3 4 5 6 7 20 19 18 17 16

For Esmée

Come away, O human child!
To the waters and the wild
With a faery, hand in hand,
For the world's more full of weeping
than you can understand.

— from "Stolen Child" by W. B. Yeats

Guatemala City, 2007

I stand in the shadowed doorway, staring at the heavy wooden door. I feel the sweat trickling down my neck. The air is hot and fragrant, the smells unfamiliar. Strong. I think the sweetness comes from the jacaranda, those trees that stand sentry along this street, an explosion of violet petals. The pavement is littered with their castoffs, like purple confetti after a parade. The impossible beauty of all that color, the cloying sweetness, brings tears to my eyes. But there is another scent, lingering beneath. Tainting it. It smells like something burned. Like something spoiled.

The phone call came this morning, to the hotel, where we have been staying. Waiting. I have learned such tremendous patience in the last five years, though sometimes I worry the line between patience and foolishness is a thin one. I have been made a fool before. Believed promises. Paid dearly for my optimism and blind faith. And yet, trust is like an affliction. Hope overriding all sensibility. This has become my religion: my faith, like all other faiths, driven by the most simple and primitive, selfish want. Accompanied by a willful and necessary blindness.

Our lawyer said to come right away. She didn't explain. I assume this means the adoption paperwork has come through, that everything has been finalized. That we are finally being offered passage from the purgatory of that hotel room with its rocking ceiling fan and stiff sheets, with the garbage smell that rises from the Dumpsters two stories below and the thin walls like placental membranes separating us from the other couple, who is also waiting. We see them in the dim hallway, at breakfast in the little café next to the hotel. They are from the Midwest, both of them tall and big and loud. We nod our unspoken acknowledgment to these, our fellow congregants, but we do not speak. And then, this morning, through these thin walls, we heard the sounds of their departure. The man's husky voice, the woman's exasperated huffs. And then the sound of a baby crying. Lying in that narrow bed, both of us were wide awake. Listening.

When the phone rang, I almost knocked it on the floor reaching for it. My heart fluttering like a bird inside my chest.

"You must come right away," she said.

And now, here we stand at that doorway again. I have been here so many times now, it is as familiar as our own heavy door with its leaded-glass window back in Brooklyn. I have studied the intricacies of it, the ornate carvings, the brass knocker shaped like a boar's head. I know the hollow announcement the brass makes when it knocks against the wood.

"Wait," you say.

And I can't believe that you are asking me to wait even another moment. I stare at you in disbelief. But you just reach out and pluck one of those purple tissue paper petals from my hair. Smile. "Okay," you say. "Go ahead."

Lake Gormlaith, Vermont, June 2015
The girls.

I see the girls first, before the camp, before the lake even. As we drive the last stretch of the winding dirt road, through the dappled light, I can see them on the wide expanse of grass in front of Effie and Devin's cabin. They are shadows at first, just silhouettes. Paper cutouts. But as we approach, they quickly come into focus. Sharpening.

They are both barefoot and beautiful. Plum, who is ten now, sits on the ground plucking dandelions, her long brown fingers nimbly weaving them into a chain. This is *ten,* I think: *grass stains, nails bitten to the quick, scabby knees.* Zu-Zu, who is thirteen, a dancer, pirouettes effortlessly across the grass. I am stunned, she is stunning: long legs, long neck, graceful hands. This is *thirteen,* I think: *precipice, flight.*

I turn to Jake, to see if *he* sees. I am so

desperate for a moment of connection, to share a single glance imbued with something. *Remorse? Regret?* Sometimes it feels that he is so willful in his refusal to relinquish anything to me, even this: a single, goddamned moment of recognition. Even now. I just want him, for once, to feel what I feel. Instead, he stares straight ahead, navigates this last turn with his hands gripping the wheel, his eyes trained on the road. I don't know why I persist. I don't know how this could fix anything. I am alone now in this endless longing, the sole proprietor of this relentless ache. Maybe I always have been.

We used to make the six-hour drive from Brooklyn to visit Effie and Devin in Vermont three or four times a year. Once a season, sometimes more. It used to be our escape from the city, from our hectic lives. But over the years, it's become an odd sort of self-torture. A masochistic game for which there are no rules. And so, over time, the frequency of these visits has decreased. It has been almost a year now since our last visit. I blame our busy schedules, our ridiculous obligations. But the truth is that it simply hurts too much; their family, this perfect beautiful family, feels like a cruel reminder of everything we've lost.

Crushed. This is what I feel as I watch the girls. A crippling heartache.

When they see us, they both stop what they are doing and come running. Jake slows to a stop in the driveway and rolls down his window, beaming at them. His face is like the sun, emerging from behind dark clouds. We have barely spoken since we left New York. But now his eyes are bright. I feel the flutter of something in my chest, but he still doesn't look at me.

"Uncle Jake!" Plum says, leaning in through Jake's open window for a hug, her feet lifting off the ground behind her. And then she is leaning across his lap and reaching for me in the passenger seat, placing the dandelion chain on my head. "Tessie!" she squeals. She is all bones and angles. She smells like grass.

Zu-Zu stands outside the car, long arms crossed against her body now, hands cupping her elbows. She is like a reed. Tall, willowy. Her hair is pulled back into a puff of a ponytail. The little glass earrings in her ears catch the light. She is three years older than Plum, but they share the same freckled toffee skin and startling green eyes, that magical, otherworldly beauty that only mixed children seem to have. Zu-Zu smiles as she waits for this ritual to end.

"Okay, okay," Jake says. "Let me out!" And Plum, like a wriggly toddler, rights herself, scooting backwards so that Jake is able to open his door.

"Did you bring my cheesecake?" Plum asks.

"Greedy, greedy little monster," Effie says as she comes out the camp's back door, wiping her hands on her apron, a bohemian housewife in her long chevron sundress. Her hair is still long and dark (as it always has been) except for one silvery strand that frames her face. She keeps it in a sloppy bun today, suspended with a single chopstick.

"Well, hello!" Devin says as he comes out of the woods. He is covered in sawdust and carrying a toolbox. He sets it down and opens his arms.

And we go through all the motions; this particular choreography is one we know by heart: Devin shaking Jake's hand and then pulling him in for a hug, Jake leaning down to kiss the top of Effie's head. The smell of pipe smoke and cedar in Devin's soft T-shirt when he embraces me. The way the girls circle us, waiting for the gifts we always bring from New York, which Jake pulls from the trunk like a magician: Zu-Zu's favorite salt bagels from Ess-a-Bagel, Junior's

Cheesecake in its striped box for Plum. The girls disappearing into the camp, clutching their respective treats, the screen door banging behind them. Devin and Jake following behind, Devin's large dark hand spread across Jake's back.

We are old, old friends.

It isn't until Effie and I make our way to each other that I forget the next move. We have been friends since we were just little girls. She is like a sister. She will know. She navigates me the way a blind person navigates her own home. She knows my configurations. Even in the dark, she knows when something is askew.

I am askew.

But she also knows better than to say anything. She will wait for me. She doesn't ask questions for which I have no answers. This is our way with each other. And today I am grateful.

"Thank you so much for offering to do this," she says instead, adjusting the dandelion crown I have forgotten is on my head. She is talking about Zu-Zu. She's been accepted into a prestigious summer ballet intensive in the city, and we are bringing her back with us when we leave on Sunday. Effie's sister, Colette, who recently retired from the same company, has promised that

16

she will be taken care of. Watched over. She will even be teaching some of Zu-Zu's classes. But I know this world feels far away to Effie, a part of someone else's dream.

Effie said she couldn't bear to go. That it would be easier to say good-bye to Zu-Zu here than it would be leaving her in New York. And because Effie is my best friend, and because she asks so very little of me, I didn't hesitate before offering to come up and get her. To take her back down with us after a nice visit. To make sure she gets settled in. *It's just a weekend,* I thought. *I miss them. The girls.*

Effie leans forward and touches her forehead to mine.

"I'm afraid to let her go," she whispers.

And I feel my throat constricting. It makes me think of a snake, swallowing a live mouse. The way all the unsaid things gather and squirm there as I try to swallow them down.

"I know," I say, nodding, eyes brimming with tears I'm not ready to spill.

Effie squeezes my hand. We are sisters, bound not by blood but by a thousand such unspoken things.

Devin and Jake grab our bags from the trunk and carry them down the narrow grassy path to the guest cottage in the woods behind the camp. I watch the leaves enclose them as they go. Jake is fairly tall, but Devin still dwarfs him. I listen to the receding sound of their voices, swallowed by the forest.

"Tessie," Plum says, grabbing my hand. "Come see my room. I have a new turtle! And I built the Colosseum out of Legos!"

"A gift from my dad," Effie says, laughing. "It took them almost a week to put it together. It took *him,* I mean . . ."

Effie's father, like my own, is a history professor, the kind of grandfather who would spend a week putting together ruins made of Legos with his granddaughter.

Zu-Zu and Plum share the larger room upstairs. It has been partitioned since I last visited, divided by colorful scarves sewn together and strung across the room on a makeshift pulley. Plum's side is oddly tidy for a ten-year-old, with shelves housing her various Lego creations, including the impressive Colosseum, and a large terrarium where Harold, the turtle, idles.

I lean over and peer into the glass. He sits on a rock directly under the glow of a heat lamp. "Wow, that is one good-looking turtle," I say.

"Shhh," Plum says. "He's sleeping."

"Oh, so sorry," I say, and tiptoe over to the divider, poking my head through to Zu-Zu's side of the room.

Pale pink tights hang from the exposed rafters; a pile of dead pointe shoes sit like some odd monument in the corner. It is a chaos of clutter that is both child and teenager all at once: ratty stuffed animals and library books, a glossy poster of Misty Copeland in "Firebird," and a mobile made from bottle caps hanging in the window. China teacups filled with jewelry, sticky tubes of lip gloss, and so many dirty clothes.

"Be careful," Effie says. "Harold is probably not the only animal living up here."

"Mom," Zu-Zu says, and plops down on her bed, clutching the stuffed baby seal, Baby Z, I gave her when she was born. I bought him at the New England Aquarium when I still lived in Boston. He is threadbare now. Every bit of fur loved away.

I sit down next to her on the bed, and squeeze her and the seal together. Her hair smells like citrus.

"I don't mind a little mess," I say to her.

"Seriously," Effie says to Zu-Zu. "Can I tell her about the you-know-what?"

Zu-Zu rolls her eyes.

"Tell me!" I say, eager for the scoop.

"So, yesterday, I come in here looking for

19

my flip-flops and smell something funky. *Rotten.* So I search and search and search. Finally I realize the smell is coming from her backpack, which is shoved under her bed. And inside is her lunch box from the last day of school, which was *three weeks ago,* by the way. So I open it up, and it's *grapes.* And they've totally fermented, turned into some kind of hooch."

I laugh. "That skill will come in handy in the dorms this summer."

"And prison," Zu-Zu says, smirking.

I love this girl.

"You can hold Harold if you want," Plum says then, coming through the place where the divider parts and handing me her turtle. "He's awake now."

Downstairs I hear the door slam shut, Devin and Jake's muffled voices below. We all sit down on Zu-Zu's messy bed, and I want to curl up with all of them, even Harold, and never get up.

After lunch, the girls want to swim, and so we all walk down to the boat access area where there is a sort of grassy beach. The clouds have parted, and the sun is bright, sparkling in the water. Plum hoists an inner tube over one shoulder and Zu-Zu carries their towels, slung over her golden shoulders. Their feet are bare, the pink pads callused. Devin and Jake walk ahead with the girls, each drinking a beer, and Effie and I hang back.

"I'm so glad you're here," Effie says, leaning her head against my arm. "It's been such a long time."

I nod.

"You okay?" she asks, pulling away from me.

I nod again, but she frowns.

"We'll talk tonight?" she asks, and reaches for my hand. And I think about how I used to be the one who fixed things. How I used to be the strong one. When did this happen to me? What have I become?

Effie spreads a soft blue blanket out on the grass, and she and I sit and watch the girls. When we were teenagers, we used to rub baby oil all over our bodies, squirt lemon juice concentrate in our hair, and lie in this exact spot, waiting for the sun. We used to swim the way the girls do now, fearlessly, out to the sandbar in the center of the lake where we stood and howled, and then leapt into the murky depths. We used to *live* in the water. Fishes. Her grandma, Gussy, called us the Mermaids of Gormlaith. But I have no desire to go into the water now. I don't remember the last time I

21

even wore a bathing suit.

The sound of the girls' voices, the joyful splashes, is the best music. I don't even mind when they bicker and whine.

"Give me!" Plum hollers as Zu-Zu steals the tube away. "That's mine."

Devin and Jake have their suits on too and both of them ease into the water, tentatively at first, and then dive under. Jake emerges, shaking his hair like a wet dog, splattering Zu-Zu, who squeals. They dive and surface after long stretches under the water, surprising the girls. Each of the guys puts one of them on his shoulders for a chicken fight. Jake has Plum. She grips the side of his head, and he smiles and smiles. But he doesn't look at me. Won't. *Can't.*

After the sun goes down, we eat outside at the picnic table, drink. Unlike at home, I am careful here, counting glasses. It is too easy lately to drink too much. To love the warm way it numbs. And I feel Jake watching me; he's counting my drinks too.

The mosquitoes bite my ankles, and I let my skin prick and tingle and itch. I wait until I can barely stand it anymore before I scratch. I am sunburned from earlier, and relish in the tender pink sting of my shoulders.

"So tell us about this new writer Tess mentioned," Devin says to Jake. "The kid."

"Charlie." Jake smiles. "He is definitely young. But he's not like a lot of the other new kids coming up. You know, all style, no substance. More concerned with how many Instagram followers they have than with their writing. He's kind of a throwback. He still writes on a typewriter, for Christ's sake. He's not on Facebook. He doesn't have a Twitter account. It's pretty incredible when you actually stop to think about it." Jake plucks a raspberry from the bowl Effie has put in the center of the table for dessert and pops it in his mouth.

He's talking about Charlie Hayden, a new client of his. Jake is a literary agent; he started his own boutique agency two years ago. We'd already mortgaged our house once for the adoption, so he had to borrow from his parents to get started. It was a gamble, one I was leery of, and the first year was a real struggle, but he slowly built a decent client list, hired a couple other young but well-regarded agents who brought their clients with them. And then a few months ago, he signed on this hotshot kid the National Book Foundation named one of the "5 under 35." At twenty-five, Charlie's the youngest of the bunch; he reminds me

23

of an overgrown baby.

We had him over for dinner one night right after he signed with Jake. He talked about Mexico, where he backpacked for a year after he graduated Harvard. He bragged about the prostitutes he slept with, the drugs he took. He was pompous. A real ass. And then, he drank too much and got sick in our bathroom. But rather than calling him a cab, Jake ushered Charlie into the guest bedroom, brought him water, aspirin. Covered him with a blanket. In the morning, Charlie sat at our table drinking coffee and scarfing down the bacon and eggs Jake had made like nothing had happened. He sent us a thank-you note two days later on creamy stationery embossed with his monogram. I don't care how good a writer he is; he's a real douche bag.

Charlie's first novel is going to go to auction on Monday, another reason why we need to get back to the city. Jake has been coddling him, as if he is an infant, or an orchid. He has held his hand from the messy first typed (yes, *typed*) draft to the finished copy, which went out on submission last week.

But as much as the kid irritates me, I must admit, I've read the book, and, if I were still in the industry, I would likely have jumped

24

on it as well. I understand Jake's enthusiasm; he and I have always been able to see promise. But something about the way Jake babies him sickens me. It's as though Charlie is his son rather than his client, and a badly behaved son at that. And worst of all, he favors him over his other, better-mannered clients. At times, I wonder if this is the kind of father he would have been. Coddling, permissive.

Jake and I met when I was still working at Norton. I actually acquired his very first client's debut novel — a writer who has since gone on to write six more novels, two of which have been made into films. For a while, we were considered a sort of power couple in the publishing world, for whatever the hell that's worth. But I left publishing eight years ago, after we came back from Central America. When words on the page became just that. *Words.* As hollow and inconsequential as dust. Empty promises made of ink, so pathetically reliant on the paper beneath them.

I make my living now as a freelance copy editor, which requires that I look at each sentence as a mechanical structure, a mathematical equation. I hardly read anything for pleasure anymore besides menus and the occasional manuscript Jake asks me to peruse. I see only artifice now, and none of the art.

I reach for my wineglass when Jake is looking away and swallow. The wine is crisp and cold. It tastes like a bite from a ripe peach.

"He's brilliant, really," Jake says, nodding, like he has something to prove.

"He's kind of a *douche,*" I say.

Plum looks up. "What's a *doosh*?"

"Excuse my French," I say, reaching for her hand. Plum has separated the delicate fish bones from the meat and laid them across the tablecloth in one remarkable piece. Fragile, yet intact. The ghost of her dinner.

Jake sips from his glass, swishes the wine in his mouth before swallowing. I study the lines of his jaw, which is always set and hard lately, muscles working under the flesh. Unlike most men his age, he's still got a full head of hair, which he wears long enough that it falls in his eyes. Now he pushes it back, and gestures to me with his chin before looking at Devin.

"What is it our folks used to say, *Never trust anyone over thirty*?" he says, talking about me as if I'm not sitting right there. "Tess doesn't trust anyone *under* thirty."

His words are sharp.

26

"He's just so *affected*," I say, though I'm not talking about Charlie anymore, and he knows it.

I look to Effie. I need an ally.

"Everything about him. Seriously, who types on a manual typewriter? And you can hear it in his writing. The *affectation*, I mean." This is not true at all, but I am feeling willful. Contrary. Emboldened by that cold, crisp wine.

Jake takes a deep breath, as if to calm himself before speaking.

"Tess hates everything I love," he says.

Effie shoots me a look across the table.

Jake stretches his neck. This is what he does to keep from lashing out.

"Hey, you guys *still* need to introduce me to Sam Mason," he says. "I just finished *Small Sorrows*. I don't know how I'd never read it before."

Sam Mason is a writer, a National Book Award–winning writer who lives in California but owns a camp on Lake Gormlaith. Sam and his wife, Mena, are friends with Effie and Devin, but we've never met them. Every time we come, Jake brings it up. Angling. It embarrasses me.

"He just did a benefit reading at the library," Effie says. "It was really fun."

"How *is* the library?" I ask, grateful to

27

change the subject.

"Broke, as always," she says, smiling sadly. "The basement flooded this spring, so the children's room had to move up to the annex. A total nightmare. It's going to cost a fortune for the repairs. But we have a few generous donors, like Sam and Mena, who keep coming through just when we need them."

Effie drives the bookmobile for the library. Devin teaches art at the college and is also a pretty successful artist himself. He makes assemblages, these gorgeous little shadow boxes. A little bit like Joseph Cornell. They met here, at the lake, where they were both spending the summer twenty years ago. They got married here as well, on the little island in the middle of the lake. Even though I've been to dozens of weddings, theirs is one I will always remember. We all had to take a boat out to the island. It was a blue-sky, brilliant-sun kind of day. Rows of white chairs were lined up underneath a canopy of leaves. Effie wore a chain of daisies in her hair. I was her maid of honor. I loaned her my grandmother's cameo (something old and something borrowed), and we painted our toenails blue. Zu-Zu was her something new, though nobody except for Devin and me knew it yet. She came six months later, followed by Plum. I drove up from New York both times, was with Effie and Devin when each of them was born. We promised each other as kids that we'd share this. Before we knew the world could be so inequitable, so unkind.

Yet every time I begin to feel that painful snag of envy, I need to remind myself that Effie has suffered too. That I hold no monopoly on sorrow. That she has earned this happiness. All of it.

"And Tess told me you're showing at Gagosian this winter?" I say, turning to Devin. "That is amazing. You must be so thrilled."

"It's not a done deal yet. But we're talking," he says. "Tessie, are you *cold*?"

I didn't realize I was shivering, my teeth chattering. It is alarming to me how lately I sometimes forget my body, about its needs. Its limits. This past winter I went out to the porch of our brownstone to get our mail and completely forgot that I wasn't wearing any socks or slippers. I stared at my numb feet, bewildered, before I realized what I'd forgotten.

I allow the wine to warm me and refuse the sweater Devin offers. "I have one in the car. I'm fine."

"The long-suffering Tess," Jake mutters.

"What?" I hiss.

"Nothing," he says, and reaches for the wine.

"I'm going to bed," Zu-Zu says, yawning. She stands up and comes around the table to stand behind me. She leans over my shoulders and hugs me. Her arms are so long and thin. I circle her wrists with my fingers. They feel fragile.

"Stay up a little longer?" I say. "We need to talk about all the fun things we'll do with you in New York this summer."

She yawns again. "Tomorrow. I have ballet early in the morning."

"On a weekday?" I ask.

"*Every* day," she says, and kisses my cheek. Her lips are warm. I close my eyes.

"Come on, Plum," she says, always the mother hen. And Plum kisses us all and then follows behind her sister, dragging her feet in the cold grass, dangling the transparent fish bones from her fingers before tossing them into the compost pile by the back door.

I watch them as they disappear into the camp. I lean back and study their silhouettes behind the curtains in the upstairs window. Jake and Devin laugh and chat. Effie reaches for my hand, and I reach for the wine, but it's empty. I reach for the second bottle, and it's empty too.

"I'll get another bottle," I say. "Anybody want to share with me?" I avoid Jake's eyes.

"Why not," Devin says.

Inside the camp, I search the refrigerator, the countertops. The cupboards. But the wine is gone. Upstairs I hear the girls' feet padding across the floor, the sound of their bedsprings as they crawl into bed. The tinkling sound of their voices. And I feel myself unraveling.

I open the refrigerator door again as if I could have possibly missed a bottle of wine the first time. And then I lean out the back door and say, "Hey! We're out. I'll run down to Hudson's." Moths flutter around the porch light. A few fireflies spark in the hedges.

"You okay to drive?" Effie asks.

"I'm fine. I've just had a couple of glasses."

This is not true. I am fairly sure I drank the last bottle almost entirely by myself. But the store is just five or six miles away. Six deserted, dirt-road miles away. And we need more wine. If I stay here, I may keep unraveling, a loose thread pulled from a sweater. The wine is the knot that will anchor me in place.

I grab Jake's keys from the pocket of his coat, feeling the same sinking quicksand

31

feeling I got when I reached into his pocket three weeks ago. And so this time I ignore what I find inside. It is better not to read the string of texts on his phone. To try and decipher the cryptic narrative played out in gray and blue, to translate the emoticons and decode the messages tapped and then trapped inside their respective bubbles.

Meet me at Palo Santo at 6?
I only have an hour.
I'll take it. XOXO
Let's skip dinner.
Go straight for dessert? ;)

Standing in the narrow foyer of our brownstone, I'd scrolled backwards. Through weeks. Months. The conversation in reverse. The affair unfolding, Jake's lies unfolding. A delicate origami bird suddenly disassembled, exposed to be nothing more than a blank piece of paper. A fabrication.

And so tonight, I simply take the keys. Do not touch the phone he has, once again, left thoughtlessly behind for me to find. It is better not to see the name in white hovering over the conversation like a ghost: *Jess.* It is best not to call the number and hear the soft voice at the other end of the line.

I have known about her for three weeks,

but I haven't said a word. For three weeks I have carried this secret, Jake's secret, around like a rock in my pocket, weighing me down. I imagine if I were to walk into the lake, I would sink. Powerless to the pull of gravity. Of this, and all the other impossibly heavy stones.

I sit in the car and turn the heater on high. The warm air blasts cold at first and then hot through the vents, and I feel the chill begin to thaw. I will go buy the wine. The guys will go to bed, and Effie and I will stay up talking. And I will reach into that secret pocket, hold out my palm, show her this sharp stone.

The dirt parking lot of Hudson's is illuminated by the neon beer signs. It is late now, nearing midnight, and the lot is empty save for a rusted-out Buick and a big white pickup truck with Massachusetts plates parked at the gas pumps. The bed of the truck is loaded down with piles of lawn bags, landscaping equipment. The passenger window of the truck is cracked open, and a block-headed black dog with crudely cropped ears presses its nose against the glass. I can hear it growling at me, and I quicken my steps to the entrance of the store.

The electronic bell announces me as I enter. Inside the shop, the fluorescent lights are bright and buzzing. It makes me squint my eyes. I wander the aisles, scan the dusty shelves, until I find the same wine we were drinking with dinner. The one that reminds me of late-summer peaches. I grab a bottle, just one, and go to the counter.

The man in front of me is buying a twelve-pack. He is wearing stained white coveralls and has greasy hair to his shoulders, a pair of paint-splattered sunglasses on top of his head. He smells of gasoline. He pays for his beer and asks the kid to put forty dollars on pump 2 before heading outside.

I set the wine bottle down, pluck a handful of miniature Reese's Cups from a plastic bucket on the counter, five cents each, and set them down next to the wine. I'll leave them on the girls' pillows while they sleep. When they were little I used to leave them gumdrops, and they were convinced there was a fairy named Star who came whenever I visited.

"That all for you?" the kid behind the counter asks. He's a teenager. His face is littered with whiteheads, his eyes shifty.

"Yeah," I say, fishing through my purse for my wallet. I swipe my debit card. "Thanks."

Outside, the guy in the coveralls is pumping gas into the white truck. He watches me as I go to my car; I can feel his eyes on my back. And the dog growls again, its throaty threat growing ominously. When the growls turn into manic barking, I rush to my car and slam the door shut, feel my heart pounding in my throat.

It isn't until I put the key in the ignition that I realize I probably should *not* be driving. This happens at home sometimes too. I'll have a few glasses of wine with dinner, and not feel anything until I lie down in bed and begin to spin. It's just six miles back to camp though, ten minutes on the road, I think, and turn the key.

There are no streetlights out here, but the moon is bright. I drive slowly, carefully, back to Effie and Devin's, the bottle of wine nestled in a brown paper bag in the seat I usually occupy. I can't get any radio stations here, so I turn the radio off and focus on the winding dirt road ahead of me. It's just a few miles.

When we were teenagers, I would come to stay with Effie's family at the camp, and we'd escape the adults by taking long walks or riding our bikes around the lake. We must have walked a thousand miles around and around the lake, up and down this road that leads away from the water and into town. I know its every turn. It is as familiar to me as the curve of Jake's spine, that geography I study each night when he turns away from me. That trench that begins between his shoulders and travels the length of him.

I know where the road bends, this place where it turns away from the lake, where the trees become as thick as a fairy tale's, as dark and terrifying as those in a dream. Strangely, I take comfort in this familiarity, in the way my whole body remembers this place.

And so I am startled when I hit a pothole and the car dips. I feel almost betrayed. By the road. By my own memory. The bottle of wine rolls off the passenger seat and onto the floor. I hear the glass crack, smell the tangy scent of it as it begins to spill. *Shit.* I slow the car and reach over, bending down to pick it up, or at least right it, with only my left hand on the wheel. But the bottle has broken. It's too late. And when I sit up again, there is something in my headlights.

I slam my foot on the brakes, the car squealing to a stop, dust from the road rising up in the headlights like smoke. The seat belt presses against my shoulder like someone telling me to stay back. My heart pounds in my throat and in my hands, which clutch the steering wheel.

In the middle of the road, just a few feet in front of me, is a child.

A little girl.

The headlights bathe her in a pool of light. She is ghostly, pale. Naked from the waist up, wearing a tattered tutu and plastic rain boots, red with black spots like a ladybug. She is maybe four years old. Her belly is round. She has curly brown hair. Wild eyes.

Catching my breath, I pull the car to the side of the road, turn it off but leave the headlights on and slowly open the door. The car *ding, ding, dings* to remind me that the lights are on. She looks startled by the noise and squints in the bright light, so I reach in and turn them off, leaving the door open so at least I have the dome light to see by.

She doesn't move.

Slowly, carefully, I walk toward her.

I can see now that she is bleeding, and I wonder if, somehow, I actually *hit* her. If I am responsible for the blood that is on her hands, dripping down her pale legs. But I know that is not possible. That the car stopped beforehand. That there was no collision. No impact.

"It's okay," I say as I move toward her as I would a wounded animal.

Her eyes dart from me to the woods and back.

"I'm not going to hurt you," I say.

I walk closer then and squat down so that I am at her level. I reach my hand out to her, tentatively, but still she shrinks back. Afraid.

38

"My name is Tess," I say. "What's your name, sweetie?"

The cut is on her right hand. It looks new, deep. The blood on her legs is wet. I can see the blue rivers of her veins, which travel across the small expanse of her bare chest. It makes her seem even more vulnerable. Her skin is paper-thin. I feel my throat growing thick. The sensation is familiar. Ancient.

Her eyebrows furrow as she scowls. She doesn't trust me.

There is an orange plastic bunny barrette in her hair. It's come unfastened, and it holds precariously on to a curl. I resist the urge to snap it closed. I'm afraid to touch her.

"Are you cold?" I ask as softly as I can, but my voice sounds strange. Too loud. Too demanding. "I have a sweater," I say. "In my car. I'll get it for you. Stay here."

I stand up again and walk slowly, my knees shaking, backwards toward the car. I fumble with the keys in my hands, trying to find the button to pop the trunk, where I remember putting my soft gray sweater. But instead of hitting the trunk release, I accidentally hit the panic button and the sound pierces the air like a scream. I scramble to find the button to shut it off, to make the blaring sound stop. The car lights flash off and on.

And she runs.

She scurries down the small embankment at the edge of the road and back up the other side, slipping into the woods. There is no light. I can't see where she has gone. I look around, as though the answer is in the trees. But I am alone here.

Something surges in me, something primitive and insistent, and I follow her. I scramble down the embankment, feel the cold shock of water soaking through my sneakers, my socks, and then I am standing at the edge of the woods, which I know are thick and deep. It is impossibly dark. I listen for clues as to which direction she's gone, but there are too many sounds — the keening of frogs, the drone of crickets, the crush and crumble of twigs. I run, but I am aimless. What am I chasing? Which way do I go?

"Wait!" I holler. "Please!" I say, but my voice is swallowed by the night.

I feel the branches scratching every bit of exposed flesh on my body. I stop when a sharp branch stabs me in my ribs. I wince. I run deeper into the woods, but it is useless. I am dizzy with the scent of pine.

I stop and stand in the cold darkness,

disoriented. The moon cannot reach me here. I turn in circles, looking for something. Some flash of her pale skin. Anything. But she is gone.

My shoulders feel hot, liquid adrenaline pooling in them in this odd aftermath. I am breathless, my heart pounding and my chest heaving. I turn toward the light of my car, which shines weakly through the trees behind me. I stumble through the brush back to the road. I leave the woods, leap across the trickling stream to the road. I go to my car, sit in the driver's seat, and reach for my phone.

Suddenly behind me, there are headlights. I get out of the car again, clutching the phone, and shield my eyes from the bright lights as the car comes toward me. I wave my hands, trying to flag it down, but it simply speeds past. And then I see; it's the white landscaping truck from Hudson's. And it leaves a giant cloud of dust in its wake.

Asshole, I think. *Masshole,* I correct myself, watching the Massachusetts plates disappear into the darkness.

My fingers are cold, fumbling, but I am somehow able to conjure the illuminated keypad, press 911. I tap *Send.* But there is nothing. No signal. Still, I hold the useless

41

phone to my ear. Try to think about how I will explain what I just saw to the operator.

And then I remember. *I've been drinking.* I am sitting here in a car, with a broken bottle of wine; the carpet drenched. The car reeks, tangy and alcoholic. What would a cop say? Could I get arrested?

My entire body is trembling now; I can barely get the keys in the ignition. I try to break down what needs to be done into manageable steps. Increments. Start the car. Drive back to Effie and Devin's. Use the landline. Call the police. Tell them what I saw. I catalog the details, recite them like a prayer. Pink tutu, ladybug rain boots. *I've been drinking.*

Then, as I start to pull away, I realize I need to be able to find this spot again. There is nothing but my own memory of this road to rely on. I need to be able to recall where I am, where I found her, where I lost her.

I search the car frantically for something, anything, I can leave behind. Something more substantial than the scraps of paper in my purse. Something that won't just blow away. But there is nothing but the broken bottle of wine. Jake and Devin unloaded everything we had out of the car after we arrived.

This time I am able to find the button to

pop the trunk without setting off any alarms, and I get out of the car and open the trunk. I find the sweater I'd wanted to give her. I pull it out and set it at the edge of the road. A marker. An offering.

And then I get in the car again, turn the key, and drive.

"Where the hell have you been?" Jake says, meeting me in the back doorway. His eyes are wide. He grabs me by the elbow, too hard. "I was just about to go after you."

Before we go into the warm, bright kitchen, he leans close to me, still clutching my elbow.

"Did you get pulled *over*?" he hisses quietly. This is the way we speak to each other lately. In hushed whispers we don't want anyone else to hear. His tone is almost always accusatory, as though I am the one at fault. If it weren't so sad, it would be laughable.

"No," I say. I shake my elbow loose from his grip and go into the house.

Effie and Devin are in the kitchen. There is a teakettle on the stove, flames beneath it. Devin is washing our dinner dishes at the sink. Effie smiles when I come in, but her

44

smile disappears when she realizes I'm frantic.

"We need to call the police. There's a girl," I start. "In the road. I found a little girl."

A collective look of horror passes across their faces.

"Oh no," Effie starts, her hand fluttering around near her throat. "Were you in an . . . accident?"

I shake my head. "No, no, she was just standing there."

"What do you mean?" Devin asks.

"I looked down for one second, and when I looked up again, she was in the middle of the road. Like a deer or something."

"Where is she now?"

I shake my head.

"You *left* her there?" Jake says.

I shake my head again, feel tears filling my eyes at the realization of what has just happened. What I saw. "She ran into the woods, and I followed her. But it's so dark out." The last three words are just a hush: "I lost her."

"How old do you think she was?" Devin asks, drying his hands on a dishtowel, and reaching for the telephone on the wall.

"I don't know, maybe three? Four?"

"Jesus," Effie gasps.

"She didn't have a shirt on. She was just

45

wearing a tutu, like for dress-up. And ladybug rain boots. But she's hurt. A cut on her hand, I think. There was a lot of blood." I can barely catch my breath. "Oh my God."

Effie motions for me to sit down on the bench in the kitchen nook. I put my elbows on the cold Formica, rest my head in my hands.

"Do you want *me* to call?" Devin asks, motioning to the phone.

"No, no." I shake my head, looking up at him. "It's okay."

Devin hands me the phone, and I dial 911.

"911. What is your emergency?"

The teakettle on the stove starts to rattle, steam, scream. Effie hurries up out of the nook and pulls it from the flame. *Sorry,* she mouths.

"There's a girl in the woods between Gormlaith and Hudson's. She's hurt." But all of the carefully rehearsed details have slipped away now. Words once again fail. "I just saw her . . . but she ran away."

"Ma'am, you're going to need to slow down," the operator says.

As I try to explain what happened, to make sense of it to the dispatcher (to myself), Effie makes coffee with a French press. I study her as she pours the boiling water into the glass cylinder, as she presses

46

the plunger and the water muddies and swirls. The intricacy, the complexity of this task seems somehow ludicrous now. Frivolous.

"Ma'am, where are you right now?" The dispatcher sounds irritated.

"At the lake," I say. "Gormlaith. At my friends' camp. I couldn't get a signal on my phone." I give her Effie and Devin's address. There is no address for that dark bend in the road, the place where she disappeared.

"Okay, ma'am, I'm sending a deputy right out. Stay where you are, please."

Devin brings a blanket and puts it over my shoulders. Effie pours us all cups of coffee, begins the process with the teakettle and French press again. And after all that effort, the coffee is bitter. Gritty with loose grounds and too strong. Still, I take a long swallow, feel as it burns my throat. Clears my head.

Jake has pulled on a long-sleeve shirt and put on pants. His cheeks are flushed with wine and sun. He looks boyish. Handsome.

"Should we drive down there?" he says to Devin.

Devin shakes his head. "Nobody should be driving anywhere."

The coffee burns in my chest.

"Do you remember exactly where you saw her?" Devin asks me gently, putting his large hand on my shoulder. It makes me feel safe. Small.

"About halfway between here and Hudson's," I say. "Maybe two, two and a half miles away? You know where the road splits and then starts to curve away from the lake?"

"That's not too far," Devin says to Jake, grabbing a flannel shirt from the back of a chair by the stove. "We'll walk. You guys stay here and wait for the cops."

Effie nods and finally grabs a cup of coffee for herself.

"You need a jacket?" Devin asks Jake, and suddenly, I remember the sweater.

"Wait. I left a sweater on the side of the road," I say. "To mark the spot."

"Oh, good," Devin says, smiling. "That was smart."

"Do you have a flashlight?" Jake asks Effie.

Effie pulls open a drawer and grabs a flashlight, tries it. The beam seems weak. She shakes it, tries the switch again, and the light surges, blinds me. "Oh, sorry," she says, and clicks it off.

"It's going to be okay," Devin says, squeezing my shoulder. "We'll find her."

Jake leads the way out the door without speaking to me. The screen door slams shut behind them, but I can hear the sound of their footsteps as they walk quickly down the road.

Plum and Zu-Zu come down the stairs then. I'd almost forgotten about them. They stand in the kitchen doorway, both of them rubbing sleep from their eyes. Zu-Zu yawns. She clutches the tattered seal under her arm, and she could be three again instead of thirteen.

"What happened?" asks Plum.

The officer takes nearly a half hour to arrive. When he pulls into the gravel driveway, Effie ushers the girls back upstairs to bed, and I go outside to greet him. Devin and Jake are still gone.

The night is dark. No flashing blue and red lights. No sirens.

He gets out of the car and slams his door shut, adjusting his holster on his hip as he walks toward me. He's a beefy guy, short but thick with red, shiny cheeks and a blond, stubbly buzz cut. He's young, maybe mid-twenties, but he moves slowly, like an arthritic old man. Like he's got all the time in the world.

"You the one called in about a girl?" he asks.

I nod, standing in the doorway, shivering.

"I'm Sergeant Strickland," he says. "Can we go inside?"

"Oh," I say. "Of course. I'm sorry."

Inside the bright warm kitchen, I motion for him to sit down, but he shakes his head and pulls a pad out of his back pocket.

I grab my coffee, which is cold now, and sit back down in the kitchen nook.

"At approximately what time did you spot her?" he says.

I try to recall the clock on the dash, but I can't remember. "Maybe eleven forty-five, midnight?"

He glances down at his watch. "And it's one A.M. now."

"Yes. I called 911 as soon as I got here. I've been waiting for you."

"Where were you going?" he asks. "When you saw her?"

"What?" I say, confused.

He is leaning against the counter. I watch a carpenter ant, fat and sluggish, crawl across the Formica. "Awfully late on a Thursday night for you to be out driving around. Where exactly were you going?"

"Oh," I say. "I was at Hudson's. Buying wine." My throat thickens. Why did I tell

50

him that?

"At midnight?" he says, one bushy eyebrow rising.

I shake my head. "We ran out," I say.

"So you were drinking?"

"No," I say, eyes burning. "I mean, yes, we had a glass of wine with dinner."

"Awfully late to be eating supper," he says.

I should have known to say *supper. Dinner* makes me sound like I'm not from around here.

"We were catching up. We're visiting, my husband and I. From New York."

I see something pass across his face, disgust, I think. He thinks I'm a summer person. A *flatlander.*

"I grew up here," I say as if I have to defend my native status. As though this has anything to do with a half-naked child in the middle of the road in the middle of the night.

"So you were having *supper,* drinking wine, catching up," he says, sneering, "and then you decided to get in your car and get more alcohol."

I shake my head. But yes, what he's said is exactly what happened.

"Can I tell you about the girl, please?" I say.

"I'm just trying to establish the events

51

leading up to the sighting, ma'am," he says, scratching his pen against his notepad. "Shit," he mutters. "Out of ink. Would you happen to have a pen?"

I stand up and go to the bookcase where Effie keeps a coffee mug full of pens. I grab one and hand it to him.

I sit back down. The bench is cold and hard. I stare into the coffee mug.

"Okay, so you left Hudson's and were on your way back here. What happened next?"

"I hit a pothole, or something, and . . ." I start to tell him about the wine bottle falling on the floor and then stop myself. ". . . I was distracted. When I looked up again, she was standing in the middle of the road."

"Lots of deer up here," he says. "Wild animals. Just last week, got a call in about a rabid raccoon."

I shake my head. "It wasn't a *raccoon*," I say. "It was a girl."

"How do you know?"

"How do I know what?"

"That it wasn't an animal? No streetlights on the road there. Could have been your eyes playing a trick on you. How much exactly would you say you'd been drinking?"

I can't believe where this is going. I want a different officer. I want to start over. My whole body feels flushed, feverish. I rub my shoulder, which is fiery now with the sunburn. I feel bruised.

"I know the difference between a girl and an animal," I say, baffled. And I wish that Jake and Devin were still here. That Effie would come down from upstairs. "I stopped the car and got out. I *talked* to her."

He scratches, scratches. Shakes the pen. "This one's out too."

I take a deep breath, get up, and grab another pen and hand it to him.

"Did you ask her what she was doing outside in the middle of the night? Did you ask her where her parents were, if they knew where she was? Probably just snuck out of the house to meet a boy."

I feel like someone punched me in the throat. "What are you talking about?" I say. "She was a *baby.*"

"Wait," he says. His smirk disappears. "*How* old was she exactly?"

"I told the 911 operator. She was maybe only three or four years old. She was wearing a pink tutu and rain boots. She had blood on her hands and her legs. She wasn't wearing a shirt."

He stands up straight, moves away from the counter. He has stopped scratching on the pad. He's listening now.

"Before I could do anything, she ran away. She got scared," I say. "Oh, wait, the alarm, I forgot. I accidentally hit the panic button, and it set off the car alarm. I think that's why she ran."

He looks at me and his face is serious now, angry even. "So she took off into the woods, a half-naked little girl who's *bleeding,* and you decide the best thing to do is to leave the scene, after you'd been drinking, and drive *home*?"

"Yes," I say, exasperated now. "I mean, *no.* I followed her. Into the woods. But it was so dark, I lost her." Something catches in my chest. Fabric snagging on a barbed wire fence. I remember the twig poking me in the rib, consider lifting my shirt, looking for proof. Instead, my finger taps at the spot, feels the tender place.

He scratches his head, looks mystified. By my story. By me.

"Did you *consider* calling 911?"

I feel like screaming.

"I couldn't get a signal on my phone," I say, taking a deep breath. "I came back *here* to call for help."

I am trying to stay calm, to be rational. Reasonable.

"Please," I say. My ribs ache. "Can you please just send someone out there to look for her? She's little and scared and hurt."

Something softens in him. For just a moment. Maybe he has a little girl at home.

"Can you give me an idea of where exactly you think you saw her?"

"My husband and our friend went back, they're there now."

"They been drinking too?"

"They *walked,*" I say. Jesus Christ.

He goes outside, the screen door slamming behind him. I can hear him on his radio, initiating a search of the area. Dispatching a team. And despite how rattled I am, I feel grateful he's finally doing something.

Effie comes downstairs without the girls.

"You okay?" she asks.

I shake my head. I feel like a child, like I've been scolded.

The door opens again, and he peeks his head into the kitchen. "Ma'am, I'm going to need you to come with me."

Effie and I go outside. The air is so cold now; it's dropped at least ten degrees. I think about the little girl out there by herself, and my chest aches.

The officer gets into the driver's side of the cruiser, slams his door shut, and turns his lights on. They paint the dark night red and blue.

Effie hugs me. I start to open the passenger door, and the officer rolls down the
window. "In the back. Pretend it's one of
your New York taxi cabs."

I obey, but I can't get myself buckled in
with the elaborate seat belts, and so he has
to come around and latch me in. The seats
are hard, plastic. As he leans over me and
locks the belt into place I feel like a child.
"You don't have any weapons on you,
ma'am?" he asks then, and I feel like a
criminal.

"It'll be okay," Effie says, but her voice is
unconvincing. "They'll find her."

I nod and nod, trying to convince myself,
and her both.

Effie reaches through the window and
squeezes my hand, but he rolls up the
window and she has to pull her hand away.
I turn to look at him but see only the pixelated blur created by the wire mesh between us.

By the time we get back to the spot in the road, that dark bend where the trees swoon, making a cavern of leaves, the other officers have started to arrive. I can't help but wonder why it took Sergeant Strickland so long to get to Effie's, when these guys seemed to materialize out of thin air.

I see Jake speaking to one of them at the edge of the road. Devin is talking to another. Within only minutes, there are police dogs straining at their leashes and the crush of boots on damp leaves. The darkness is filled with red and blue lights, the bright beams of flashlights cutting through the darkness. And then a helicopter buzzes overhead. As I get out of the cruiser, I feel like I've stepped onto the set of a movie.

It is only June and so cold; I tremble thinking of her out there by herself.

The dogs bark, and their voices echo. When Effie and I were kids, we loved to holler our names out toward the water, listen as they bounced back to us. A magical call and response. I have watched Plum and Zu-Zu do the same.

Strickland goes over to another officer, who is standing outside his cruiser. The other cop towers over him. He could be a former Marine; he has that ex-military air about him. Strickland looks back at me and motions for me to come over.

"Ms. Waters, this is Lieutenant Andrews. He's the officer who'll be in command of the search."

"This the RP?" the lieutenant asks Strickland.

"RP?" I say.

"Reporting party," he says. "You the one who called it in?"

"Yes." I nod. Finally, someone in charge around here. Someone taking this seriously.

"Problem is, ma'am," he says, and clucks his tongue, "we haven't gotten any calls in about a little girl."

I shake my head. I don't understand. *I* called in about a little girl. *I* called. "What do you mean?" I ask.

"You say you saw a girl out here, but nobody's called in to report a missing kid."

"Maybe they don't know," I say. "Her parents. Maybe they don't realize yet."

I think about all those stories of girls who go missing from their beds, stolen away in the middle of the night while their parents are sleeping. Oblivious until morning when they go to their child's empty room.

I am shaking now from the cold. My whole body is trembling, my teeth are chattering. Bone hitting bone.

"Can't you put out some sort of Amber Alert or something?" I say.

"Not without a missing persons report," the lieutenant says.

I am so confused.

"Wait. So I found a girl. But she's not *lost,* because no one has called in to say they lost her?" I look at him in disbelief. "She's four years old. She's bleeding. Somebody has to find her." I spin on my heel to look for someone, anyone to back me up here. I feel crazy.

The helicopter is so loud overhead now, I can barely hear the lieutenant when he speaks again. The carnival lights and the sound of panting dogs are too much; this feels like a dream. A nightmarish, fever dream.

"We've got dogs out," he says. "And there are heat sensors on the helicopter. If there's a girl out there, she'll be glowing."

"Glowing?" I think of her standing in the

yellow light of my headlights. I recall the blue rivers that ran under the surface of her paper-thin white flesh. The way she seemed somehow illuminated.

"Infrared. It picks up body heat. If she's out there we'll find her."

"Oh," I say. "Okay."

Jake comes to me then and puts his arm across my shoulder. I realize I am still just wearing a T-shirt. I am freezing. Because I am cold, I forget for a minute that I don't want him touching me. About how strange this gesture of his feels. How forced.

"Hey, what did you guys do with my sweater?" I say. I can barely talk. I am so cold; my whole body is trembling.

"Your sweater?"

"Yeah, the gray one I put on the road to mark the spot."

Jake shakes his head. "Oh, shit. I forgot about that. This is the place though, right?"

I nod, speechless. I do recall this bend in the road. I know it the same way I know, when I wake in the middle of the night (without even opening my eyes), what time it is. I know the nuances of darkness. It is no different here.

"Where are you going?" he asks.

I walk away from him, down the road,

60

looking for the sweater I remember putting out here. Where the hell is it? And then it hits me.

She came back for it.

Time passes. How much time, I have no idea. The sky begins to soften with light, though it will be another hour or two before the sun comes up. The officers traipse through the woods. The dogs bark. The radios crackle, disembodied voices speaking a language I don't understand. A code of numbers. The secret language of emergency.

I sit with Devin and Jake at the edge of the road. Someone found a blanket and I wear it over my shoulders like a cape. Effie pulls up in Devin's truck, parking next to us. She jumps down out of the cab and passes Devin a Thermos.

"Coffee," she says. "And muffins." She hands me a warm paper bag. I unroll the top, and my face is hit with steam and the heady scent of wild blueberries.

"Where are the girls?" I ask.

"Back at home," she says. "They're still sleeping."

"Alone?" I say, feeling my stomach flip.

"They're fine."

"But what if there's someone bad out there? What if this little girl somehow got away from someone?" My mind is spinning. I think about Plum cartwheeling across the grass. About someone taking her.

"Tess, they're fine. The camp is locked. I'm headed back now, but you need to eat something. *Please,* eat a muffin."

I reach into the bag and pull out a muffin, but by the time I get the paper peeled from the bottom, I can't remember feeling hungry.

After Effie leaves, a van with WCAX-TV emblazoned on the side shows up. They set up large bright lights, and the female reporter primps and preens in front of a mirror her assistant holds up for her. Her heels sink into the soft grass at the edge of the road. I notice a run in her stocking.

Someone directs them to me. Tells them I am the one who saw the girl. It happens so quickly. Before I can even think about saying no, the bright lights are in my face. The dreamy feeling of déjà vu rushes over me, disorienting. I have been here before.

But it is too late now, and before I can even think of what to say, how to appeal to everyone watching to keep an eye out for her, the cameraman takes aim at me, and the reporter says, "Just try to relax. Tell us what you saw."

She turns to the camera then, juts her chin out and tilts her head.

"We're here with Tess Waters, who is visiting from New York. Earlier tonight, she says she was driving back to a camp on Lake Gormlaith where she's staying, when she found a young child in the road. According to Ms. Waters, the girl appeared to be wounded, but ran off into the woods before she had a chance to help her."

The reporter, whose lipstick is smudged on her front tooth, turns to me then, as if I have suddenly appeared. Like I haven't been standing there the whole time.

"Can you tell us a little bit about the girl you saw?"

I repeat what I have been saying all night. *Pink tutu. Ladybug rain boots.*

The reporter nods, holds the microphone to my face.

"She was scared," I say. "She's just a baby."

She nods again. Scowls. "You said she was hurt?"

"Yes, her hand. Her hand was bleeding."

The reporter tilts her head again, smiles in some odd approximation of sympathy or

64

pity, and then turns back to the camera. I can see every pore in her face. The orange line of her makeup at her jaw. I notice that one of her earrings is missing a back. It makes me anxious, reminds me of something, though I can't pinpoint what.

"Officers say that there have been no reports of a missing child and no other witnesses. But the search will continue. For this lost little girl."

When the lights turn off, I say to her, "You're missing the back of your earring. You should take it out before you lose it."

She looks confused and then fumbles with her earring. She nods. "Oh, thank you."

And then she is climbing into the back of the news van, her dirty heels disappearing inside. The van stays put though. Someone says something about a press conference being scheduled, and then there are other vans pulling up. WPTZ, WVNY. I go through the same routine with three other broadcasters. I am seeing spots from the bright lights.

Other people seem to come out of the woods then. There is suddenly a crowd. Cars park at the edge of the road. It is like an impromptu parade. Part of me would not be surprised at all if a marching band arrived next. Majorettes. Balloons. I am delirious. Dizzy and exhausted. There's a terrifying sense of excitement buzzing and humming among the people who walk up and down the road, as if she might just wander out again and reveal herself. As if this is only some elaborate game of hide-and-seek.

When the sun fills the sky with light, my head starts to pound. The wine, I realize. The alcohol has run its course, metabolized into pure sugar, depleted my body, and now I will pay with the headache. Nausea. I am hungover. This is the part I usually sleep through. A bottle of ibuprofen on the night-stand, a glass of water.

I need water. I am overwhelmed with a terrible thirst.

"I need water," I say to Jake, who is cracking his neck. He nods, and I stand up, cross the road, and go to where I saw someone passing out water bottles to the officers earlier. I drink as if I haven't had water in days. In years.

Sergeant Strickland and Lieutenant Andrews are standing just a few feet away, near the tree line. They are talking loudly enough for me to hear them. Strickland is being scolded.

"We've been out here for three hours now. The helicopter isn't picking up anything.

The dogs aren't picking up anything. You think maybe you jumped the gun a bit, Sergeant?"

"She says she saw a naked little kid out here. What was I supposed to do, sir? It's SOP."

"You're supposed to talk her off the ledge, is what you're supposed to do. And now she's talked to the media" — he gestures to the crowd — "we've got a full-blown circus on our hands."

Strickland's face is red, his thick neck straining at his uniform collar. I feel something like rage growing in me.

I stand up and walk over to them. My legs feel weak, useless.

The lieutenant seems surprised to see me and reddens a bit. Then he stiffens his posture, pushes his chest out, and clears his throat.

"Ms. Waters . . ." he says.

"I'm not crazy. She's *real*," I say, as calmly as I can. "I saw her."

"Of course, ma'am," the lieutenant says, smiling at me condescendingly. "And we're doing everything we can to locate the juvenile. But if you could please refrain from conducting any more interviews, we'd appreciate it. We'll hold a press conference in a few hours. In the meantime, how about we don't feed the lions?"

I nod, feel tears stinging my eyes.

I peer up at the sky then, at the helicopter, which circles and circles overhead. At the weak glow on the horizon that will eventually become the sun. At the last few stars pulsing like fireflies in the sky.

Back at the camp, Jake stretches, yawns. "I'm sorry, I need to go to bed. Just for a little bit."

It is dawn. 5 A.M. The sky is overcast, and mist hovers over the lake like ghosts. The surface of the water is still, though the air is not still at all. The loons are crying out, their wings beating against the water as they take flight. They seem disoriented by the helicopter that circles over the lake.

"Come to bed?" Jake says, motioning for me. "You need sleep too. Just an hour or two. Then we can figure out what to do."

"What did the lieutenant guy say?" Effie asks softly. She is enclosed in Devin's arms. Like a nesting doll. "What's next?"

"He says they'll keep searching," I say. "There are a lot of empty camps, abandoned buildings. Places where a little kid might hide." This is what Andrews promised me before he told me to go home. I worry now he would have said anything to get me to leave. That he would have done anything, said anything to pacify me. *To talk me down off the ledge.*

"If she's little, I imagine she couldn't have gotten very far," Effie says.

I nod. "He said the farthest a child her age could go in twenty-four hours would be less than two miles."

I imagine the circumference of this invisible circle. Two miles, radiating out from that spot in the road where I found her.

"They didn't see anything with the helicopters? The dogs?"

I shake my head. "I don't think they believe me."

"That's ridiculous," Effie says. "Of course they believe you. Why would somebody make something like that up?"

I shake my head.

Devin says, "I spoke with some of our neighbors who came out when they saw what was going on. Folks are really shaken up about this. I don't think it'll be hard to organize some volunteers. I'm going to talk to Billy Moffett, see about using the back room at Hudson's to set up headquarters. People are going to want to help."

"Does anybody have any idea who she might belong to?" Jake asks. "It's so weird nobody's reported her missing."

Devin shakes his head. "No idea. Nobody I talked to seems to know of any local kids that fit that description. Could belong to one of the summer families, but it's still pretty early in the season. Most folks don't come up to the lake until the Fourth of July."

Jake yawns again. "Sorry," he says again and shakes his head. "Man, I am so tired. Come to bed," he says to me. "Just for a little bit."

"Go," Effie says, reaching for my hand. "We should all get some sleep. There's nothing we can do right now. The police are still looking. If they find something, I'm sure they'll call."

And because I am exhausted, delirious, I agree. I don't have the energy to argue with her. With anyone.

I follow Jake along the narrow wooded path to the guest cottage. He looks thinner lately, his clothes hanging just a bit looser on his already lean frame. He's been running more, eating better. The subtle changes in his appearance feel like glaring clues now. Something I should have noticed. How could I have been so inattentive? So stupid?

I study the familiar back of his head; he's

71

grown his hair out a bit lately as well. It's more like it was when we first met now: softly curling over the back of his collar, framing his face. I remember I used to marvel at the color of his hair. It's brown, but the individual strands are a thousand colors: blond, auburn, and the occasional deep amber. Unlike many of his peers, there are no gray hairs in that spectrum. He still has the same boyish grin he's always had, though he wears a trimmed beard and mustache to hide the scars that remain from the cleft lip he was born with. The methotrexate his mother took for the crippling rheumatoid arthritis she suffers from is to blame. Though he never talks about it, I know he was teased as a kid; his mother told me one night not long after I met her. Her eyes filled with tears as she talked about the way he would come home from school crying. Sometimes, when I feel angry with him, I need only to focus on that scar, and all of a sudden, I feel an inexplicable tenderness toward him. There's a vulnerability there still, I know, a persistent wound that won't heal.

Birds flutter and sing in the trees. The sun burns through the mist. The dew is already evaporating from the grass.

Inside the cabin, it smells like cedar. There

is a small desk, a bookcase stuffed with discarded library books. A record player and a collection of albums. Our suitcases sit waiting at the foot of the Hansel-and-Gretel-style cupboard bed, which is made up with clean white sheets and a heavy down comforter. I kick off my sneakers and peel off my socks before climbing up the built-in steps and into the bed. I don't bother to take off my clothes. I am too tired. And as wound up as I am, I cannot resist the pull of the feathers, the pillow that cradles my head.

Jake peels off his clothes except for his boxer shorts and climbs in next to me. He gets too hot for pajamas when he sleeps. At home, he sleeps naked. And even then, he throws all of the covers off in the middle of the night, his body like a steaming furnace.

Now, he curls around me, and it takes my breath away. First, because his body feels unfamiliar. He is *much* thinner, his muscles wiry and taut. Second, because I don't remember the last time he has enclosed me like this. I know it is because the bed is small, because there is no place for him to go. At home, in our king-size bed, I sometimes cannot find him in the middle of the night. My limbs search for the familiar sharp bone of his ankle, the hot spot of flesh of his hip. But now, we are forced together. And I try to take comfort in the way his chest rises and falls against my back. The way his fingers interlace with mine.

I am too tired to feel sadness. To feel anything but exhaustion.

And I fall instantly and deeply asleep.

"Try to think of something else," you say. I lie on my stomach on the bed, peering up at the TV. I hear the crackle of the paper in which the syringes are sealed. My entire body clenches in response. I will each muscle to relax, try to concentrate on my breath.

"Ready?" You are straddling me, your knees on either side of my back.

For four months now we have gone through this ritual, two, sometimes three times a day, yet I am still startled by how cold the needles are. I close my eyes when the first one goes in. Try not to think of the sting but only of the drugs that are entering my bloodstream, the magic elixirs that will turn my body into a vessel rather than this barren wasteland. Everything I have read suggests that visualizing can help. Dreaming the hormonal cocktail's journey, imagining the bursts of testosterone and estrogen as they make their way through to my reluctant ovaries.

"Almost done," you offer, and I can hear the apologetic smile in your voice. I squeeze my fingers into fists.

For four months, we have found ourselves here. Me facedown on the bed, you straddling me like a horse. In the morning after breakfast, during our lunch breaks from work, and as soon as we get home at night. We have become accustomed to this. We are like junkies, I think. Addicts stuck in a futile ritual.

We sit, breathless on the bed, hold hands. Wait.

Because after the needles, there is hope. Hope: that rush, that euphoric buzz. Hope like an opiate.

And later, we make love. We make love with intention, with a purpose. And despite what I have heard about couples losing their passion when sex becomes just a means to an impossible end, I feel more passionate than I ever have. My entire body tingles and pulses with desire. But the desire is bigger than flesh.

I have wanted this my whole life. I realize this now, only now that I am not able. Now that we have waited too long, assumed too much. How did I become so distracted? How did I convince myself that this didn't matter? That the very core of my being could be ignored? Do I blame you for this? Do I blame you for blinding me to my own wants?

Maybe. Maybe a little. Sometimes when I think about the needles, I wish that you were the one who had to go through this. That your body was the one to be punished in order to make up for our ambivalence. I dream the cold needle slipping into your flesh, the hands reaching up inside your body. The dyes injected into my failing fallopian tubes filling your body instead. Because you were the one who assured me that we had plenty of time. That tomorrow, tomorrow we could chase this particular dream. That if we put that boiling pot on the back burner it wouldn't burn out. That possibility wouldn't simply evaporate, leaving only the black-bottomed pot behind. Hot to the touch and empty.

Is this why you agreed? To taking out a mortgage on the house? To walking me into the lab each and every morning for the last four months where the phlebotomist stuck me with a needle, pulled my blood from me, all in the name of Hope? Of sorry? Was this your grand apology? Did you know, even as we sat, breathless on the bed, my back aching from the sting of the needles, that it was too late and that it was your fault?

I try not to think about this. Instead, as the needle pricks and the drugs rush in, I squeeze my eyes shut until I see a constellation-filled sky. And then I make the same wish on a zillion imaginary stars.

I wake with a start, sweating, my heart pounding, and sit up, disoriented. I don't know where I am. The pale curtains in the window are aglow with the morning sun. The bed is empty. Jake is not here.

Overhead I hear the helicopter, feel the way it makes the walls of the cottage shudder and hum, and suddenly I remember. I feel crushed by the realization of what has happened, of what I found last night. Of what I lost. I take comfort in the sound of the helicopter though, because it means they are still searching.

I am drenched in sweat. I pluck the wet cotton of my T-shirt from my skin. Brush the damp hair away from my face and twist it into a ponytail. My neck feels clammy. I look at my watch. It is 9 A.M. I open up the little Dutch door of the cottage to a bright June morning.

There are sounds coming from the camp.

A television? Voices. I slip on my sneakers; they are still wet from my plunge into the little stream at the edge of the road. They squish and squeak as I make my way back up the path to the camp.

Inside, the girls are sitting in the kitchen nook eating leftover blueberry muffins and bacon. Zu-Zu's hair is pulled back into a tight bun. She is wearing her leotard and tights, a thin cotton blouse that reveals one knobby shoulder. She is sitting on the bench, one leg curled under her, a pair of purple warm-up booties on her feet. Plum is still in her pajamas. I notice a smear of blueberry on her cheek and resist the urge to lick my thumb and wipe it away.

"I heard the helicopters last night," Plum says, her mouth full. She motions upward. "It sounded like they were right over our room!"

I don't know how much Effie has told them, and so I just nod. "I know. It's loud."

In the living room, Jake and Devin are watching the TV. The news is on, and they are talking about the girl, showing the clip of me talking to the reporter.

"You're up." Jake turns to me, smiles. It feels like an apology. Every gesture of kindness he offers lately a small and futile recompense.

I sit down next to him on the couch, an unspoken acknowledgment of his effort. But when he reaches and puts his hand on my knee, it is too much, and so I move away. Lean forward, study the TV.

"Officers say that there have been no reports of a missing child and no other witnesses. But the search will continue. For this lost little girl," the reporter says, shaking her head.

No other witnesses.

Wait. How could I have forgotten this? How could I have failed to tell this to the police?

"There *was* somebody," I say. "I saw this guy at Hudson's. And then he drove past after I saw her."

"What are you talking about?" Jake says.

I walk to the TV and shut it off.

"There was a man at Hudson's who drove past me after I saw the girl. He blew past me on the road. She was already gone, but maybe he saw something."

Devin scowls. "Do you remember what was he driving?"

"It was a big white pickup truck. I remember there were a lot of lawn bags in the bed of the truck. And Massachusetts plates."

"That's odd," Devin says.

"It seemed like he might be a landscaper

81

or something," I say.

"From out of state?"

That is strange.

"He was buying beer, and he paid for gas." And for some reason this reminds me of the Reese's Cups I picked up for the girls. I forgot to put them on their pillows. I shake my head. Everything feels thick. Confused. "His dog was growling at me. A pit bull, I think. It had clipped ears."

"Did you get his license-plate number?" Jake asks.

I look at him in disbelief. "No," I say.

"Do they have security cameras at Hudson's?" Jake asks Devin. "Maybe there's some footage of him."

Devin snorts.

"You should tell the cops what you saw," he says. "It shouldn't be too hard to track down somebody with out-of-state plates if he's still close. Maybe he's got a camp up here. Could be he's just getting it ready for the summer."

"I've got Lieutenant Andrews's number," I say, digging in the pocket of my jeans. He'd given me his business card before we left the site. "But I won't be able to get through on the cell number if he's still down the road. Do you think he's still down there?"

"I don't know," Devin says. "My plan is to help get things set up for the volunteers at Hudson's. Effie is taking the girls into town. Jake, why don't you and Tess take your car and stop by and see if Andrews is still there. And then you can both meet me at Hudson's?"

Jake sits wringing his hands. "I *hope* somebody else saw her too. It seems like with only one witness, there's just not enough concrete evidence. To keep a full-blown search going, I mean."

"You don't believe me?" I ask, feeling anger welling up. "You think I'm making this up?"

He shakes his head and scowls. "I didn't say that. I'm just saying that guy Andrews seems like he thinks maybe you were confused. That maybe it was an animal or something."

"It wasn't a goddamned animal," I say. "Jesus Christ. I know the difference between a little girl and an animal."

"Hey," he says, his hands up in mock surrender.

"I know exactly what I saw," I say.

"Let's just calm down," he says. "Seriously."

And my eyes widen. "Don't tell me to calm down," I say in that soft, awful language we speak. "Don't ever tell me to calm down."

Jake and I get in the car.

"What is that smell?" he asks. "God." He covers his face with his T-shirt.

I remember the broken wine bottle.

"Hold on," I say, and pull the drenched floor mat out of the car, toss it on the grass. I will rinse it out with the hose later. Let it soak in a bucket of soapy water.

He backs up and drives us down the road.

She is with us in the car. *Jess. Jessica?* Her scent is stronger than the acrid wine. More potent than the silence between us.

She's nobody I know. Just one of his assistants (one of a million who come and go). And while I've never met her, I know *exactly* who she is: a bright-eyed girl from Brandeis or Wesleyan or Vassar. It doesn't matter. She's young and hungry. She's come to New York with her diploma and her aspirations and her work ethic. She survives on ramen noodles and Two-Buck Chuck, but she lives in an apartment paid for by her parents and shared with another Vassar grad whose rent she takes and deposits into a checking account whose balance she never bothers to check. She's probably had an eating disorder and overcome it. Or, more likely these days, she's a girl who embraces her curves. Not swayed by societal demands, by media (she most certainly does not have cable, though she does subscribe to Netflix, to *Vogue*). She has dark hair, because she is serious. She drinks too much at parties. She is not fascinating but wishes she were. She wants and wants and wants something she is not yet able to articulate. And so when Jake, her boss, the guy whose phone she answers all day long, asks her to get a drink after work, she has to stop herself from saying yes too quickly. It is her job to remain elusive and aloof. She makes him wait three days before she agrees.

That night, in that claw-foot tub, that sulfurous bath, she shaves her legs and rubs them with scented oil. Wonders if she should shave her pubic hair; she still isn't exactly sure what she's supposed to do about that.

When she sleeps with him, in that shabby apartment that costs more every month than she and her roommate make together, she tells herself that she wouldn't be doing this if he had children. If he were a family man. Assures herself that this is somehow less despicable because there are no children involved. She sets aside her father's own indiscretions. Separates herself from those women, those home-wrecking women who didn't know that you don't sleep with men who have little girls at home. Who have families.

And she is able to do this because she is young, and when you are young the world is a big and remarkable thing, and your actions don't seem to have consequences that extend beyond your own fingertips. And because there are no children involved. He is only a husband, not a father. Because while one can quickly cease being a husband, it is nearly impossible to cease being a dad.

No children involved. This is what she thinks. Because she doesn't know. (And I forgive her this. I forgive her stupidity and shortsightedness and the simplicity with which she sees the world). Because she cannot possibly know what happened in Guatemala.

Jake pulls over to the side of the road behind a row of police cars.

"I'll wait here," he says.

"Okay," I say. "It'll just be a minute."

What felt private, personal last night now seems to have become public. This little girl with her tangled hair and transparent skin belongs to the world now. She is the lead story on every news station. Everyone who lives within a twenty-mile radius has a theory about where she came from, and where she has gone. Everyone is looking for her, staking claim. But *I* am the one who found her, the one who knelt down and tried to help her. I am the one who lost her too. She belongs to *me.*

And yet, here is a man riding a horse like some medieval knight. He has arranged for a whole group of men on horseback to comb the woods, to seek her out. The horses swish their tails, and fat green flies buzz and plunder in their wake. One horse lifts its tail and shits in a steaming pile. The other rears its head. They huff and grunt, their noses dripping snot on the dirt road. Everything smells like horseshit. My nose tickles and burns.

I walk toward Lieutenant Andrews, who is standing near the edge of the woods where the yellow tape is woven in and out of the trees like a ribbon in a child's hair, talking to a woman I assume is a neighbor. She is in her fifties, short, dressed in a powder-blue cardigan and a straight black skirt, wearing the kind of sensible black shoes you see on waitresses.

It becomes clear rather quickly that she's not a neighbor at all, rather some sort of psychic who has come from Burlington to try to help find the girl. *To commune with her spirit,* I overhear her say to Andrews.

Jesus Christ.

I have the inexplicable, childlike impulse to kick her in her shins, which are knotted with varicose veins. Yet Andrews listens, nods. It pisses me off that he is more attentive to her, less dismissive of her, this quack, than he was of me last night.

"Okay then, let's take a little walk. See what you pick up," Andrews says.

"I'm sorry," she says, pressing her palm against the air in front of her. "I need to be alone. Undistracted. If the area's contaminated, I won't be able to get a good read. There are too many people here." She is shaking her head.

I approach, ready to tell Andrews about the man in the truck, when the woman reaches out and touches my arm, startling me. I pull my arm away.

"Did you keep anything?" she asks.

"Excuse me?"

I don't know what she's talking about. For

a moment, I am confused and think of the jacaranda. I recall the purple petals, how I kept finding them later in my luggage, in my hair, their scent nauseating and pure all at once. How six months after we left Central America, when I came here to see Effie, to get as far away as I could from Guatemala, from Jake, the sight of fallen lilac petals nearly brought me to my knees.

Her oddly coiffed hair does not move when she tilts her head and studies me. Her glasses are smudged. Her black bangs are speckled with dandruff.

"From the little girl?" the woman insists. "Did she leave anything behind?"

I have no idea how she knows I was the one who found her, that she is mine. It renders me speechless, and I shake my head, *no, no.*

"I saw you on the news," she says, answering my unasked question.

Of course. How stupid of me.

She clutches a tattered hanky. And I wonder if this is some odd talisman she carries, or perhaps just some sort of prop. Then she sneezes loudly, violently into it, and I realize that it's neither. "Allergies," she explains.

"Lieutenant?" I say, shaking my head as if to clear it. "I was hoping I could talk to you for a minute?" I am trying to be polite, trying the honey-versus-vinegar approach with this particular fly.

"Sure, what is it?"

"Has anyone called in about her yet? Her mom and dad?" I ask.

He looks at me and shakes his head. "No MPR," he says.

Every time he speaks to me, he seems increasingly more leery and frustrated.

"We'll keep looking, but if a report of a missing kid doesn't come in soon, if we don't pick up on something, we're going to have to assume the report was false."

"False?"

"That you were mistaken, ma'am. About what you saw."

"I *saw* her," I say. "Jesus."

I look around for support. For someone to help me out. But Jake is in the car, nose buried in a manuscript.

"*They* believe me," I say, motioning to the crowd of people in the road, to the army of horses and neighbors and even to the psychic who is still blowing her nose. "If you give up on this, they'll be furious with you. With the entire police department."

"Or," he says. "They will be furious with *you*. Out-of-towner getting the locals upset with a false report." He is threatening me.

"I'm *from* here," I repeat. "I grew up here. This is my home too."

"Well," he says snidely. "Welcome home."

I look to the group of neighbors in the road as though they will rally behind me. As if I can summon them, evoke an uprising with a single glance. But they are strangers. They don't know me. To them I *am* just some flatlander. What they care about is the little girl. She is one of them, she belongs to *them* now.

I remember why I came then, but just as I'm about to tell him about the guy in the landscaping truck, the radio at his hip goes off.

Again, the muffled scratchy voices speak in code.

"Excuse me," he says before I get a chance to speak, and he walks away, leaving me with the psychic.

"I see water," she says, her eyes closed.

I roll my eyes. I see water too. There's a freaking lake right in front of us.

"There's so much red," she says ominously, eyes fluttering. And then her eyes shoot open wide. *"Underground."*

"I'm sorry," I say. "I need to go."

Andrews is sitting inside his cruiser now, speaking into his radio. I think about interrupting, tapping on his glass. But I can already imagine how pissed off he'd be at me for disturbing him. Better to stay on his good side. I'll just come back later. I'm pretty sure the guy in the truck didn't see anything anyway. She'd already slipped into the woods by the time he blew past me.

I walk back to the car. Jake has stopped reading the manuscript he brought with him and is thumbing through Charlie's file. He's got at least a half a dozen editors who are vying for Charlie's book. It could be the biggest deal he's made in his career. He barely notices as I get in the passenger side and sit down. My presence barely registers. Sometimes, lately, I feel like I am only a ghost.

Despite the crowd forming by the woods, the formal volunteer search has not begun yet. Devin has suggested all volunteers congregate at Hudson's at noon. There, in the back room, they will be fed donated sandwiches, outfitted with reflective vests, given maps of the area, and a description of the girl. *My* description of the girl.

Effie took Zu-Zu and Plum into town, ostensibly for Zu-Zu's ballet class, but I know she wants to keep them both away from the circus that is growing outside for as long as possible. Plum has already asked if they'll be allowed to search with us, but Effie offered her a playdate with her friend Maddy instead, and that seemed to distract her.

In town, Effie's going to pick up the food for the volunteers; the Shop 'n Save has offered to supply coffee and donuts, sandwiches and sodas. She's also picking up the reflective vests. I imagine they were originally made for hunting: to help differentiate the hunter from the animal. She asked if I needed anything from Quimby, but I couldn't think of what I would need now. What else exactly might be missing.

She also has to run her bookmobile route this afternoon: delivering books to the shut-ins and those who are unable to travel into town to the library. She thought maybe if I came with her, we could use the opportunity to canvas as well. Distribute flyers. Maybe somebody, somewhere, saw something.

Devin is already at Hudson's meeting with Billy Moffett, whose father has owned the store since we were kids. Effie and Billy used to sneak off to the woods together to make out when we were teenagers. Now he has a full beard and six kids. I wonder if she ever told Devin about him. It's incredible to me the things that one cannot know about another person. How easy it is to keep such large parts of one's life a secret. How readily we overlook entire portions of our loved ones' pasts. Dismiss those things that do not fit into our visions of them.

When Jake and I met, he'd just broken up with a long-time girlfriend. They'd dated in college, and started their lives together in New York. But while he'd gotten a job in publishing, she'd pursued a career in journalism and unexpectedly gotten an opportunity to be a foreign correspondent for a major cable news network. I see her on TV sometimes, reporting from Afghanistan, Iraq. She is so different from me physically: pale, diminutive, birdlike. She'd slept next to him for nearly seven years. They'd even been engaged briefly before she broke it off. Yet, we never talked about her. I didn't know her middle name, what she smelled like. What he loved about her. He must have felt deeply for her. But out of sight is out of mind. It is incredible to me how willing we are to forget. It makes me wonder how quickly I too might be forgotten, dismissed.

"So, what are we going to do if they don't find her by Sunday?" His voice startles me.

"What's that?" I say.

The car still smells sour.

"I just mean, we've got to get Zu-Zu down to the dorms on Sunday. She starts the program Monday morning."

I shake my head. The idea of going back to New York seems strange now, ludicrous.

"I don't know," I say. "We can't just leave. I mean, if they don't find her."

"Charlie's book is going to auction on *Monday.*"

I turn to him, look at his face, a face more

familiar to me than my own. For three weeks now I have been trying to imagine what she must think, feel, when she looks at him. How he might return her gaze. I have tried to remember what it was like to love him.

"Couldn't you handle it from here?" I ask. "If you needed to?"

He sighs. "Without cell reception?"

"Effie and Devin have a landline," I say, and know even as I say this how absurd the idea is. I think of the ancient wall-mounted phone, the curling cord. The rotary dial. I try to imagine him conducting a publishing auction in the kitchen nook as the world swirls around him.

"I need to be at the office," he says.

"Then go," I say. "Go home."

"Don't do that," he says.

"Don't do what?"

"That thing you do," he says, sighing. "It's passive-aggressive."

I feel a knot forming under my breastbone.

"How so?" I ask.

"You want me to stay. To say that this is more important than work. But instead of just coming out and saying that, you give me this false permission to leave. It's passive-aggressive."

"You don't need my *permission* to do

97

anything." I bristle.

He rolls his eyes then. Just a little. But he's not looking at me. He's looking at the road. And he's not speaking.

"I am not your keeper," I add. "Clearly."

We pull into the parking lot at Hudson's and leave the windows rolled down. The smell of the wine-soaked carpet is strong even without the floor mat. The wine must have seeped into the carpet beneath. I will need to have the car detailed when we get back to New York.

New York. It feels so far away now. A place I dreamed of once, instead of the place where I have lived the last fifteen years. Where I made and then abandoned a career. A place where I have friends, a routine, a life. I often feel this way when I come to visit Effie and Devin. The lake has that effect. When I wake to the sounds of the loons on the water, to the light filtered through the soft natural lens of leaves, I become an amnesiac. As if my entire life leading up to the moment has been a sort of waking dream (one of asphalt and hissing buses, of crowds and glass and concrete). There have been a hundred times that I have imagined staying here. Of never returning to Brooklyn. It would be so easy, I think, to buy a little house here, a plot of land. To find a job and start over. How simple it would be to just come *home.* As I told Andrews, I grew up here, though I don't have family here anymore. After my mother passed away, my father retired from the college and moved back to Maine, to the small island where he was raised. Still, I could stay here. I could come home. I could just slip back into this life. I think this happened to Effie too. Except instead of waking up, she just gave in to the pull this place has. Refused to wake up. I envy her this delicious acquiescence.

I am surprised to see that Hudson's parking lot is completely full. Cars also line the edge of the road for a quarter mile in either direction. I see the bookmobile parked around the side of the building. That means Effie is already back from town.

Jake's phone rings. He gets cell reception here.

He grabs the phone and glances down at the screen. "It's the office," he says. "I've got to get it. I'll meet you in there."

I wonder if it's her. Would she be that careless? That needy?

I take a deep breath and get out of the car.

A small group of women huddle at the doorway holding steaming cups of coffee and smoking cigarettes.

"What if it's like that Jaycee Dugard girl?" one woman says. "You know that one was livin' in the backyard of that house? With that monster all those years and nobody knew. I read her book."

"You mean like somebody's been *keeping* her?" another woman says. Her eyebrows are pencil thin and rise up high, making her look surprised.

"It could happen. Way out here in bumfuck nowhere. That man that took that Dugard girl got her pregnant twice. What if it's like that? Like one of them babies escaped. How else do you explain that there ain't nobody called her in missing? Maybe don't nobody know she exists."

"Or maybe she *don't* exist," the lady with the eyebrows says.

"Like she's a ghost?"

"Like maybe that lady, the one from New York, didn't really see nothing at all."

"*Excuse* me," I say, and, as I push past them, a look of recognition crosses the second woman's face. I can tell she's searching for words, smiling stupidly at me.

"Hey, wait," she says. "You're the one who found her. I saw you on the news."

I nod. What else am I supposed to say?

"We're here to help," she says. Nodding, smiling sadly. As if it's my own child that's lost. "We'll do whatever we can."

"Thanks," I say.

They part then and let me pass. I can hear their whispers behind me. I feel my skin grow hot, like I am in middle school again and these are the mean girls.

I enter the store and make my way through the crowd of people to the back room, where Effie and Devin are waiting for me. Effie offers me a sandwich: wheat bread, turkey, bland cheese. I eat it, because I know I should, but it barely registers on my tongue. She hands me a cup of coffee as well, but I refuse it. I am jittery enough already without more caffeine. Devin is distributing vests, flyers, and maps.

"Excuse me," Devin says loudly, standing up on an overturned milk crate, a makeshift platform. People stop talking, turn to him. It's incredible, despite how soft-spoken he is, how easily he commands attention.

"First, I want to thank Bill Moffett for offering up this space. And to the folks at the Shop 'n Save for generously donating lunch," he says. "What I need for you all to do now is to sign in. It's very important that everybody sign in so that we know exactly who is out there looking. We don't need to lose anybody while we're searching. When you finish for the day, please come back here and sign out. Effie's got vests and maps. If you are able to distribute flyers, please take some. We'll caravan back to the site in about a half hour. The police are already there. They'll explain to you exactly what you should do. Thank you again."

Devin returns to his spot behind the folding table where the stack of flyers and the sign-in sheet are.

"Where are the girls?" I ask Effie.

"Zu-Zu has a private lesson after her regular class, and Plum's at Maddy's. We can pick them up after we do my route. You still want to come with me, or do you want to go search with the others?"

"I'll go with you," I say.

She squeezes my hand. "You okay?"

I nod. But I am not okay. I ate the entire sandwich, but I still feel empty.

I go to the table and wait in line to sign in and grab a flyer. The tall guy in front of me turns around and smiles. His teeth are tobacco-stained, his gums red. His eyes are bulging, prominent, with fleshy pockets beneath them. He stares at me for several seconds too long. In New York I am accustomed to being ignored, to invisibility. His prolonged gaze makes my skin crawl.

"Sure is a shame," he says, still grinning. And when he speaks, I can smell the nicotine and stink of those rotten teeth in his breath. "Sounds like a sweet little thing." He grabs a flyer from the pile and hands it to me.

"Thank you," I say. He keeps grinning.

I walk away from him, clutching the flyer, but I can still feel his gaze on my back.

Missing, it says in a bold font. *Caucasian girl, approximately four years of age with brown curly hair. Last seen wearing a pink tutu and ladybug rain boots. Possibly injured. Seen along Lake Gormlaith Rd. at 11:30 P.M. on Thursday night. Please call 911 with any information you might have.*

The first photo of her that we receive from the agency is black-and-white. Blurry, pixelated. She is so small. Almost two years old, but stunted. She looks more like an infant than a toddler. Her eyes, though, are enormous. Pupils like a baby doll's. Light catching in them, like sunlight on dark water.

Child's Name: Esperanza Sophia
Child's Age: 22 months
Sex: F
Developmentally Handicapped: NO
Physically Handicapped: NO
Medical history: The child will visit the MD later this week. Blood work and medical report will be available soon.

"Esperanza," you say.

"Yes?"

"Her name means *hope*?" Your eyes widen with the implications of this: that the humility and yearning born from our bodies' failures is somehow, suddenly, manifest in a two-year-old child. This filthy, hungry girl. Her head likely infested with lice, one eye rheumy with infection, her limbs emaciated. This is how Hope materializes: as need. As hunger. Esperanza.

We are sitting at the coffee shop around the corner from our house, the place where they serve hot scones with raspberry jam. Coffee in mugs as heavy as stones.

"Does it matter?" I ask you.

You look confused.

"HIV," I say. They have told us there are no guarantees of her status.

You shake your head, but I sense hesitation.

"No," you say. "Of course, it doesn't matter."

But it makes me angry — that sliver of a moment, that fraction of time in which you paused. Your uncertainty, no matter how small, feels like an affront. Like a confirmation that your heart is not fully in this. That you are afraid, when I need you to be courageous. I do not ask for much. I have never asked for much. But this, I need.

I hang the flyer on our refrigerator, next to the collage of photos of Effie's girls. She is the same age as Plum. This is *two,* I think: *wide eyes, small hands.* Mine. Mine.

Effie's bookmobile route takes us around the entire lake as well as down each of the dirt roads that branch off the main road like spokes on a wheel.

When she first got the job, the bookmobile was simply a modified Ford Econoline van, but when the van finally died, the town raised funds to buy the new state-of-the-art bookmobile, commissioned a famous local artist to paint a mural on the body, and decked out the inside not only with shelves but comfortable seats as well. You could practically, happily, live in it.

Most of the people she delivers to are elderly. Shut-ins. They are the same people who get home deliveries from the Shop 'n Save, from Meals on Wheels, from the mobile clinic. Vermonters are headstrong people; many folks in their eighties and nineties here refuse to leave their homes for assisted living facilities, nursing homes. Effie's grandmother, Gussy, lived in her own home in Quimby until the day she died. She even chopped her own wood until well into her eighties.

There are others she delivers to as well: the families who have unreliable vehicles, those who simply wouldn't go to the library on their own. She visits the small schools that don't have their own libraries. Home day cares. Effie used to deliver books to a younger woman, a midwife, who was agoraphobic. After her little boy was killed in a car accident on the old covered bridge, she never left her property, a little house down by the river. Then Hurricane Irene came. Thankfully, her daughter managed to get her out of the house before the river swept it away.

Today we stop at a dozen houses, dropping off books and flyers, asking if anyone has seen the little girl, pleading with them to keep an eye out, to spread the word.

"*That* place is creepy," I say, pointing to a house set back from the road, obscured by trees. The house itself is fairly typical, a shoebox of a ranch house. But surrounding it are a half dozen rusted-out trailers, windows blocked with sheets of plywood. Weeds grow up around them, enclosing them, strangling them with their thorny vines. I think about the women back at Hudson's, about that poor kidnapped girl they were talking about, the one who'd been kept in that guy's backyard for eighteen years.

"Who lives there?" I ask.

"I don't really know," she says, shrugging. "It's not on my route."

"Should we try to deliver a flyer?" I ask.

She gestures to the BEWARE OF DOG signs stapled to the trees. The NO TRESPASSING signs duct-taped to the trailers that face the road. She looks at me, grimaces a little. "Do *you* want to go in there?"

She slows the bookmobile, and I peer through the trees, struggle to see if there are any vehicles in the driveway. But the gravel path leading to the garage is empty.

"Doesn't look like anybody's home," I say, and I can practically hear Effie's relief.

"I've just got one stop left," she says, pulling off the road and onto a long drive. She parks next to a beat-up black Honda.

As we get out of the car and walk toward the house, my stomach flip-flops.

The yard is littered with toys: ride-on toys, a plastic toddler's playhouse, baby dolls, and toy guns. It looks like there has been an explosion, the way these filthy artifacts of childhood are scattered. You can hear the

109

sound of the children through the closed door as Effie and I walk up the cracked sidewalk, sidestepping plastic bats and mud-splattered bouncy balls. Naked Barbies missing limbs and heads.

Effie knocks on the door, turns to me, and smiles.

"They must be eating lunch. Usually the kids hear me coming."

A woman answers the door, looking frazzled and confused. There is a baby in a diaper on her hip. The baby leans against her chest, twirling its finger through a blond curl. The woman is probably younger than she seems, but her face is long, drawn. She's wearing a Metallica T-shirt and jeans. She is barefoot.

"Oh, wait, is today Friday?" she asks.

Effie smiles. "It is. Are the kids eating lunch?" she asks, leaning forward and peering into the house.

"Just finishing up," she says.

"Listen," Effie says, reaching for a flyer from the stack she's got under her arm. "You probably heard this on the news, but there was a little girl found wandering alone in the road here last night. She ran off into the woods though."

The woman takes the flyer and nods. "I saw it on the news this morning. I could hear the helicopters last night. Really scary. They said nobody's reported anybody missing though? Seems kinda fishy to me. Like some kinda hoax."

I bristle.

Effie persists. "Does she sound familiar at all? Do you have any kids who fit this description?"

The woman studies the flyer. "Sounds like half the kids I take care of," she says. "The girls anyway. Wearing dress up clothes and boots. I got one girl who wears a tiara and pink cowboy boots every day. But no. None of 'em with curly hair."

I look at the baby in her arms, at its mane of curls.

"Oh," she says. " 'Cept for Stevie here."

"You do drop-ins sometimes, right?" Effie asks.

I have no idea what this means.

"Every now and again."

"Have you had any new kids come in lately?"

She shakes her head. "No, nobody I don't know anyway."

"Is that the Book Lady?" a voice trills behind her. And then there is a stampede of little kids, all scrambling to get out of the doorway to the bookmobile, whose back doors are wide open, beckoning. I back up to make way as they push past. I study each one, as though she will be among them. As if she might just emerge as she did last night, in her tattered tutu and rain boots.

"I should go to the van," Effie says to me. "So they can check books out."

I nod. "Okay. I can help."

The woman says, "I got the ones to return in the other room. I'll bring 'em out as soon as I get Stevie down for his nap."

She slips into the house, but leaves the door to the kitchen open.

Effie follows the group of children to the bookmobile, but I hang back. I peer into the kitchen, see the table littered with breakfast dishes. Bowls filled with colored milk, sippy cups of juice. A cat comes to me and cries, winds itself around my legs.

"Well, hello," I say. I squat down to pet him. He arches his back, pushes his head hard into my thigh, and then starts back into the house.

And then I see them. Ladybug rain boots on the mat just inside the door. They are in a tangle of tiny sneakers and sandals. I didn't notice them before when I was standing. My heart pounds in my chest as I gesture in disbelief at the tiny boot. I reach into the house and pick it up.

The woman comes back then, without the

baby this time. Hands on her hips, she studies me.

"This is her boot," I say, looking up at her.

"What's that?"

"Her rain boot," I say. I stand up, still clutching the boot. "The little girl. The flyer. This is what she was wearing last night."

The woman shakes her head, smiles. And my jaw falls open.

"This is *her boot,*" I say again, feeling my eyes sting with tears now.

"Then she's a four-year-old with the biggest feet I've ever seen," the woman says, laughing. "Those are my niece's. She's ten." And then I see the same look pass across her face that passed across the deputy's face last night.

My head pounds and I nod, muttering apologies as I back out the door.

We get into the bookmobile after the children have all picked out their books. They stand on the porch of the house, clutching their colorful selections to their chests, waving at Effie, who leans out her open window and blows kisses to them. It makes me think of a video I saw on YouTube not that long ago of a missionary leaving an African village. As his helicopter lifted off, the children shielded their eyes from the sun and peered up at him waving, jumping. It's as if Effie connects them to some distant civilization.

"That was the last stop," she says. "How many flyers do you think we distributed?"

I look at the stack on the seat.

"A lot," I say. "Maybe forty or fifty? Should we make some more copies?"

"Sure. I'll make some more. I need to get the bookmobile back to the library and grab the girls from in town. Do you want to come with me, or should I drop you off at Hudson's?" Effie slows the van and looks at me.

I am staring at the flyer, at the words that have distilled the little girl down into parts. Like she's a little puzzle made of interlocking pieces.

"You okay?" she asks.

I look up at her. She's the closest thing I have to a sister. She will know if I am lying.

"What's going on?" Effie asks, reaching for my hand. "I mean, other than this."

"He's sleeping with a girl at work," I say. Though this is not what is going on in my mind at all. This is not what is making my skin crawl, making my heart race and my head pound.

Effie takes a deep breath and looks at the road again. Her eyes well up with tears.

It takes me aback. This is not what I

expected. I expected her to get angry. To say, *What the fuck? That asshole.*

But instead, there are tears in her eyes.

And something about seeing her crying, about how completely blindsided I am by her response, makes me want to cry too. She scoots across the seat, and puts her arms around me. I feel my body tremble and then the tears come. It feels like a dam has broken. And for some reason I think of that woman Effie told me about. The woman whose house was swept away in the raging river during the hurricane. I worry that if I'm not careful, I might be carried away as well. That I might just get caught up in this awful current. That I could drown.

And so I pull back, wave my hands in front of my face, swatting away the tears.

"It's fine," I say. As if words are enough to make that true. But it's not fine. None of this is fine.

"What are you going to do?" she asks. "Are you going to leave him?"

It feels like someone has just sat on my chest. All of the air goes out of me.

Jake and I have been together for almost twenty years. I barely remember who I was before I met him. In the last three weeks I have imagined a thousand scenarios about how all of this would play out, but in none

115

of them did I imagine *me* leaving *him.* Where would I go? I'm afraid I don't remember who I am outside of this anymore, outside of *us.*

"God damn it," she says then, wiping at her own tears with the back of her hand. And then she shakes her head, and gives me exactly what I need. "What the fuck, Tess? What an asshole. How did you find out? Did he tell you?"

And I am so grateful for this, I feel myself starting to cry again.

We go together into town. I am not ready to deal with Jake and the police and the media again yet. I just want to see the girls, to go get ice cream with Zu-Zu and Plum. To sit at a picnic table and ask them about their lives. I think about the rain boots, about my mistake. How could I have thought a ten-year-old's boots belonged to a toddler? I want to study Plum, to know what *ten* looks like.

Watching her grow up has been agonizing. Because of the girls, maintaining my friendship with Effie has demanded more from me than I knew I had. We had dreams, she and I. About our children, about watching them grow up together. I came here, not long after we received the referral from the adoption agency, proudly clutching the photo just as Effie had held on to the sonograms of her daughters. How was this different? It's all dreaming then, isn't it? It's all imagining until it's not anymore.

We sat at the kitchen nook, and I unfolded the photo, pressed the worn creases flat with my fingers. We studied her, peered into her face, dreamed what her skin would look like. Zu-Zu was five at the time, but Plum was two. The same age as Esperanza. A living, breathing *two*.

We would have shared everything, we promised. At exactly the same age, they would have been like sisters. They would have learned to ride a bike at the same time, how to tie their shoes, how to read. We would have taken them swimming in the lake with plastic floaties on their arms. They would have learned to climb the ladder to the tree house together, scurrying tentatively behind Zu-Zu, who would have loved Esperanza like a little sister. She might have held her hand. I thought about when they were older, when Plum would come to visit us in New York. How I would buy them matching dresses and take them to the Met to see the ballet. Effie and I joked that they would be Country Mouse and City Mouse. Esperanza would teach Plum how to ride the subway, the trick of the turnstile. She would teach her how to hail a cab and how to sleep in the sticky heat of our house, with the sounds of sirens and honking horns outside the window. She and Plum would grow up together the way Effie and I had.

But then, one day I woke from the dream. And Plum became a ghost to me, the remembrance of what was lost. Of what should have been.

We go to pick up Zu-Zu first. She takes ballet lessons at the same place where my mother sent me when I was little: Miss Gracie's Dance Studio. Miss Gracie had little patience for me and my flailing limbs though; I didn't make it through even the first year. This is where Effie's sister, Colette, learned to dance as well. It's a little converted garage off of Gracie's house. Gracie's oldest daughter, Sara, has taken over the studio now. Sara worked as a professional dancer for many years before coming home to help her mother.

We stand at the window and watch as Sara adjusts Zu-Zu's hips, gently turns her heel forward, her knee out. Taps her butt and then her stomach. Holds Zu-Zu's head and tilts it a fraction of an inch. Sara motions for her to go to the center of the floor and searches for the music on her iPad. And then Zu-Zu is dancing the variation she's been working on: the Lilac Fairy from *Sleeping Beauty.*

She is thirteen years old, but her entire body seems to have a wisdom that far exceeds those years. Every muscle is informed by the music. I shake my head. She is not only perfect, flawless, and precise, but there is also such tender emotion imbued in every gesture, though it is nuanced. Controlled. If her movements were words, I'd describe them as *articulate,* but the prose of her limbs and spine are also, somehow, luminous.

I turn to Effie and watch her watching her daughter. There is a moment when I realize that Effie doesn't even remember that I'm here; she is so focused on this beauty before her. And it isn't pride exactly that I see, but wonder.

She turns to me, refocusing. As though she's just woken up.

I shake my head. "I had no idea," I say.

She shakes her head as well in disbelief.

"I *have* to let her go, don't I?" she asks.

I nod. And then I remember why we are here. Jake and I have come to visit and then to bring Zu-Zu with us to New York. To deliver her to the teachers who will take this talent that is somehow both raw and refined and shape it further. We are going back to New York. Back to our house in Prospect Heights. Jake is going to go back to his job.

120

Back to our lives.

It feels far away now. So much has happened since I found the texts, since we loaded up the trunk with our suitcases and the treats for Effie and Devin's girls. Since we drove in silence for three hundred miles. Since we sat outside under the twinkling lights strung in the trees, drinking wine, pretending nothing had changed when, in fact, nothing was the same. Between the time before the girl wandered out of the woods and disappeared back into them.

What do we do now? How do we go on? It seems like my entire life has been a series of these strange moments, which have changed the entire trajectory of my life. A pinball in a machine, trying so hard to simply get from one place to the next, but at the mercy of the flippers and spinners and slingshots.

Zu-Zu finishes the variation and then notices us in the window. She smiles, sweat beading up on her hairline. She motions for us to come in. Sara sees us and smiles as well, turns off the music, and opens the door.

While Effie and Sara chat, Zu-Zu flops down on the floor to remove her pointe shoes. She slips them off and tosses them into her dance bag. She peels off her filthy toe pads, and wiggles her damaged toes at me.

"Aren't my feet pretty?" And she is thirteen again.

I smile. "That is disgusting," I say.

Her feet in the shoes were beautiful, but now they look disfigured. Damaged. Boney-looking bunions, and pulsing veins. Her toes are callused and blistered. The nails cut short and one toe caked with dried blood.

"I'll see you in September," Sara says, hugging her. "Remember, don't be afraid of the Russian teachers. They just *seem* scary. Text me some pictures. And have fun."

And then we are in the bookmobile again, all piled into the front seat.

"Did they find her yet?" Zu-Zu asks, leaning her head against my shoulder as we pull out of the small parking lot. I turn and kiss her forehead. Her skin is salty.

"No," I say.

"She must be really scared," she says.

She is old enough to understand all of the terrible things that could happen to the girl, and I can only imagine what she is thinking as she gazes out the window as we drive to the library.

We drop off the bookmobile, get Effie's car, and go to pick up Plum at her friend

Maddy's. They've been playing in the sprinkler. She is wet and muddy when she throws her whole body around me.

"Can we please get ice cream?"

And I am grateful she isn't thinking about the little girl. That she is so easily distracted.

Back at Gormlaith, I have Effie leave me at the search site. "I can drop off the girls at home and come back here," Effie says.

"No," I say, turning and smiling at Plum, who has fallen asleep in the backseat of Effie's car. She leans against Zu-Zu's shoulder. Zu-Zu looks out the window, studies the yellow tape.

"Stay with them. It looks like Devin's still here." I motion to his truck, which is parked down the road. "I'll get a ride back with him and Jake."

There are only two police cruisers now. The news vans are still here though. A Fish and Game guy sitting in his truck. A fire truck and a half dozen cars I assume belong to the volunteers are parked on the edges of the road. I can hear the distant sound of leaves crushing under their feet, imagine them traipsing through the forest, looking under rocks, inside hollowed trees. The officer who spoke to the volunteers said that the search should start within a small perimeter and slowly grow wider. Imagine a pebble thrown in the water, he'd said. Start with the small circle and then span out in ripples.

I get out of Effie's car and stand in the road, aimless. The air is swarming with black flies. I swat them away, wish I'd worn spray. I remember noticing a rusty can of Off! on the windowsill in the guest cottage.

Effie leans out of her open window. "You sure you don't want to come back with us? We could go for a swim. Cool off a little? It keeps the black flies away anyway."

"I'm making brownies!" Zu-Zu says.

I go to the passenger side, and she rolls down her window.

"I'll see you back at home in just a little bit," I say. "Will you save me a corner piece?"

Zu-Zu nods. I can see her eyes are glassy with tears.

"Do you think they'll find her?" she asks.

I nod.

"What if they don't?" Plum says sleepily, rubbing her eyes. Yawning.

My chest constricts. "We'll all keep looking until we do. I promise."

■ ■ ■ ■

This time, when I scramble down the embankment I am careful not to step into the little creek. No one seems to notice me as I slip into the woods. I follow what I think I remember as the path I took through the trees last night.

It's like I am now in a different place entirely though. And I wonder if I am somehow mistaken. Maybe this is *not* the spot at all. I look at the moss-covered log and can't recall seeing it before. The area I stand in is not at all familiar. Even the strong smell of the woods seems different than it did last night. Was it really here?

I close my eyes and try to visualize where I would go if I were a scared little girl. Where would I run? I try to imagine being four and terrified, alone. And something about this very act of imagining makes my heart begin to race. I feel sick. I wonder if this is some delayed nausea from the wine last night, my body only now remembering it ought to be hungover.

I come to a small clearing where it looks like someone has recently had a campfire. There is a clumsy circle of rocks, the charred remains of a couple of logs in the center.

126

Beer cans, cigarette butts. The air smells charred, feels charged. I don't know which is worse: thinking that she is alone out here in the woods or that she isn't.

Panic informs every muscle of my body, and I feel like I might pass out. I sit down on the ground, feel the dampness from the needles and leaves seeping through the fabric of my shorts.

I put my head in my hands, feel my blood pulsing in my temples.

Then I see something on the ground, obscured by pine needles. Orange tip, plastic cylinder. I kick at it, uncovering it, and suck in my breath.

It's a *syringe.* What the fuck?

And for one confused moment, I think of the needles. Of Jake, of that old futile ritual. But then I realize how absurd this is.

I look around, as though whomever it belongs to might still be there. But I am surrounded by trees. Jesus Christ. I've seen discarded needles in New York, but here? What is wrong with people? I try to figure out how to pick it up, to dispose of it, without pricking myself. I think about the girl again, wandering around out here. Could whoever left it here have seen her?

Then, as I bend over to pick it up, something touches my shoulder.

"Jesus!" I say, sitting up, pressing my hand against my chest.

It's the psychic.

"You okay?" she asks softly.

I nod, gesture at the syringe on the ground. "Nice, huh?"

"Shit," she says, then rolls her eyes and shakes her head. She sits down on the moss-covered log next to me and stretches out her stubby legs.

I swat at a mosquito that buzzes near my ankle.

She reaches into a fanny pack she's wearing and hands me something that looks like ChapStick. "It's citronella oil and lavender. Put this on your wrists, and the bugs will leave you alone," she says.

I do as she says and hand it back to her. She smells powdery. Like church, I think strangely.

"So have you, um . . ." I start, not having the vocabulary for this. "*Seen* anything? Like visions or whatever?"

She smiles. "It doesn't really work like that."

"Then how *does* it work?"

She tilts her head, as if she is deciding whether or not she can trust me. I smile weakly. A poor assurance.

"I'm mostly an empath," she says. Her

voice is deep, somber. "Which means that I am able to sense both the missing person's emotions and bodily states. But I am also a psychometrist."

"What's *that*?" I ask.

"*That*'s why I asked if you kept anything from her. I can gather information from objects. Things in the physical world. They can lead me to the person they belonged to."

I think of the sweater I left by the road. The tutu and boots. But there is nothing. I have nothing.

"So if you don't have an object, then how do you find her?"

"Have you ever had déjà vu?" she asks.

I nod. "Sure."

"It's like that. Like a sensation. A vague feeling, but also sort of specific. Like trying to remember a dream."

"How does that help anybody?" I ask.

"Well, dreams slip away; they get fuzzier and fuzzier the more you wake up. I've taught myself how to stay in that dream state long enough to hold on. To remember."

"Have you *remembered* anything then?" I ask.

"A little. I see red, and water. I have the feeling of something being underground. But there's a word I keep hearing too.

Sharp."

"What does that mean?" And I think of the cut on her hand. The blood. The red could be blood?

"I don't know. It's confusing. I also feel hunger and fear. I think she's very afraid."

My eyes sting. This woman is a crackpot, but she's all I've got.

"Then you think she's alive?" I ask.

"Yes," she says, and stands up, brushes the leaves from her ample bottom.

"What are we supposed to do?" I ask, choking back tears now, feeling gullible and stupid.

She shakes her head. "I guess just keep looking," she says, bending over and gingerly picking up the syringe, which she seals inside her fanny pack.

We leave the woods together, make our way through the trees. Strickland is standing at the edge of the tree line, as if he's been waiting for us.

"There's a campsite," I say, a little breathless. "In the woods. Somebody's been out there. We found beer cans . . ."

"Yeah, lots of teenagers party in the woods here. No place else for them to go."

"We found a *syringe,*" I say.

His eyebrow rises nearly imperceptibly, but then he just shrugs. "Drug of choice

130

these days," he says. "Listen, the lieutenant needs to speak with you."

When we fully emerge from the woods, I sense right away that something is very, very wrong.

Then I realize what it is. It's the *silence.* The helicopter has disappeared. The constant whir and buzz that I have grown oddly accustomed to since last night is gone, and the absence of sound feels like a hole. As I strain to hear, I realize that the wild sound of the dogs, the jangling of their tags, their insistent breath, has also faded.

I feel anxious, panicked. My entire body is filled with a new, horrific fear.

Even before I see Lieutenant Andrews motioning for me to join him at the edge of the road, I know what has happened.

"Where is the helicopter?" I ask. "The dogs?"

"We're scaling back the search, ma'am," he says.

"What does that mean?" I say, and my voice sounds foreign to me, strange. Almost childlike. "You're not looking for her anymore? It hasn't even been twenty-four hours."

"I didn't say that, ma'am," he says, and smiles condescendingly. "I said we are *scaling back* the search. We've still got officers

131

out. We've got divers scheduled at the lake tomorrow. But if I'm going to be honest with you, the story just doesn't hold water."

Water. I think of the psychic. At least *she* believes me.

"How so?" I say.

"Any trouble going on with you at home?" the lieutenant asks.

My eyes widen. I think of her, *Jess,* of her voice on the other end of the line. I shake my head. And I wonder if the lieutenant is some sort of *empath* too. "What the hell do you mean by that?"

"I've been a cop for a long time," he says. "I've seen just about everything there is to see."

I have to resist rolling my eyes. This is *Vermont.* He's acting like he's some jaded cop from Detroit, Chicago. I have watched the nightly news here. Read the papers. Just last night the headline was TRACTOR TRAILER STRIKES DEER ON I-89.

He continues. "And believe it or not, this isn't the first time I've been sent on a wild goose chase."

I am using every bit of self-control I have not to tear my hair out. Or his.

"Most of the time, it's because something's going on at home. It's a cry for help. I had a woman who faked her own kidnapping. Turns out her husband was about to leave her, and she figured her getting kidnapped might make him stick around."

"Did he?" I seethe.

"Long enough to help get her admitted to Waterbury," he says. *The state mental institution.*

Something about this feels like a threat.

"This has nothing to do with me," I say.

Again, that patronizing smile. "Ms. Waters, please consider what we have. No kid reported missing. No evidence found at the site. No witnesses." He ticks each item off with his thick fingers and then curls those fingers into a zero. "We've got nothing."

"Wait," I say, feeling my heart throbbing in my temples. "There might be another witness. There was a truck, a white pickup truck with Massachusetts plates that passed me right after I saw her."

"And you're just now remembering this?" he asks.

"No," I say. "I came to tell you earlier but you were on your radio."

He sighs, rubs his face with his hands. I can see the shadow of a beard. He probably wants nothing more than to go home and shower and shave.

"I remember, because I thought it was strange that a car with out-of-state tags

133

would have landscaping equipment in the back. I saw the guy at Hudson's earlier when I stopped. He had overalls on and long hair. My friend, Devin, the one who lives here, said maybe it's somebody with a camp at the lake. Maybe he was getting it ready for the summer."

"So he was inside the store?"

"Yes," I insist. "You can ask the kid who was working last night. I think it's Billy Moffett's son. Check the register tape. He bought forty dollars' worth of gas and a twelve-pack of Bud longnecks. And when he drove past me, he was headed toward the lake, not away from it. So he wasn't headed out of town."

He sighs again. It's as if he's been waiting for my permission for him to call off the search. My confession that I made it all up. But like a child caught up in a lie, I keep insisting that it's the truth.

"Please," I say. "I'm not doing this for attention. I'm not *insane."* The word makes me stiffen, and I hope he can't see the way my entire body reacts to it.

That night, Jake goes to the cabin not long after dinner, says he needs to prep for the auction, though I know he's been over all of the editors' most recent acquisitions. He's ready, but I don't argue. Instead I stay with Effie and the girls in the camp. Devin disappears upstairs to read, leaving us alone.

We play a game of Clue, but Zu-Zu and Plum are bickering. Plum doesn't get the deductive reasoning aspect of the game, and Zu-Zu's patience is thin.

"I want to make an accusation!" Plum says gleefully, clapping her hands together. "Miss Scarlet, in the library, with the revolver."

"You already know it didn't happen in the library," Zu-Zu says, exasperated. "Remember? I showed you the library card the last time."

"You don't know everything, you know," Plum says, pure sass.

135

"I know it didn't happen in the *library.*"

"Stop," Effie says, rubbing her temples. "One day without fighting. That's all I ask."

"Well, I'll be gone soon, and then there will be nobody for her to fight with," Zu-Zu says dramatically, crossing her arms.

"Good," Plum says. "Because you're mean."

"Whatever, Plum."

"Seriously, stop," Effie says. "We've got company."

"I'm not playing anymore," Plum says then, and slips under the table. I can feel her at my feet. I reach under the table, fingers poised to tickle.

"Get out from under the table, Plum," Zu-Zu says, the little mama. "Don't be such a baby."

"I'm not a baby," Plum starts, and then there is a hard knock under the table, a brief moment of silence, and then wailing.

Effie sighs heavily and then ducks under the table. Plum crawls out, crying and clutching the top of her head. Plum crawls up into Effie's lap and Effie studies the spot on her head. Kisses it.

"I need to pack," Zu-Zu says, rolling her eyes. "Are we still leaving on Sunday? I mean, now that all this stuff is happening?"

She's asking me, but I look to Effie for help.

"We'll make sure you get to New York on time," Effie says.

"But what about that little girl?" Plum asks. Her eyes are red, her cheeks streaked with tears.

"People are looking for her. She's probably just found a safe warm place to hide," I offer.

"Who does she belong to anyway?" Plum asks.

"We don't know yet, punkin'," Effie says, and buries her face in Plum's hair. Something about this makes my chest hurt. "She's probably just lost."

"Well, if I was ever lost in the woods, I'd stay in the same place. That way you could find me. Or I'd use my echo."

"You don't use an echo," Zu-Zu corrects. "Your voice *makes* an echo."

"Mom, she's doing it again."

"Stop correcting," Effie says.

"Where are the tights you ordered?" Zu-Zu asks.

"Upstairs, with the pointe shoes and slippers."

Zu-Zu stands up and starts to head upstairs but then stops, goes to the freezer, and pulls out a bag of frozen raspberries.

She brings them over to Plum and gently rests them on her head before skipping into the living room and then up the stairs.

After the girls have gone to bed, Effie and I sit outside in two Adirondack chairs facing the lake. My feet are bare and the grass is cold, but I don't want to hunt for my shoes.

"You have good girls," I say.

Effie nods. "Thank you. I need to be reminded of that every now and again."

"Sometimes, I wonder how things would be different . . ." I say. I don't even need to finish my sentence, because she knows exactly what I am thinking about. This is the same conversation we've been having for eight years. "Maybe if we had a child, if we were a real family, then Jake wouldn't have done this." This is what I have to think, because the alternative is even worse. What if we had a child and he did this anyway? What if his selfishness, his lack of regard, extends beyond me? What if he is capable of hurting everyone?

"How did you find out?" Effie asks quietly, pulling the comb that holds her hair up and letting it tumble down.

I take a sip of beer from the bottles she brought out for us. It's bitter, but the only thing that seems to be taking the edge off.

The sharp edge that seems to border everything now.

"Texts," I say. "A whole string of them. He didn't even bother to delete them." But this is not how I know. I think now that I knew long before the note. I sensed it, the way you can smell rain before it comes. I felt it in my skin, smelled it in the charged air between us.

"Who is she?" she asks. "Anyone you know?"

I shake my head, and wonder if I have met her. I'm sure I have, though all of the assistants blur together. They all have the same hungry eyes, the same eager smiles. They share the collective longing, the marvelous ache of ambition and youth.

"I'm going to stay here," I say.

She turns to me, her eyes widening. She thinks I mean forever. "Of course you'll stay here. Stay as long as you like. We'll figure out what to do."

"No," I say, smiling. "I mean, yes. But I just mean until they find the girl. I know Jake is going to say he has to go back to New York. But I can't go. Not until they find her."

Effie reaches out for my hand, and I let her take it.

The sky is filled with stars. I look up, feel

dizzy. Disoriented.

"I still dream about her," I say. "The same dream. I must have had it a thousand times."

And Effie knows exactly what I mean now too. I don't have to explain. This is friendship, I think. This is sisterhood.

The first part is real.

I am alone in Guatemala City, staying in that roach-infested hotel: the one with the elevator that terrifies me, with its ancient accordion gate and sticky floors that smell of piss. I have been here for almost a month already. You will come later, though as the days go by, I begin to wonder if this is true. There is always something keeping you. And you are beginning to feel so very far away.

Each morning I sit on the small balcony, which looks out over a terracotta colored courtyard, eating plantains and black beans, fresh cheese and eggs. Drinking the strong Guatemalan coffee. I have acclimated. To this food. To this climate. To this world that does not belong to me.

Please come, I say at night into the phone that tenuously connects me to you. But there is always a new client, a new contract, another conference. Work, work, work.

141

From my hotel room, I speak with the Guatemalan attorney nearly every day, with the agency, though neither one has anything new to offer me. We have done everything we can do on our end: the home studies, the interviews. We have paid the dossier fees, been fingerprinted, had everything, our entire lives it seems, notarized. There is nothing left to do, they say, except to wait.

"When can I see her?" I ask them. I was told that up to six weeks prior to the finalization, I would be able to visit her in the orphanage. That if we "establish rapport" she can come home with us on a 1-9 visa. I am waiting for the call that tells me it is time.

After breakfast, I wander the streets of Zona 10, careful to stay within the safety of this neighborhood. I carry the photos that we have received once a month for the last five months. I study them, looking for clues. Already, she is changing. Growing. I worry that the clothes I have brought her (those tiny dresses and leggings I worried over in store after store) will be too small. In the marketplace, I buy more clothes, starched white cotton dresses with colorful, embroidered flowers.

My hotel is ten blocks away from the orphanage, but I take a different route. The one time I walked by, I heard the infants crying and I fell instantly ill. I had to slip into a little café.

"Baño?" I pleaded, and a group of old men at the bar snickered as I rushed past them to the filthy bathroom where my bowels emptied in a watery rush. I couldn't get out of bed for three days, and my fevered dreams were all accompanied by the soundtrack of wailing babies.

And then the call comes.

"Ms. Waters?"

"Sí?"

"You come visit Esperanza today. Ten o'clock."

I search through the pile of trinkets I have bought as I wandered the streets. The colorful tiny bracelets, the little dolls and tiny shoes. I search frantically through the bags in the closet. Finally, I find the toy dog, the impossibly soft and tiny animal I bought after three hours at FAO Schwarz one blustery afternoon last winter.

I study the most recent photo. Will I know her?

At 9:59, I push the buzzer as the church bell across the street rings out the hour.

A tiny woman opens the door and ushers me in.

I follow her soundlessly through the dark corridors. It is remarkably quiet here, and I wonder if I only imagined the keening.

We come to a door that opens to a small,

enclosed courtyard, and I see her.

She is sitting on the ground, legs splayed out in front of her. She is playing with one of those plastic cones with the stackable color rings. I had one as a child. Such a strangely American thing. The yellow one encircles her small wrist, and she is chewing on the red one. I clutch the stuffed dog tightly.

I look to the woman to confirm that this is her, though it is only a formality. It is her. This is Esperanza.

When she sees me, I feel my entire body hollow out as though making room for her. And when she holds her arms out to me, waiting for me to lift her up, I feel like I might faint.

Her legs wrap tightly around my waist, and I bury my nose in her thick, dark hair. The tears falling from my eyes make her hair wet. She buries her face in my chest, and I can feel her heart beating through her delicate rib cage. Esperanza. My daughter.

But this is where the dream defies the truth. Denies the truth.

In the dream, I walk with her, back through that dark corridor, her body clinging to mine. I give her the tiny stuffed dog and she clutches it. In the dream I sing the lullaby I have memorized: *"A la roro niño, a lo roro ya, duérmete mi niño, duérmete mi amor."* Lullaby baby, lullaby now, sleep my baby, sleep my love. And I walk with her out that heavy door into the blinding sunlight of the afternoon. And together we stare up Into the canopy made by the jacarandas, into a purple sky.

Mama, she whispers in the dream. *Bella mama.*

On Saturday morning, I wake long before Jake does, which is rare. He is usually the first to rise; his alarm goes off at least an hour before I finally pull myself out of bed. But here, in these woods, I wake with the dawn that spills softly through the pale curtains. I feel energized. Purposeful.

I climb out of bed quietly, careful not to wake him. If he does wake up, he feigns sleep, and I am grateful not to have to make conversation. I pull on a sweater and slip on my sneakers and make my way up the pathway to the camp, the wet grass tickling my ankles. The birdsong is cacophonous, louder than the morning sounds of the city even. There's an odd peace in New York on a Saturday morning. A hush and lull that has always seemed suspect to me. Like the whole city is keeping a secret.

Instead of going to the camp, I make my way quietly across the long expanse of green lawn toward the lake. The sun has yet to burn through the hazy mist, and it encloses me as I make my way down the dock that wasn't here when Effie and I were kids. I walk all the way out to the edge, and it could be the edge of the universe.

But still, through the haze and fog, I hear voices, a humming motor. And as the fog slips and shifts across the water, I can see the boat. It says STATE POLICE on the side, and there are two men in vests on the boat. Swimming next to them are three divers, their backs laden with oxygen tanks. They bob in the water like bath toys.

Please don't find anything, I say. I pray.

I feel the dock shifting underneath me, and turn around as I hear heavy footsteps. It's Devin, holding two steaming mugs of coffee.

"Hey," I say, smiling and accepting the mug he holds out to me.

"Want some company?" he asks.

"Sure," I say, and scoot over to make room for him next to me.

He lowers himself down and peers out at the boat, at the divers. His sister drowned in this lake twenty years ago. She'd come here for the summer as part of the Fresh Air program. This must be excruciating for him to watch.

147

"How old was she?" I ask. "Keisha?"

"Eleven," he says, smiling sadly. "Just a little older than Plum is now."

Silently we watch together as the boat moves slowly across the water. Listen to the muted sounds of the radios. An egret perches on a rock at the shore, observing.

"Effie says you want to stay here," he says. "If they don't find her by tomorrow."

I nod.

"I'd be happy to drive Zu-Zu down with Jake," he says. "That way you can still have your car here. He won't need it in the city, right?"

I turn to him, my eyes filling with tears. I don't know what Effie has told him.

"Are you sure?" I ask.

"Absolutely. It's a good opportunity to do some face time with the folks at Gagosian anyway. See my family too. It's been a while since I've been in the city. And as much as Zu-Zu insists otherwise, I have a feeling she'll be happy to have me there."

"Thank you," I say.

"Of course."

We sit together until the coffee is gone, and the boat continues its slow trawl, its agonizing, though thankfully futile, crawl.

"I'm heading down to Hudson's in about an hour. Do you want to come with me? I

148

think we're going to get a lot more people searching now that the weekend's here," Devin says, standing up. The entire dock rocks with his movement.

"Yes," I say. "I want to come today too."

At Hudson's Devin organizes the crowd of volunteers into groups of five, distributes vests, and repeats the instructions. I am grouped with two men and two women. One of the women looks really familiar to me, but I can't place my finger on why. I rack my brain trying to think where I've seen her before. The Miss Quimby Diner? The bank in town?

"Tess?" she says softly. "Tess Mahoney?"

My maiden name.

I study her face again. So strangely familiar.

"It's Rose," she says. "Rose Lund. *Mrs. Lund?*"

Oh my God. She's my sixth-grade English teacher. Mrs. Lund. I adored her. She used to give me books, picking out ones she thought I would like.

"Oh my God," I say. "Wow." I embrace her, transformed into an eleven-year-old girl again. I used to stay in from recess, and we'd talk about books together. When I was eleven I loved her more than almost anyone else. And now, hugging her, I am transported. I am a child again.

"I heard on the news that you were the one who found her," she says. "You here visiting Effie?"

I nod. Effie and I had been in the same class together.

"I can't tell you how happy it makes me what each of you girls have done. Effie and all the good work she does at the library. And you, you fancy editor in New York."

I don't tell her that the only editing I do now is freelance copyediting. That I am a glorified mechanic, fixing all the broken sentences. She had gripped my hand once and told me that I would make a difference in the world.

"It's so good to see you," I say. "But I wish it weren't for this."

She scowls. "I know."

I go outside to get some air before we head back to the site to search. Outside the store, there's a man smoking a cigarette. I cough as I walk through the cloud of smoke he is generating.

"Mornin', neighbor," he says. It's the man who was here yesterday, the one ahead of me in line for the flyers. His face is red, his cheeks chapped. His thin hair combed over a freckled scalp. He drags heavily on his cigarette and blows it out of his long, thin nostrils.

"Excuse me," I say, and push past him out into the dirt lot. I pretend to check my phone, though I am not expecting to hear from anyone. And then the rest of my team joins me.

I am the youngest person in my group; Mrs. Lund, *Rose,* must be in her seventies now. Her best friend, Ruth, the same. They link arms and walk slowly, as if they are headed to church rather than deep into the woods to look for a missing child. The two men are both my father's age. Griff is a retired plumber and avid hiker, and Marcus is a professor at the college in the math department. He says he knew my dad. For some reason, their collective seniority makes me feel like a child instead of a grown woman.

It is easily ten degrees cooler in the woods, and each time we step into the shade, my bones feel hollow. I'm not sure what we are looking for. Is the hope that she'll simply stumble out of the brush just as she stumbled out of the woods the other night? That she'll come to us? Of course, the alternatives are worse: that we won't find her at all. Or that we will, but not alive.

We get to a spot where there is a large moss-covered boulder.

"Okay," Griff says, leaning against the enormous rock, and studying the map that another volunteer distributed this morning. (We can't get a GPS signal here; those of us with smart phones have already tried.)

"Let's stick together at first, and then we'll break off into two groups. Sound good?"

We all nod.

Marcus adjusts the backpack he's wearing (he's volunteered to carry our supplies: granola bars, bug spray, sunscreen, et cetera). "You all have your water bottles?" We all nod and raise our bright yellow plastic water bottles, courtesy of the Dollar General in town. And as we stand there in a circle, it feels like we are giving a toast at some sort of grim celebration.

Lieutenant Andrews came and spoke to us this morning, gave us explicit instructions regarding what to do if we find any sort of "evidence" (*don't touch*) and what to do if we encounter her: either living or dead. He asked us to assign a team leader to each group, and our group elected Griff. Griff has hiked the entire Appalachian Trail, and was also the only one to volunteer for the job.

Our area is in the woods just south of

where I found her. I was under the impression that we'd do some sort of grid search, lining up in a row and holding hands like I've seen on TV. But Andrews explained that grid searches are less effective than you'd think, that our energies would be better spent simply combing through our assigned areas, looking under rocks and fallen trees, noting anything that seems suspicious: evidence that she was here.

We walk together through the woods, our eyes trained on the ground. Griff leads the way, followed by Marcus. Rose, Ruth, and I follow behind. I can hear Ruth's labored breathing and wonder if she's up for this. The last thing we all need is for one of us to have a medical emergency out here in the woods.

Something darts out in front of us, and Rose lets out a scream.

"It's just a squirrel," I say, touching her back. She presses her hand against her chest and takes a deep breath.

And I remember the time in the sixth grade when she read *Where the Red Fern Grows* aloud to our class. I remember sitting on the red square of carpet I'd been assigned. I hated sitting cross-legged (*Indian-style* in those days before *crisscross applesauce*), because my legs always fell asleep. All I wanted to do was stretch out, get the prickling sensation to stop. I was distracted, and so when Mrs. Lund began to cry, I was startled. I remember looking up at her in the rocking chair where she sat, and watching her shoulders tremble and her face flush red. Her voice cracked as she read. It was the first time in my life I'd seen an adult cry. And I remember thinking that all I wanted to do was to stand up and go to her, to give her a hug, to make her feel better. But instead, I just sat there. Just like all the other kids. Later, I remember justifying it to myself by thinking that my legs were pins and needles. I couldn't have stood up. But I knew that I'd just been afraid. That weakness in others terrified me. And that in the face of other people's pain, I would always fail.

We keep walking quietly, the only sound the leaves under our feet, the urgent call of the hermit thrush, and Ruth's labored breaths.

"So, Rose says you live in New York," Ruth says.

I nod and smile. "Brooklyn."

"And you're a writer?"

"No, no, I'm an editor," I say reflexively. "A copy editor. Freelance."

"Does that mean you work from home?"

she asks. Her face is the powdery pink of a plastic baby doll.

"Yes," I say, smiling. "In my pajamas if I want."

"That must be so nice," she says. "And a wonderful way to be able to stay home with your children."

It feels like a blow to my chest. Every time.

"I don't have any children," I say.

"None?" she asks, as if this is inconceivable.

I scowl. *No, none, not even one.*

"I can't," I say. And I don't know why I am telling her this. Why I feel compelled to explain. "I mean I'm not able. My husband and I . . ."

She leans toward me and whispers, "I had three miscarriages before we finally had our son. Sometimes you just need to keep trying."

I feel like I am being scolded. She's questioning my efforts, as if this is because I simply gave up. But I don't know what to say to make her stop. To shut her up. I fear that even the truth would not faze her.

"I'm forty-five years old," I say.

"Oh, dear," she says, as though I've just told her I'm dying. "I'm sorry. It's just that you look so much younger."

I take a deep breath, and feel my heart

sputtering. I try to take deep, calming breaths, but it skips again, and I need to get away.

"We should maybe fan out," I say, loud enough for the guys to hear. If I have to stay here for even one more minute, I may pass out.

Everyone stops.

Deep breaths.

"I mean, if we're in two groups then we're covering a lot less area than we could be covering if we were each on our own."

Even Marcus the Mathematician can't argue with this.

"And I'm actually okay by myself. I know these woods," I say, nodding. "I grew up here." My ridiculous refrain.

Marcus shakes his head. "We're supposed to stay together."

"It's *fine*," I say. "Ruth and Rose, maybe you ladies should stick together. But I'll be okay on my own."

"You really should stay with us," Mrs. Lund says. "It's safer if you stay with us."

"It's *okay*." I try hard not to sound exasperated.

Griff looks at his watch, a complicated affair with all sorts of knobs and buttons. A compass even.

"I have a compass app on my phone," I

say brightly. "I'll be fine."

They look at me dumbly. None of us have any experience with this. And despite Andrews's helpful little lecture, nobody really knows the rules. But somehow, I am suddenly the dissenter, the renegade.

"I'll meet you back at the big boulder in a half hour," I say, and start to walk away before anyone can stop me.

I stumble through the brush, following a vague path mottled with sunlight. I am both purposeful and aimless. The bugs are so thick, I wish I'd sprayed myself with the Off! in Marcus's backpack before abandoning them. I swat at the mosquitoes that are relentless this deep in the woods. But still, they bite, and welts raise on my skin like a disease. I X them out with my thumbnail, this habit a relic from childhood. I'm wearing shorts and a T-shirt, wishing I'd worn something to cover my apparently delicious skin.

I try to imagine that I am a child again, feel the wild abandon in my legs and arms as I push and push, almost running through the woods now, the voices of my search group fading into the thrum and hum of the forest's other noises and the sound of my own breath. I try to think like a child.

Where would she go? What would she be drawn to? Where would she go to feel safe?

I have only been lost in the woods once, and I was with Effie, not alone. When she and I were twelve or so we decided to hike the Nature Conservancy trail, the trailhead about halfway around the lake from her camp. It was impulsive. We saw the sign as we were riding our bikes one day and decided to stop. We did that all the time back then: rode around looking for adventures, dropping our bikes at the first sign of one.

That day we had been searching for wild blueberries, but all the usual spots had been ravaged by animals, the bushes plundered for their delicate fruit. We were wearing sandals and hadn't even brought water bottles. Still, we jumped off our bikes and made our way from the road into the forest.

There was a wooden pedestal with a laminated map of the trail, a roughly hewn bench. We studied the one-mile circular trail on the map, and shrugged. We could probably walk the whole hike and be back to our bikes within an hour.

It was hot that day, and I remember thinking we should have brought some water. That we were probably pretty stupid not to have some with us. Then again, we were close to the lake. But fairly soon, the path curved far away from the water, and the woods grew cold.

"Are we still on the trail?" I said. Because now, the well-worn path was not so well-worn; instead it was riddled with branches and roots.

"I think so," she said, but I could sense just a little bit of fear in her voice as well.

"Well, let's keep going," I said. The hike was a simple loop. Soon we'd be back at the map and the bench. And then we could make the short hike back to the road.

But the bright red arrows that had been appearing on trees at regular intervals earlier had stopped.

"How long since you last saw an arrow?" I asked.

Effie shook her head.

"Are we lost?" I asked.

"No," she said. "I've hiked this trail before. It takes a while to get back around."

And so we kept walking, trusting that we were headed in the right direction. But as the sky darkened, I knew something was wrong. Effie could sense it too. She reached for my hand, and I squeezed it. We stopped and stood still. I remember thunder rumbling in the distance, and my entire body flushing with the heat of fear.

"Let's turn back," I said.

But Effie shook her head. "No," she said. "We should keep going. I swear this is the trail. If we just keep going, we'll get back. It's a loop."

I nodded, even though I worried that we had somehow gotten off the trail, or maybe somehow onto a different trail altogether. One that had nothing to do with the Nature Conservancy loop. What if this was some other trail, some ten-mile trail? Part of the Appalachian Trail that wandered all the way from Maine to Georgia?

We had no water.

And it was starting to rain.

We didn't speak for the next twenty minutes as we forged ahead, hoping, praying that we would wind up where we had started. That the promises made on that map would be kept.

My entire body was buzzing with all of the possible disasters. I thought about our parents waiting for us at home. How long would they wait before they started to get worried? I wondered about our bikes, hidden in the foliage so that no one would steal them. How long would it take them to find the bikes? Thunder rumbled again, and I imagined what would happen to us when the rain came. When the breakfast we'd

161

eaten no longer filled our bellies. I thought about dying out here. About Effie and me suffering slow, painful deaths.

I could barely breathe when all of a sudden Effie started running, motioning for me to follow her. And there was that damn bench. That map. And I felt so foolish. So relieved.

It took all afternoon for my body to stop trembling. I could barely pedal my bicycle when we finally emerged out of the woods. Effie and I didn't talk about that afternoon again. I know her mind must have traveled the same places mine had. Must have considered, maybe even for the first time, the possibility that we were not impervious to danger. We'd been wild kids, careless kids. Carefree kids. But after that day, there was a certain caution that informed everything we did. I always had water with me after that. And we always left our bikes where they would be seen. And I noticed Effie almost always checked in with her mom to let her know where we were going.

I remember that panic now, that hot flush of fear that I felt. And I hope that this little girl is not yet old enough to speculate about all the terrible things that can happen to her. That she still trusts that someone will find her. That the world is a safe place.

I come to a small cavern and realize I have been running. I am breathless, my heart beating hard in my chest. I bend over at the waist and put my hands on my knees, waiting for my body to calm.

When I stand up again I feel dizzy, disoriented.

A dragonfly flitters in front of my face and I am momentarily mesmerized by its iridescent wings, by the way it hovers, suspended in the air.

"Pretty, huh?"

I whip around at the sound of his voice, my eyes wide.

The man is standing by a tree about ten feet away, smoking a cigarette. His face is in the shadows, but I can see that he's wearing an orange vest. Another one of the searchers.

"Jesus Christ," I say. "You scared the shit out of me."

He emerges from behind the tree, and I realize it's that creepy guy again. Is he following me?

He takes a drag on his cigarette and then drops it to the ground, grinding it into the mucky leaves.

"Know why they call 'em darners?"

"What?" I say, already assessing how far I have gotten away from my group. Listening for the sound of their voices, of anyone's voices.

"Dragonflies. They're called *darners* in some parts."

"No," I say, backing up a little as he walks toward me.

"When I was a little boy, my daddy told me that if I was bad, the darners would come in the middle of the night and sew my ears shut. Sew my mouth shut too."

"What a terrible thing to tell a child," I say.

He laughs then, and his chest rumbles like it's full of wet leaves.

"Maybe if you follow the darner, it'll lead you to the little girl," he says. "If she's been naughty, maybe it's looking for her."

I back up again, and start running.

I can hear him hacking behind me. As if his body is turning itself inside out. I don't glance back; I just keep running until I see orange through the trees. Until I see Mrs. Lund and Ruth standing together, drinking from their bright yellow water bottles. I hear Griff's low voice and see Marcus scratching on his pad of paper. I could cry; I am so relieved. It feels exactly like that time I was lost with Effie. Because the relief I feel now is tempered by fear. That man is out here in

164

the woods, looking for her. What if he finds her before I do?

We search all morning, emerging from the woods at noon as though waking from a dream. The bright light blinds us, and we stumble from the foliage onto the dirt road. One after the other, the rest of the volunteers materialize in the road and silently climb into the waiting vehicles, which will bring us to Hudson's for lunch before we return and keep looking.

No one speaks, but it is obvious. No one has found anything. She is still lost.

When we pull into the parking lot at Hudson's, I see the news vans that had been parked at the site are now here. The police cars are also here. There are state police as well.

Huddles of people in orange vests congregate outside, smoking cigarettes, stretching, waiting for whatever is about to happen. I push through the crowd, go into the store, and head straight to the back room, where

Effie and the girls are laying out sandwiches on a long folding table. Plum is carefully arranging the napkins like this is a party, and Zu-Zu is lining up cold sodas in tidy rows.

Devin and Billy Moffett are standing together, talking, in the back of the room.

"What's going on outside?" I ask Effie. "Did they find her? Did somebody find her?"

"I have no idea," Effie says. She hands me a brown paper grocery bag filled with wrapped sandwiches and motions for me to put them out on the table. "I don't think anybody knows. Somebody said they're going to have another press conference at one fifteen."

"Where's Jake?" I ask, glancing around, as if I could have missed him somehow in this small room. He promised to meet me here at lunch. That he'd come with us to search this afternoon.

"I think he might have gone into town? He said he needed to send out some e-mails," she says.

"He could do that from here on his phone," I say angrily. As if this is Effie's fault. As if she's the one who's jumped ship.

She ignores my raised voice and nods. "He was doing something on his laptop. I told him there was Wi-Fi at the library. I think he might have gone into town."

I take a deep breath. And she reaches out and squeezes my hand.

"Are you hungry?" she asks, motioning to the sandwiches. "There's tuna." Effie and I lived on tuna sandwiches when we were kids. Tuna sandwiches with salt-and-vinegar potato chips crumbled up inside. Comfort food. If she had a can of Country Time lemonade and a foil-wrapped Ding Dong too, this could be the summer of 1976.

I shake my head.

"Let's just see what the police have to say. Maybe it's good news," she says. "If it isn't that she's been found, then at least maybe someone's come forward and knows who she is. Maybe they found that guy."

I remember the man in the woods then, and I shiver. But how would they know about that guy? I scowl. "What guy?"

"The one in the white truck?" she says. "The one you saw here that night?"

"Oh," I say. I'd almost forgotten about him. "Right."

"Maybe he saw something too."

I nod, but I'm thinking about the *other* guy now. The one in the woods.

"Hey," I say. "There's this guy in the search party. Totally creeps me out. He was alone out in the woods earlier, not in a group, and he scared the shit out of me."

"What did he do?" she asks.

"He told me this awful story about dragonflies sewing naughty children's ears shut," I say.

"What?" She looks horrified. *"Why?"*

I shake my head, thinking of the wings of the dragonfly. Iridescent and shimmery, like the little girl's tutu.

"I have no idea," I say. "I got a strange feeling from him. He kept grinning. Almost like he's enjoying this."

Effie hands me a Diet Coke, and I pop it open. I need the caffeine.

"Hey," I say, getting an idea. "Who holds on to the sign-in sheets?"

"I think Billy's keeping them. I can ask Devin. Why?"

"I want to find out the guy's name," I say. "Do the cops do any background checks on the volunteers? Or can any nut job just join in the search?"

Effie smiles. "I'm sure he's just a concerned neighbor. People are weird. Especially some of the folks who live out here in the woods. Not always the best social skills."

Plum comes up to us with a big chocolate-chip cookie poised at the edge of her lips.

"Did you have a sandwich yet?" Effie asks, gently grabbing her wrist before she can bite. Plum shakes her head sheepishly. "Okay, give me the cookie then. You can have it *after* you eat a sandwich."

Plum relinquishes the cookie and then comes to me. For comfort, I suppose. I pull her close to me. I can feel her ribs under my fingertips.

I bend down and whisper. "I want to have a cookie for lunch too. But your mom is totally making me eat a sandwich first."

She nods. Commiserates.

"But I can teach you something cool," I say.

I grab two tuna sandwiches, then a bag of chips. I demonstrate how to crush the chips inside. She takes a bite, giggles, and then runs off to join Zu-Zu, who is sitting on a metal folding chair in the corner, tapping away on her phone.

Effie is making herself a special sandwich too.

"Can you maybe find out who he is?" I ask. "His name should be right before mine on the sign-in sheet from yesterday. He was ahead of me in line."

"Sure," she says, shrugging. "I'll find out."

Time passes slowly. I wind up having not only the sandwich but three cookies and two Diet Cokes as well, just to pass the time. I text Jake, **Where R U?,** and he texts back, **In town. Getting an e-mail out. Meet u back at camp. No apologies.**

At 1:10 the crowd assembles outside in a strange semicircle around an empty podium in the parking lot. The news media scurries about affixing microphones, laying down cables. 1:15 comes and goes. Effie is inside with the girls still, and so I find my search group and stand with them.

"How are you holding up?" Mrs. Lund asks and pats my back, the same way she did one afternoon when I was eleven and had thrown up in the bathroom at school. I remember feeling so grateful for her in that moment, for the soft small circles she made on my back.

I nod. "I'm okay. I really hope all of this means they found her."

"Me too," she says.

Finally, Lieutenant Andrews appears, with Sergeant Strickland at his side, and a man I don't recognize. Looks like state police.

"Good afternoon, everyone," Andrews says, and a collective hush falls over the crowd.

"I'm Lieutenant Roger Andrews, and this is Vermont State Police captain Nielson. I first want to thank you all for your efforts in the search for the juvenile reported missing

171

on Thursday evening.

"We have performed exhaustive searches of the area, using all of the resources available to us. Over seventy rangers have combed the surrounding area. We have had a team of trained search-and-rescue dogs, and we have utilized infrared technology in the helicopters. And this morning, we had a team of divers searching the lake."

My heart stops like a plug in a drain. I look over at Devin, who is standing in the doorway of Hudson's. I think of his sister.

No, no, no, please no.

"I want to thank you as well, the tireless volunteers who have responded to this report by canvassing neighbors and searching for clues. This is a testament to a community that cares deeply about one another."

I close my eyes, hold my breath. *Please no.*

"However, I am here this afternoon to announce that our efforts are turning from one of search and rescue to investigative."

My eyes fill with tears. I feel like I might collapse.

Mrs. Lund continues to rub my back. I am nauseated. I concentrate on staying upright, because every impulse I have is to fall.

Andrews pauses, ready to deliver the bad news to the crowd. He seems to be choosing every word carefully. I will him to hold his silence. Time slows.

He coughs into his hand and nods.

"It is our belief," he says, then pauses. "That there is no missing child."

The crowd begins to hum and buzz. Heads swivel, whispers hiss. And I feel the blood begin to drain from my body.

"After significant investigation, we firmly believe that the reporting party was in error."

The crowd turns to look at each other, and then, it seems, they all turn to look at me.

"There is simply no credible evidence of a missing child. There are no missing persons reports. No secondary witnesses. And after an exhaustive search, no physical evidence has been recovered in the area."

I feel like I am about to collapse. My blood pounds hot in my ears. My head throbs.

The reporters push forward, barking their questions like dogs. Their voices, their questions tumble together. Indistinguishable from each other. Until one loud voices demands:

"Was it a hoax?"

The lieutenant ignores the question, but looks through the sea of faces straight at me.

"At this time, we will be ceasing all search efforts, though we will continue to investigate the report in the event that new information comes in. But again, it is our belief that the report of a missing juvenile was a false one."

I am breathless, trying not to cry. My entire body trills. I storm through the crowd, ignoring their glances and hissing whispers. By the time I reach Andrews, I feel explosive.

"What are you *doing*?" I say to Andrews.

He takes me by the elbow and ushers me to the side of the building. "Miss Waters," he says. "It's over. You just need to go back home."

My body stiffens.

"You have to keep looking," I say, shaking my head. "You can't stop now."

"Miss Waters, listen. Sergeant Strickland gave you the benefit of the doubt. You're lucky it was him and not me who showed up that night. But I'm in charge, and I've got a few more years under my belt than Strickland does."

"But there has to be some sort of law

about this. You can't just ignore me," I say, feeling desperate now. Unhinged.

"Ma'am," he says "We conducted a full-scale search. Went above and beyond protocol. You've gotten this entire town worked up into a frenzy over a figment of your imagination. And now it is time for you to let it go. To let these good people get back to their lives. And let us get back to our work."

I shake my head even as he turns and starts to walk away. "I'm not crazy," I say loudly. Several people turn to watch. "She's real. And you are leaving her alone out there."

Someone snickers. And I realize I am making a spectacle of myself. That I am in the center ring of this circus. The main attraction. *Again.*

"What?" I say to no one in particular. To everyone. *"What?"*

We watch the press conference again on the five o'clock news.

Jake sits down next to me on the couch, puts his arm around my shoulder, but I don't want him touching me. Where was he earlier when I needed him? Where was he when I had to walk through that angry horde of people? Where was he when the news reporters started shoving their microphones in my face?

"So that's it?" he says softly.

On the screen Lieutenant Andrews said, in no uncertain terms, that the search would cease unless some concrete evidence of her existence materialized. I watch now as Strickland stands, nodding his head knowingly, as if they are in cahoots. As though I *am* crazy.

"That's ridiculous," Effie says. "So they're just going to pretend like this didn't happen."

"They don't believe me," I say. "You heard them. They think it's a hoax."

"That doesn't make any sense," she says. "Why would somebody pretend to see a child in the road?"

"For attention, I guess?" Jake offers.

"That's absurd," Effie says angrily. She's held her anger toward him in check so far, but I can see her cracking now.

He seems to sense this and stands up awkwardly.

"We'll keep looking," she says, taking his spot next to me. Squeezing my hand. "None of this means the volunteers need to stop searching. The people here aren't going to just let this go."

"They will if the cops say I'm lying," I say.

"I believe you," she says. "Devin believes you."

What she doesn't say is that *Jake* believes me. And the irony hurts. *He* is the liar. He is the one who has willfully deceived me again and again. I cannot begin to get a handle on the depth of his deception.

But I am telling the truth.

I saw her. She is *real.*

"Well, I guess this means we can go back to New York together tomorrow," Jake says coldly, and my whole body tenses.

Effie squeezes my hand so tightly, my bones ache.

"Let's go for a walk," I say to Jake, and stand up.

He follows me as I make my way through the kitchen and out the back door. I don't slow to wait for him, but I can hear him behind me. Devin has taken Plum down to the access area to swim. I can hear the sounds of their voices echoing. The splashes and Plum's squeals. We walk in the opposite direction, away from them, clockwise around the lake.

Jake shoves his hands into the pockets of his jeans, head down, like a scolded child. "So then what now?" he asks.

I shake my head.

"I mean, it seems like we *should* probably just head back home, right?"

I stop. We're in front of an old battered dock. I think it used to belong to the Foresters, the family that had taken in Devin's sister all those summers ago, but that camp is abandoned now, the foundation crumbling, the building falling slowly into the water.

"You can always come back up if they find something. That guy in the truck or whatever. If they need you," Jake says.

My throat feels thick. "I don't know what

the rules are," I say. "What I'm supposed to do next."

"Well, we can find out. Call that Strickland guy maybe?"

"I'm not talking about *this*," I say, gesturing ridiculously toward the woods that surround us. My eyes sting.

Jake looks confused, but then his face pales.

"What are you doing?" he asks.

"What are *you* doing?" I almost laugh.

Jake shakes his head. Did he really think he could get away with this?

Ten years ago I might have felt anger. I might have felt rage at this injustice. This audacity of his. The vulgarity of it. Perhaps, if there were a child. If there were a *family* in jeopardy, then I might feel outrage. A mother bear protecting what is hers. But now, I feel only profoundly disappointed. When you have suffered betrayal by the universe, a betrayal by a man is not only unsurprising but expected.

So when I found the phone, the texts, I didn't feel angry but foolish. And there, perhaps, lies the problem. I am more upset by being made a fool than by his sharing his affections, by his fucking someone else. Maybe even loving someone else. And so when I picked up my phone and dialed that

179

number (I do admit the tremble in my fingers, a sinking sensation, a certain sort of drowning), and she answered with her cigarette-Sunday-morning voice, it wasn't jealousy I felt at all but rather simple sadness. God, pity even. Understanding.

You have no idea, I had said. *What you're doing.*

She thinks there are no children involved, that she is not destroying a family. She can't possibly understand that we *were* a family. A family cobbled together out of a want bigger than anything this girl, this stupid girl, can possibly know right now (when her biggest concern is her relationship status on Facebook — *It's complicated,* she settles on).

She cannot know the smell of jacaranda, the hollow knock of eager knuckles on a large wooden door. The sound of ten babies wailing. The way my chest heaved when I entered that filthy room with its crumbling walls and dim light, and saw the babies, a sea of babies with their mouths wide open like naked, featherless birds in a nest, reaching, pleading, screaming. That the woman assured me that they were held twice a day after their changings. *Twice a day* they were touched. She can't know the scent of a dozen dirty diapers. Muted by the smell of burning plantains and jacaranda. She

180

doesn't know the way that bile tasted in my throat at the chorus of *mama-mama,* the word the same in nearly every language. A word so primitive it only has one sound. That universal glottal evocation.

She cannot know when she traces her manicured nails down his chest, that I once watched Zu-Zu cling to him. Once press her hot wet cheek to that same chest. And the way he told me it made him feel. *Like a father,* he said. Almost. Our bodies carry no evidence of those who have loved us. If they did, if they bore the imprints of everyone's hands, every child's wet cheek, every mother's palm, if our flesh carried the ghosts of all the hands that have touched us, then we might be more careful.

This is not her fault. She doesn't know anything more than what he has told her. And I know that he could have told her anything. Or nothing. And so it doesn't matter who she is, because in the end this has so very little to do with her (though I suspect she thinks it has everything to do with her).

Who is this? she'd asked. *What do you want?*

And I didn't confront Jake. I didn't have to, because I knew she would come to him eventually. She would shudder and cry and apologize. I could picture him closing his office door, and her wide eyes. The way she'd probably say, "Fuck, Jake. What the fuck? I can't do this anymore. If you're going to leave her then leave her. But I'm done being somebody's mistress." Because she fancies herself independent, even though her parents still come from upstate once a month and load her refrigerator with lactose-free milk and fresh fruit and the same cereal she's loved since she was little. Even though she is still too afraid to take the subway after dark. Even though she wants nothing more, in the end, than a house somewhere filled with her own babies (though she doesn't know it yet). But I forgive her this even. Because she is so very young.

It has been three weeks since I discovered the texts on his phone. Since I spoke to her, as she broke down on the other end of the line, apologizing like a child who got caught stealing candy. For three weeks, I have kept my silence, though it's a simple enough question to ask: *What do you want?* It's as easy as this. But I haven't asked, because I know he has no answers. I am so tired of his lack of answers.

I hear Plum's voice echo across the lake. "Da . . . dee!"

"Well, what do *you* want to do?" he asks. Always depending on me to make the hard decisions. For once, I'd like him to just stand up and be a fucking man.

"I want you to go back to New York," I say.

"And?" he asks.

"And that's all, for now. I'm not making this decision for you. Go back home. Decide what the hell it is that you want. When you get that figured out, you let me know."

I walk out to the end of the dock now, and he doesn't follow. It feels precarious underneath me, and so I am careful. The sun is still bright in the sky. Now that the helicopters are gone, the loons have returned and are peacefully gliding across the surface of the lake. I see one not far from where I stand. Usually they travel in pairs this time of year, but this loon is alone. Or at least it seems she is alone until she swims close enough for me to see. It is early in the summer, and so the baby is young. She rides on her mother's back. I scan the surface of the lake, waiting for the father to poke his head up from the water. He must be fishing, finding them food. But the surface of the lake is still. And they are alone out there. He is nowhere to be found.

I have come alone. Despite your pleas for me to wait for you. For the paperwork to be finalized. Even when I told you about how many children there are in the nursery, offered you the ratio of caregivers to child as though this were some secret formula. When I told you that they are held only twice a day, you didn't respond in the way I expected. You weren't horrified. It did not make you weep, the way it did me. This is not incomprehensible to you the way it is to me. I don't understand how you are not enraged. This is our *child*. Our daughter. And she is being left alone to cry. No one is holding her. She is completely alone.

Besides, you said, you couldn't just up and leave work. Not indefinitely. *Who will provide for her if neither of us is working?* And when you say this, I hear your words laced with resentment. I have left my job. As soon as we were given the referral, I gave my notice. An extended leave of absence, I said. Maternity leave. Maybe you could wait until there's actually a child, you'd said, as if she were any less real just because she wasn't in our arms yet. Maybe wait until we have a buffer, you'd said, in our account.

And I hate that this always comes back to money. I see you silently calculating: the cost of the failed treatments, the IUIs, the IVFs. Our account dwindling with each visit to the pharmacy, each bill that arrived from the clinic. And then the money we have sent to the agency, the amount staggering. I fear you have a running total in your head, that when we finally get her, you will be measuring her against what we have spent. Seeing if she was worth it. If the value of this warm flesh in my arms matches this second mortgage it will take another thirty years to pay off. I know that there is a part of you that thinks we are purchasing her, and this makes you uncomfortable. There is some primitive place inside of you that wonders if human flesh should be for sale. And of course, I agree, but I would do anything. You don't understand this. I cannot seem to make you understand this.

"Wait," you said.

But I could not wait. She was being held only twice a day.

And so while you were sleeping, I sat in the

darkness in the other room, the laptop on my lap, my face illuminated by the screen. I searched the Internet and found the hotel in Guatemala City. In Zona 10. I used Google Earth and zoomed in on the address I found after they finally gave me the name of the orphanage. I studied it so intently, I could find my way through those streets from the hotel to the orphanage with my eyes closed. I speak only a small amount of Spanish (recollected from high school), but I am learning. I listened to the lessons online with headphones on, pretended I was only listening to music.

And it is music, this language that belongs to her. I learn a lullaby so that when she finally comes home, I will be able to sing to her these familiar words. *"A la roro niño, a lo roro ya, duérmete mi niño, duérmete mi amor."* Lullaby baby, lullaby now, sleep my baby, sleep my love.

But now, here alone in this shabby hotel, I wonder if you were right. Leaving my job, coming here all by myself. I am in a city where I do not speak the language, and the food has made me sick. For three days I can't leave the bed, because I am feverish and vomiting. This city is rejecting me.

Outside my window I hear music, and laughter and sirens. Life goes on all around me, but I am enclosed in a cocoon of cold sheets

186

and a threadbare blanket. I hung the DO NOT DISTURB, NO MOLESTAR sign on the door. When the maid comes, I poke my head out and whisper, *"Estoy enfermo. Hay servicio de limpieza."* I am sick. I think I have told her I do not want housekeeping. I am relying on Google Translate on my laptop.

I text you photos of the hotel, of the city.

And I wait for you.

Back at camp, there is a flurry of activity. Zu-Zu is running around, grabbing things from the washing machine, from the closets.

"Oh my God, *Mom,* where's the box of pointe shoes?" she asks, frantic.

"They're already in Daddy's truck," Effie says.

Devin and Plum come into the kitchen through the back door, and Zu-Zu almost knocks him over.

"Slow down." Devin laughs.

Jake is outside loading up the back of Devin's truck with his own stuff. Early tomorrow morning, Devin will drive him back to Brooklyn and drop off Zu-Zu at the dorms in the city. Effie and Plum and I will stay here. After that, I have no idea.

I sit on the daybed on the porch, looking out at the lake, while the others hustle about. I feel like a stone in the water, every-one moving around me as I remain immovable, unyielding.

"Want some company?" Effie asks. She's wearing her bathing suit top and a pair of sweats. She still looks like a kid.

She sits down on the other side of me, puts her arm across my back, and holds me. I shudder. She leans into me, squeezing me as hard as she can, and I remember. She was there when everything fell apart before. When I fell apart. It was Effie who put me back together, who gathered the shattered pieces of me, who made sure none of the shards were forgotten. Discarded. Swept away.

"You okay?" she asks.

I nod, though I am not okay, not okay at all.

Sunday morning. For the girls we pretend that everything is okay. Zu-Zu is trying to be brave, blasé about leaving, but I can see how nervous she is. This is the first time she's left home. Effie too is pretending that everything is fine. Just a normal morning. She makes pancakes, bacon. But Plum is the only one who can eat.

I take my coffee outside as we gather around Devin's truck to say good-bye.

Zu-Zu curls up into her mother's arms, and I have to look away. Effie's eyes are filled with tears, which makes my eyes fill as well.

"I'll be down in a couple of weeks," Effie says. "Do you have Baby Z?"

Zu-Zu nods.

"Bye, squirt," Zu-Zu says, reaching for Plum.

Plum is the only one who isn't misty-eyed. She hugs Zu-Zu and then wriggles out of her arms. "When we come visit, I want to go to the Statue of Liberty. And to see the Rockettes. And to that big toy store, what's it called, Mama, Effie-O?"

"FAO Schwarz," Effie says, laughing. "We'll do all those things. I promise."

Devin comes and gives Effie a hug and then hugs me too. He pulls away but keeps holding on to my shoulders. "Listen, Billy is going to keep the search going. There are at least fifty people planning to go out today. I'll be back in a few days, and we'll figure out where to go from there. Okay?"

I nod. I am so grateful to him.

Jake comes out of the camp and barely speaks to me as he gets into the passenger side of the truck, Zu-Zu sandwiched between them.

"I'll call you when we get there," he says.

I nod. I don't wish him luck with the auction. I don't say anything. I have no words for this moment.

And then the truck is backing up out of the driveway and onto the dirt road. But instead of feeling sadness or fear, I only feel relief. I am startled by this; by the peace, by the *release,* of this moment.

"Let's go finish up breakfast," Effie says, reaching for my hand.

It's Sunday, so she doesn't have to work. She has promised Plum that she'll take her strawberry picking at a local farm, and that they can make a strawberry-rhubarb pie to have with supper tonight. I offer to make dinner for them: homemade mac 'n' cheese, Plum's favorite.

"Are you going to join the search today?" Effie asks quietly.

Plum has slipped back into the kitchen nook, where she pushes what's left of her breakfast around her plate. I think it might just be hitting her that her sister will be gone all summer.

"Yeah," I say, shrugging. "I figure I'll go down to Hudson's and see if anybody else shows up." What I don't tell her is that I'm worried that instead of a group of eager volunteers waiting for me, I might be facing a lynch mob. Devin assured me that just because the police have given up doesn't mean that the community will. He said that

Billy Moffett is taking over the volunteer efforts, that the search headquarters are still open. That most folks still believe what I said I saw. And they won't stop searching until they find her. But I felt their anger at me as I walked through the crowd. I felt their suspicions, their disbelief.

"Hey," I say when Effie slips into the nook next to Plum. They both look so sad. Effie's eyes are puffy, and I have a feeling she was up crying last night.

"Maybe we can watch the DVD of Zu-Zu's recital tonight. *Coppélia,* right? That's the ballet she did this year?" I suggest.

Effie nods. "That would be nice. God, I miss her already."

"Me too," Plum says.

"Me three," I say.

The phone jangles on the wall, startling me. It's early, really early.

Effie stands up and grabs it. I can tell she's worried it might be Devin. That something could have happened, though they just left a few minutes ago.

"Yes, hold on one moment. Let me see if she's available," she says stiffly.

I cock my head at her as she covers the mouthpiece.

"It's Lieutenant Andrews," she says softly. "Do you want to talk?"

I feel my skin flush hot. I think of how awful it felt having all eyes on me in the parking lot at Hudson's. At the humiliation. At the frustration.

"Yeah," I say, nodding, and take the phone from her. I stretch the cord into the living room, but I can feel Plum straining to hear.

"Miss Waters?" he says.

"Yes?"

And then I wonder if maybe he's calling because some new evidence has come in. Something to prove I was telling the truth. Maybe they've found her.

"Ma'am, I'm going to need to have you come into the station. Can you make it into town this morning?"

"What is it?"

"I'm not at liberty to discuss this on the phone," he says. "I just need you to come by the station at your earliest convenience."

"Can you just tell me what this is regarding? Did they find her?"

But he's hung up before I can even finish my sentence. Effie comes into the room.

"What's going on?"

I shake my head. "I don't know."

In small towns, Sunday mornings belong to the faithful. There are four churches in Quimby, and each of their respective parking lots is full, but the sidewalks are empty. Deserted. None of the shops are open on Sundays. The banks and businesses are all dark. Only the Miss Quimby Diner is open. I can see its neon sign from here, and in about a half hour the churchgoers in their Sunday best will file from their cars into the restaurant to load up on chicken-fried steak and biscuits and gravy.

I drive down Main Street and turn off onto the street where the police station is. It's a small, two-story brick building. And in all the years I lived in Quimby, I've never once set foot in here.

Inside the doors, I am greeted by a sickly looking ficus tree and a counter like at the doctor's office. The architecture inside is gorgeous though; it looks more like a library or old train depot than a police station. The woodwork is cherry, and there is a winding staircase that leads to the second story.

I go to the counter, where a woman who looks vaguely familiar is on the phone. I struggle to remember how I know her as she finishes up her conversation, gesturing that she'll be right with me. And then I realize that she's my prom date's mother. The last time I saw her, she was snapping photos of me in a green monstrosity of a dress.

"Mrs. Gagnon?" I say, smiling when she gets off the phone.

"That's me," she says. "And you are?" Her tone is short, as though she'd like me to get to the point. And then I remember where I am; a police station is probably not the place for friendly chitchat.

"I'm Tess Waters," I say. "Tess Mahoney? Your son, Mark, and I went to the prom together."

"Junior or senior?" she asks.

"Senior."

"Oh, that's right. You're that girl who went off to Boston." It's a simple fact, but it feels like an accusation.

"Yes, but I actually live in New York now," I say, as if this can somehow remedy whatever it is about Boston that has upset her.

"You're also the one that got everybody

riled up about a missing little girl," she says, raising a single eyebrow skyward.

"Yes," I say, bitterly. "I'm the one who found her."

What I want to tell her is that her son is a pig. That he got wasted on peach schnapps before we even got to the prom and kept trying to grab my breasts all night. That he ditched me when I wasn't receptive to his groping, and I had to walk the whole way home in that stupid dress.

"About that," she says. "Lieutenant Andrews said that you'd be in. He's expecting you."

And then she is on the phone, letting him know.

Two officers enter the building, a woman handcuffed between them. Her face is gaunt, pony-like, her hair thin. She is bra-less in a man's ribbed wifebeater, and her thin, bare arms are mottled like bruised fruit. I think of the syringe I found in the woods. She catches me looking at her and stares back; her face is defiant, her jaw grinding. I look away. Ashamed.

Andrews comes out into the waiting area all smiles, reaching out to shake my hand. I wonder if this is his MO: butter me up before giving me the bad news. Jake does that too.

He leads me to an office with his name on a brass plate on the door and ushers me in.

He sits down behind his desk and motions for me to sit in the chair across from him. Outside the door, I hear commotion (raised voices — the woman's? — a slamming door, and squawking radios), but it doesn't seem to register with him.

"Thanks a whole lot for coming down here on a Sunday," he says. "Hope I didn't wake you up this morning."

I shake my head. "No," I say. It already feels like entire days have passed since Devin, Jake, and Zu-Zu drove off in the truck.

"Why am I here?" I ask. "Did you find her?"

He grimaces.

"Still sticking to your story, huh?"

"My story?"

"Listen, ma'am, I understand that this has all been pretty exciting. What with the whole community rallying to find this kid. I'm sure your adrenaline is still going. All this attention. All this drama."

"What are you talking about?"

"I know how intoxicating it can be. To have the media hanging on your every word. To be the center of attention. Hell, I can't say I blame you. It's only human nature."

"I'm sorry, sir, Lieutenant. I'm not sure I'm following you?"

I glance around, as if someone is going to come in and help translate what he's saying to me. But we are alone. It feels like he's a cat, toying with me. Batting me around before he pounces.

"Ms. Waters," he says. "We've done a little bit of . . . *homework,* shall we say? And it's our understanding that this isn't the first time you've been in the limelight."

I shake my head, feel my stomach plummet.

"That about eight years ago you got yourself caught up in a bit of a media frenzy too."

My heart starts to pound hard in my chest, knocking against my ribs. Jesus, of course he'd do some digging. Find that specter that is always, somehow, hovering, haunting me. I have to will myself to stay seated. Not to run.

"I don't see what any of that has to do with this," I say.

"That's funny, because I think it has everything to do with it." He sits back smugly in his seat and strokes his mustache. "I've seen it before. Somebody gets a little taste and wants the whole cake."

"I'm sorry, and with all due respect, none

of this is *cake.* Two nights ago, I found a child, a little girl, wandering around, by herself, hurt. Just because your team wasn't able to find her, doesn't mean that she doesn't exist. Or that I somehow conjured her up for my own amusement."

He grins as if *I* am amusing him.

"Your search lasted less than twenty-four hours," I say.

"And cost this town thousands of dollars, never mind the manpower that could have been dedicated to other, legitimate, concerns."

"So this is about *money*?" I say.

"It's about resources," he says. "And funny thing. People around here don't like to see resources wasted. And when resources are squandered, somebody's got to pay up."

"I'm not sure I understand what you're trying to say."

"Well, let me make it crystal clear for you then," he says, and his expression changes from one of mild amusement to accusation. "You lied to this community. You lied to the police. It cost this town a whole lot of money it simply does not have. And now the pressure is on me to make things right."

"So you want me to pay you back?" I almost laugh.

"What I want you to do is admit that you

lied. Because the DA is considering pressing charges against you."

"Pressing charges against me for *what*?" I am seething now.

"*I'd* like to see prosecution for knowingly making a false report of an emergency. And even if the DA decides to shit-can the case, our department is going to pursue a cost-recovery suit. To pay back this community."

"Are you fucking kidding me?" I say, standing up.

Andrews stands up too, puts his hands up in a sort of mock surrender as though I might strike out, attack him.

"I'm going to contact my attorney. This is bullshit," I say. I feel vertiginous, my legs weak.

"Meanwhile, I think it's best that you stick around town."

"*Meanwhile,* there is a little girl out there in the woods," I say, shaking. "If anything happens to her, I hope you can sleep at night knowing that you did nothing."

And with that, I storm out of the building and into the bright and beautiful Sunday morning.

I drive back to the lake in a fugue state. My mind is spinning, imagining everything that will happen next, *could* happen next. I try and fail to come up with a plan for how to deal with this. Earlier I was happy that Jake left, but I now worry about how I will handle this on my own.

I know I need to contact a lawyer, but it's been years since I needed a lawyer. *Eight* years. And I haven't spoken to our "counsel," Jake's best friend, Oliver, since. Things went so badly, I couldn't bear to even see him afterward. I know he and Jake have maintained their friendship, but that it is strained now. A delicate, tenuous thing.

I can't call him. And I certainly don't want to talk to Jake about this. He's likely not even on the Jersey Turnpike yet, and my entire world has been turned inside out. A pocket plucked from a pair of pants, the pale lining exposed. Shaken and empty.

My hope is that Effie will know what to do. Know someone I can speak to. I will need someone local who can help me sort this out. There has got to be someone with legal qualifications here. Someone to defend the drunk drivers, the wife beaters, the junkies who seem to be proliferating here.

Andrews's accusations feel like beestings.

But though my brain is swirling, I feel a new sense of resolve and purpose as I round the lake and see the camp through the trees. I will talk to Effie, find a lawyer, get some help. Deal with the cops. Keep them from pressing charges. Find the girl. *Find the girl.* How has this fallen so far down the list?

But when I pull into the grassy driveway, Effie's car is gone. And I remember: strawberry picking. It's already almost noon. I have been gone for hours.

I let myself into the camp, using the key she leaves behind the window's wooden shutter, and it is quiet inside. Still.

Sunlight spills through the windows in the breakfast nook. The kitchen is bright and clean. I think of all of the conversations that have occurred in this room, all the lives that have been lived within these walls. Effie's grandfather built the camp with his own father in the 1940s. It has been a haven for the people in her family for decades now.

When we were kids, we'd pore through the albums that were filled with photos of all the people who have come here. It belongs to her now. And someday it will belong to Zu-Zu and Plum. Her grandmother came close to selling the camp only once, back when we were just out of college. Back when Effie came home when her ex-boyfriend, Max, died. That was the summer she met Devin. And just a year later, I met Jake.

When I think about the trajectories of our lives, I imagine an infinity symbol, endless, looping, converging and then separating again. In the years after college, we diverged. She stayed here with Devin, made a quiet, happy life, made a family. And far away, I built a career. Got married. Tried and failed to have children. Ached. Longed for what she had, though I never told her this. We lived at the edges of each other, though always knowing that we would be pulled toward one another again. When Max died, at each other's respective weddings, at the birth of Effie's girls, and after Guatemala. And now, here we are at that center place. That confluence, where our worlds merge. It has happened again and again in our more than forty years of friendship. There is comfort in this truth. I will always have her when I need her. I can't say the same about anyone else in the entire world.

There will be a note. Because there is always a note. Scrawled in Effie's terrible handwriting on a lovely homemade piece of paper, some pulpy thing she and Zu-Zu made last summer. I have gotten handwritten thank-you cards on this same thick confettied paper.

"Gone berry picking. Pie later! Also . . . found the name of that guy from the search."

I pick up the paper, try to decipher what it says next. Her handwriting has always been atrocious. Small and tightly slanted.

Lincoln . . . then something with an *S*. It looks like S-h-a-m-q, but I know that can't be right.

Sharp? Lincoln Sharp? I catch my breath. *Sharp.* That's what the psychic had said. Jesus Christ.

Effie and Devin don't have Wi-Fi at their house. No Internet access whatsoever. Not even dial-up. And no cell service. And so I drive down the road to Hudson's, sit in my car in the parking lot, trying to search Google on my phone.

There are a few volunteers milling around in the parking lot: those who didn't bail after the last press conference. Devin said there were a good number of people who would continue to search. Who thought the police were full of shit. I am grateful to them all, every last one of them, but I sink down into my seat. I'd rather not have a conversation with anyone at this point, not even those benevolent folks who don't think I am insane.

Lincoln Sharp, I type.

The first thing that pops up is the *Peter J. Sharp Theater at Lincoln Center,* and I realize I forgot to put quotations around the name. When I click again I get a few hits, but none of them seem relevant. I scroll down, squinting at the small screen of my phone, but there's nothing. Of course, there isn't. He's some hermit living in the woods. He doesn't exist as far as Google is concerned.

I try the local paper's Web site then, thinking maybe I can find something there. Again, nothing comes up. He has no Facebook profile. No Twitter feed, no LinkedIn account.

I am about to give up when I remember the site I'd checked religiously, daily, when we were going through the adoption process. Family Watchdog. The sex-offender site. It's a long shot, I know. But better to ease my mind.

Back then I had plugged in the address of our brownstone every day, looking at the squares that pocked the map. Blue was for sexual battery, yellow for rape, and red for crimes against children. I clicked on each menacing red square, scrutinized each profile. I memorized the names of the offenders, printed the photos of their faces. I was both grateful for and terrified by this wealth of information about the perverts and criminals living among us. I didn't tell Jake. There were so many things I couldn't tell him then.

In Brooklyn, I had searched simply by address, *our* address, but now I actually have a name. Trembling, I click on the Search by Name tab and enter: *Lincoln Sharp.*

The signal here is weak, and the search stalls. I have to click out of the site and back in again. It takes forever to load, and I feel myself tensing with impatience. I re-enter his name. Figure it will not show up here either. Wonder even, if he, like the girl, is just some sort of ghost.

And then there it is.

LINCOLN MICHAEL SHARP.

I blink my eyes, look again to make sure I am not mistaken. Then I look up, out the window at a group of orange vests piling into a minivan. And shaking, I click on his name.

His face appears. Those wild eyes, the freckles. The thinning hair. The photo is pixelated, grainy. But it's *him.*

"Jesus Christ," I say out loud.

I click on the Map tab, and a map slowly loads. It reminds me of the map that Marcus had of the search area. And there is the terrifying red square. I click on it, and the address appears. 195 Lake Gormlaith Road.

My entire body shaking, I click on the Convictions tab.

LEWD OR LASCIVIOUS ACTS WITH A CHILD UNDER 14 YEARS OF AGE.

Someone taps at my window. My whole body startles, like one of those dreams where the earth gives way beneath you and you wake with a start, grasping at air, trying to hold on.

It's the psychic.

I turn the key enough to roll down the window.

"Hi there," she says. She's so short, she barely needs to bend over to see into the driver's side.

"Hi," I say.

"Sorry to startle you."

"It's okay," I say, though my heart is still rattling around in my chest. "I was actually just thinking about you. About something you said the other day."

"Yeah?"

"Yes, about something *sharp.* Do you remember that?"

She nods. "Sure. I remember."

"I think it's someone's name. Last name. One of the volunteers."

She scowls.

"Is that possible? That you were thinking of someone's name?"

"I suppose," she says. "But it might just

be a coincidence."

I shake my head. "There's somebody named Sharp who lives near where I found the little girl." I look out the window, making sure that he's not lurking out there somewhere. I haven't seen him since we were in the woods.

"I got a bad feeling from him the other day. And I was just now looking him up," I say, motioning to my phone. "He's a registered sex offender."

Her small eyes widen.

"Look," I say, holding out my phone to her. She is wearing a pair of glasses on a beaded necklace. She puts them on and studies the screen.

"You told the cops?" she asks.

"Not yet," I say.

"They're sending me home, you know," she says. "Now that they've called off the search."

I nod. I actually expected she'd already be long gone.

She leans forward and whispers. "But I believe you," she says. "I came over because I wanted to give you my business card."

I take the card from her. It's not what I would have expected: no glossy purple card stock with a constellation of stars, no loopy script. No clip art crystal ball. It is simple, cream-colored stock embossed with her name: *Mary McCreary, Psychic Detective.* And her phone number.

"Thank you," I say.

"What are you going to do now?" she asks. "Are you going back to New York?"

I don't know *what* to do next. I could tell the police about Lincoln Sharp, though shouldn't they know about him already? Wouldn't this have been one of the first things they checked? I imagine I could let them know, but then I think about the look of disgust on Andrews's face earlier. Think about the accusations that he is making against me. I imagine he'd dismiss this little tidbit the same way he dismissed me. He might even use it as further evidence that I'm just some wing nut. Especially if I mentioned the psychic.

"I guess I'll just keep looking, with the other volunteers," I say. And suddenly the three or four remaining orange vests seem to mock me.

"Well, let me know if you find anything. I can be back here in a couple of hours, if you need me," she says. "I drive a Mustang."

For some reason I think of those men on horseback who were at the site the other morning. I wonder where they have gone. All those people who came crawling out of the woodwork seemed to have crawled right back into it again.

"I don't have any way to pay you," I say, anticipating the hourly fee for a lawyer is going to eat up most of the money I have stashed away in my emergency account.

"There's a little girl in those woods," she says. "It would be criminal if I was able to help and didn't. Sort of like the Hippocratic oath."

With that, she walks over to a beaten-up cherry-red Mustang convertible that is missing all four of its hubcaps. And then she is peeling out of the parking lot, Foreigner's "I've Been Waiting for a Girl Like You" blasting from her speakers.

I return to my phone, looking at Lincoln Michael Sharp's pixelated photo and profile again. I start to Google his full name, thinking I might find a news article about an arrest, something, when Effie calls.

"Hey, we're back. Making pie. Wanna help?"

"Go ahead and get started. I'll be there in just a bit."

I click my phone off and start the car. I back out of the driveway and wonder where Lincoln Sharp is now. I feel cold and hollow. I need to tell Effie there's a registered sex offender living down the road from her.

Here she has crafted this perfect life, this safe world for her girls. She's been living this idyllic dream, cradled in nature. And meanwhile, Lincoln Michael Sharp is living, lurking, among them. A predator. My throat constricts. *The girls.*

I drive slowly along the road between Hudson's and the camp. I peer at the address numbers affixed to a few of the camps along the way. They are in ascending order. 191, 193, the road curves. The yellow police tape flutters in the trees. A few volunteers sit at the edge of the road, nod and wave as I approach. Solemn.

I drive slowly, slowly down the road, the trees becoming thicker, blocking out the sunlight. And then I see the same house Effie and I passed yesterday. That shoe-box house set back from the road, the one with the collection of rusted-out trailers, the one with the yard choked in weeds. My throat feels thick.

There must be a half dozen trailers littering the front yard. Old appliances, a rusted-out patio swing with a tattered canopy and faded cushions. A BEWARE OF DOG sign hangs precariously from a tree that looks like it might topple over if a strong gust of wind came along.

I stop the car and idle. I squint, trying

hard to see if the house number is affixed to the house, but it's set back too far from the road. When I see the truck in the driveway, I start moving again. He's home this time. And then just as I'm about to give up, I see the mailbox. Standing like a sentinel at the edge of the driveway. My heart thuds.

In metallic letters it says:

L. M. SHARP. 195 LAKE GORMLAITH RD.

My stomach roils, and I feel sick. I press my foot on the accelerator and my tires kick up dirt behind me as I race toward Effie's camp. By the time I pull into the driveway, I realize I am going to be sick. I don't want to scare Plum, so I quickly and quietly get out of the car and run down the path toward the guest cottage. I kneel down behind the building and vomit. I haven't eaten anything since last night though, and so it's just fizzy bile that splatters the leaves.

Effie and Plum are in the kitchen slicing strawberries. Effie is showing Plum how to hold the paring knife, and Plum concentrates as she slices the berries into pale slivers.

I force a smile as I come into the kitchen, but I can tell Effie knows something is wrong.

"Plum, honey," she says, wiping her stained hands on a dishtowel. "Can you go out to the laundry room and look for Mommy's apron? I'm getting strawberry juice all over my skirt."

"Okay," Plum says, setting down the knife.

As soon as she skips away, Effie reaches for my hand.

"What did the police say?"

God, the police; that was so long ago.

"Did they find her yet?" she asks. Her hand is small in mine, I can feel the architecture of her bones.

I shake my head.

"Then what's going on?"

I listen to make sure Plum isn't coming back. "Andrews is threatening to press charges against me for making a false report."

"What?" she says. Too loudly. "That's insane. Are you kidding?"

I shake my head. Feel tears come to my eyes.

"It's fine. I just need to get a lawyer to help me deal with this," I say.

"Mama, where is it?" Plum says from the other room.

"Not sure, honey. Look in the dryer. If it's not there, check the hamper?" Effie turns back to me. "I can find someone. We'll go into town first thing tomorrow morning. I'll see if Devin knows anybody."

I shake my head. "There's more," I say.

"What?"

"That guy, the one I told you about? The one in the woods who told me that fucked-up thing about the dragonflies?"

"Yeah?" she says.

"Mama, it's not *here*," Plum says, and I can hear her feet padding around the laundry room.

I lower my voice and continue, "He lives in that messed-up house with all the trailers. That one we drove past?"

Her eyebrows rise up; her eyes widen.

"And he's a registered sex offender," I whisper. "Lewd and lascivious conduct with a child under fourteen."

Effie's hand flies to her mouth. *"What?"*

Plum stands in the doorway holding out an apron. "This one okay?" she asks.

And for just a moment we both turn to Plum, look at her bare feet, her skinny legs. At the drips of strawberry juice that run down her arms. I feel swollen, helpless.

"What's the matter?" Plum asks.

Effie motions for her to come and pulls her in close. "Nothing, baby. It's perfect, thank you."

As the pie bakes, Plum disappears upstairs to play with her dolls. Now that Zu-Zu is gone, she has reverted back to being a ten-year-old again. No pressure to impress her older sister, to keep up.

Effie and I grab a bottle of wine and go outside and sit in the Adirondack chairs facing the water. It is early evening, but the sun is still bright. I realize that today is the solstice, the longest day of the year. It certainly feels like it.

I pick at the peeling purple paint on the arm of the chair. The violet scales drift onto the grass like petals.

"Did you hear from Devin yet?" I ask. Jake hasn't called, and even though I wouldn't know what to say to him, this stings.

"Oh, yeah. He called when you were still in town. They got to Brooklyn around lunchtime. Devin will take Zu-Zu into the city tomorrow to get her set up at the dorms. He said he'll be back here Wednesday or Thursday, depending on when he can get a meeting in at Gagosian."

I study the dizzying pattern of daisies on Effie's skirt. At the few drips of strawberry juice that mar the pristine white cotton. I imagine her later, dabbing at the spots with a Q-tip and bleach.

"What are we going to do?" she says. "You need to tell the police about this. Doesn't it seem like this is something they should be looking into?"

"I *can't* go to the police," I say. "They're seriously pissed at me. They're convinced I'm some sort of psychopath who made up this whole story for attention."

"Is that what he said to you?"

"In so many words," I say. "I think they saw the video."

Effie sighs. "Shit."

I shake my head, rub my temples.

"Wait, is that guy, Sharp, is he even al-

217

lowed to live there?" she asks. "I mean, there have got to be kids living around there. Isn't there some sort of law about that?"

"I think it's just schools and day cares," I say. I don't know the rules here in Vermont. In New York they can't live within one thousand feet of a school or day care center. I was so grateful that our brownstone was two doors down from a preschool.

"Wait," I say. "There *is* a day care center. That place where you deliver the books."

That home day care couldn't have been even a quarter mile from his house.

"Oh shit," Effie says. "I bet Lisa has no idea."

"I'll call Andrews tomorrow," I say. I take a long, slow swallow of the wine, feel it warm my chest. "They may not believe me about the girl, but they can't ignore somebody who's breaking the law. And if they pay him a visit, then maybe they'll find something."

"You mean find . . . her?" she asks.

I shake my head. "God, I hope not."

I had promised to make mac 'n' cheese for supper, but when the pie comes out of the oven, we are tipsy on wine and don't want to bother going through the motions in order to eat dessert. And so we eat pie for dinner. With everyone gone, it feels like the rules have gone out the window. Effie lets Plum load up her steaming piece with vanilla ice cream. And I eat two pieces myself while we watch the DVD of Zu-Zu's performance as Swanhilda in *Coppélia*.

It is only nine o'clock when I make my way to the guest cottage; I am full and sleepy with wine and exhaustion. The sun has just now finally gone down, the last faint glow of this day, the longest day, has finally slipped away, and I too slip away.

In the morning, Effie and I go into town. She slows as we approach Sharp's, and I stare down that gravel driveway, at the collection of trailers in his yard.

"There?" Effie says softly. I nod.

The truck that was in the driveway yesterday is gone. I wonder if he has a job. How one even goes about getting a job after being convicted of something so vile.

She keeps driving slowly, and as we pass the search site, it looks abandoned. It's Monday. Everyone has gone back to work. The yellow police tape looks like tattered ribbons in the trees.

"Do you think we should talk to Lisa?" Effie says. "It kills me that this guy is living so close to her day care. That can't possibly be legal."

What she doesn't say is that this guy is also *her* neighbor too. I think about Plum and Zu-Zu riding their bikes down this road alone.

"Let me talk to Andrews first," I say, forcing a smile. "No need to sound the alarms until I get more details about this guy. Who knows, maybe he's just some sort of exhibitionist. Like a flasher or something. Remember that guy who used to hang out in the cemetery near the high school?"

"Oh my God, I totally forgot about him."

In high school, there was a guy who lurked in the cemetery, smoking clove cigarettes. He was notorious for whipping out his penis every time the high school girls took a shortcut through the headstones. Back then, we just considered him a creep, didn't even think about going to the police about it. It seemed like there was something wrong with him, beyond the flashing. Some sort of mental delay; he probably had Tourette's or something, because he barked at us too. I used to feel a little sorry for him.

"*Lewd and lascivious* could mean lots of different things. I couldn't find anything in the newspaper archives. If it was a big crime, wouldn't people know about it?" I say.

Effie nods, but it's one of those nods that is meant to reassure herself. To convince herself. It is well intended but unconvincing.

"And seriously, why would he bother to volunteer for the search if he had anything to do with the girl?" I say, this time to reassure myself.

Effie has to work at the library this morning, covering for the children's librarian, who is out sick. Normally, Plum would stay home with Devin, or, if necessary, alone with Zu-Zu, but they are both gone, so she comes with us. Last night Effie filled Devin in on everything that transpired with Andrews, and he gave her the name of an attorney, a friend of a friend: a small-town lawyer who handles everything from DUIs to divorces. A sort of one-stop legal shop, is the way Devin described him. I also plan to pay Strickland a visit. I am hoping that if Andrews won't listen, Strickland might. Plum will hang out at the library while I'm running errands, and then I promised her I would take her to the public pool afterward for free swim.

In town, we park, and after Effie and Plum skip up the steps and disappear inside the library, I walk down the street with the address for the lawyer in hand. When I called earlier this morning, the receptionist was able to schedule me for a consultation right away. It makes me wonder though, how good this guy is if his schedule is so wide open.

The attorney's office is in one of the Victorian buildings on the park in the center of town. Some of these gingerbread-trimmed monstrosities have been converted into apartments; these are the more run-down of the houses that circle the park. But some of them have been maintained and lovingly restored; out-of-state folks came in when the market crashed and scooped them up. A few, like this one, now house an eclectic mix of small businesses: dentists, financial advisers, computer repairmen, a yarn shop.

This building is silvery gray with a brick-colored roof and trim. There is a widow's walk at the top of what I believe is the third floor, turrets, as well as a wraparound porch that encircles the entire, enormous building, and is adorned with an American-flag bunting. The Fourth of July is still two weeks away, but the whole town is at the ready with an army of flags lining the main street, as well as a banner stretched across Main Street, reminding everyone of the scheduled parade and fireworks.

I open the heavy wooden door, step into the cool, dark foyer, and study the building directory hanging on a dark wood paneled wall. The offices of Hughes & Leighton, Attorneys at Law are on the third floor. There is no elevator here that I can see, and so I make my way up the winding mahogany staircase.

The door to the office is open, and I poke my head in, worried I am in the wrong place.

"You Waters?" a gruff voice says, and then there is a deep glugging sound. A man emerges from behind a water cooler, holding a paper cone of water. He's tall and thin and about my age, I guess. Prematurely gray, but handsome: a good, strong shadowed jaw and dark eyes. He's wearing blue jeans and a button-down white shirt. Kind of casual for a lawyer, I think, but it also puts me at ease.

"Yes," I say, smiling and offering my hand. "Tess."

"Ryan Hughes," he says, and shakes my hand, and I worry for a moment that my bones will crumble in his grasp. I surreptitiously shake it out when he finally releases it.

"Wait a minute," he says. "Were you Tess Mahoney?"

"Yeah," I say. "Once upon a time."

"I *knew* you looked familiar!" he says, and

smiles a broad warm smile. "Did you go to White Mountains Arts Camp?"

"Um, yeah?" I say, surprised. I haven't thought about that summer camp in ages.

"I did too! Eighty-three through eighty-six. I remember you! You were the poet," he says.

I grimace and then laugh. "Also once upon a time."

"I was there for music," he says. "Piano. I grew up in Putney."

"You have an amazing memory," I say.

"I remember you reading a poem about a chicken?"

"Oh my God," I say, feeling my cheeks grow hot. "I was in a William Carlos Williams phase. Red wheelbarrows and plums in the icebox and all that."

He smiles, and his eyes crinkle up at the corners. "Tess Mahoney," he says, shaking his head.

I look around the room, feeling awkward.

"Oh, my receptionist's kid got sick at day care. She had to go pick him up," he says, gesturing to the empty reception area. The Leighton of Hughes & Leighton is also apparently absent.

"You want coffee?" He motions to a pot sitting on a little console table in the waiting room.

I shake my head. I've already had enough coffee to make my hands a bit shaky, my stomach tight.

"Well, come on into my office then."

He leads me down a long corridor and into an office that looks more befitting a college professor than an attorney. There are floor-to-ceiling bookshelves, with primarily fiction titles: ones I know well. I even note one I edited myself, though I don't mention this. His desk is beaten up, its raw wood surface patterned with cup rings, endlessly interlocking circles. He motions to an overstuffed chair facing his desk, and I sit. He plops down in a ratty office chair behind the desk and reaches for an empty manila folder. I can see that someone has typed up a label with my name. He plucks a pen from his desk and scratches it at the edge of a yellow legal pad, checking for ink.

"Why don't we start at the beginning," he says, smiling, and it's the kind of smile that makes me feel like he's actually listening.

I begin by telling him everything that happened that night. I figure honesty is the best policy in this situation, and so I tell him about the wine. That I probably shouldn't have been driving and about how Strickland kept pushing the issue with me, how he kept insinuating that maybe I'd just imagined her because I'd been drinking. I tell him about stopping by Hudson's and then describe what happened on the drive home, when I looked up and saw the girl standing in the bright beam of my headlights. I blink hard and recall the details: tattered tutu, ladybug rain boots. I feel my throat grow thick as I recall the sway of her back, that round toddler belly and tangled hair.

"And then she was gone," I say, the word *gone* catching in my throat.

He pushes a box of tissues from the corner of his desk toward me, and I pluck one out. My nose is running, my eyes full.

"And you were alone?" he asks. And for some reason, the question is like a hook in my heart.

I nod. I was alone. I *am* alone. Jake is gone, and here I am dealing with all of this shit by myself.

I take a deep breath. "I don't know. There was a truck that passed me after she disappeared into the woods, after I went in looking for her. It was a white truck with landscaping equipment in the back. Massachusetts plates. I told the cops, but they don't seem to have done anything about it. They think I'm making it all up. That I'm just some sort of crackpot looking for attention."

He nods, takes a moment. "Now, please don't take this the wrong way, but do you have anything in your background, in your history, that might lead them to think this?" And I wonder how much he knows. How much homework he's been able to do in the last two hours since I called. It doesn't feel like an accusation, but I know I need to tell him. If I want him to help me, he needs to know what sort of dirt they're likely to drag up. And he seems kind. Like someone I can trust.

And so I tell him about Guatemala. About what happened when we got back to New York. About the media frenzy that ensued. About the way I couldn't even leave my house for a month without some reporter shoving a camera in my face.

"Is that all?" he asks, and I consider nodding. Lying. But he needs to know. If he's going to be able to defend me, he needs to know what he's dealing with.

After a moment of hesitation, I take a deep breath and direct him to the video on YouTube. I continue to breathe deeply and slowly as he watches the worst two and a half minutes of my life.

When it's over, I half expect him to shake

his head, send me away. Politely suggest I find someone else. This is what Oliver had done after. But instead he just scratches down some notes in an illegible script on the yellow page.

"So the police initiated a search, and it didn't turn anything up. And now they're putting the blame on you, because of your . . ." He pauses. "Your *history.*"

I nod.

"But they're ignoring a lead that might support your case. And they've publicly denounced your story, made you look like a liar in front of this entire community."

"Yes," I say. "I feel like a criminal. It's insane. It's like all of a sudden I'm in a Kafka novel or something."

He smiles. "You haven't wavered in your story, have you?"

"What do you mean?"

"I mean, you haven't given them any indication that you, yourself, have doubts about what you saw?"

I shake my head. "No," I say. "Not at all. I *know* what I saw. She is not some figment of my imagination. She's real. And she's still out there somewhere."

I remember then the second reason I've come into town.

"I'm actually on my way to the police station after this," I say. "I did a little digging myself. It took about ten whole minutes. There's a registered sex offender living right near where I spotted her."

His eyes widen. "Do you know what he was convicted of?"

"Lewd and lascivious acts with a child under fourteen," I say, and I feel my skin crawl. "He showed up to help with the search, and I got a really bad feeling about him. And there's a day care center right down the road. Isn't that illegal?"

He shakes his head, grimaces. "Not in the state of Vermont. Unless he's still under the supervision of the Department of Corrections, there are no restrictions on where he lives or works. Likewise, if he's from out of state, after he registers, there aren't a lot of requirements."

"So the neighbors weren't notified? And he can live within *walking distance* of a day care center?" I feel nauseated.

"Yep," he says.

"I need to talk to Lieutenant Andrews," I say, shaking my head. "This is crazy."

"No," he says, lifting his finger up. "I would advise you not to speak to the police at all. If they're seeking to press charges against you for making a false report, you don't want to give them any ammunition.

230

And if they question you again, you notify them that you've hired an attorney. But the most important thing is that you stick to your story."

"It's not a story," I say. "It's the truth."

"Then you keep telling them the truth. Without an admission, there's no way the DA will pursue charges."

"What about the civil suit? To get back the money spent on the search?"

"That's a bridge we'll have to cross later," he says. "Right now, let's focus on getting them to drop this."

"Wouldn't finding the girl solve all of these problems?" I say. "I mean, God forbid, if that man . . ." My stomach turns, and I can't finish my sentence.

"You cannot go to the police. This guy, Sharp? He hasn't done anything illegal. There would be no grounds for a search of his property." He is looking at me intently, his eyes warm and concerned. He is not going to budge, though.

"But what if he has her?" I ask. "What if something terrible is happening inside his house?"

I sit in a plastic chair at the edge of the pool and watch Plum swim. Because of his sister's accident, Devin insisted that both girls learn how to swim as babies. I remember watching him dunking Zu-Zu under water when she wasn't even walking yet, amazed by the instinctual closing of her eyes and holding of her breath. The way her tiny arms and legs propelled to keep her from sinking. As a result, both girls are practically amphibious: as at ease in water as they are on land.

The pool is filled with children this afternoon; it's one of the few places in Quimby where kids can hang out all day in the summer. There are only a few parents here, the ones whose children are still swimming in the baby pool. One mother blows up a pair of bright pink water wings while her diapered toddler splashes her chubby hands in the water. Her friend sprays down a little towheaded boy with sunscreen. Most parents just pull up to the gate and drop their kids off with enough money to pay the admission fee, and for a snack from the snack bar. Effie and I spent most of our summers here when we were kids as well. I learned how to swim in the cold blue depths of this pool, got my first kiss in the playground beyond the gate.

"Aunty Tess, watch!" Plum hollers and dives into the water, doing a handstand, her skinny brown legs sticking out of the water like a frog's. I smile and clap as she emerges, triumphant, and then slips into the water again.

For hours, I sit and watch her. Feeling the sun on my back, wishing I'd brought sunscreen. The sky is bright today, though in the distance I can see some dark clouds moving slowly toward us. I suspect it will be another hour or so before they cover the sun, and we might get some rain.

After Plum is done, shivering inside her beach towel, teeth chattering like the clacking keys of a typewriter, I bring her to the ice cream truck that is parked in the parking lot. She is overwhelmed by the colorful signs plastered to the front, takes forever to make up her mind before ordering an ice cream that looks like Tweety Bird's head.

233

It's one of the same milky pastel treats offered when I was a kid, and I have the fleeting thought that maybe it's some sort of relic of the past, having sat in the truck's freezer for the last thirty years.

"What are you getting?" Plum asks, licking at the already-melting confection.

"Nothing for me," I say.

As we drive back to the lake, I think about what I should do next. I had planned to go to Strickland, to get him to at least look into this guy Sharp. But now that Ryan, Ryan Hughes, fellow camper, my *lawyer*, has insisted I not go to the police, I feel aimless, restless. Like I need to do something, but my hands are tied.

I remember Lisa, the day care, and think that at least she should know. It seems crazy to me that the state doesn't require anything of these criminals beyond simply checking in with law enforcement. I know all of the information is available online, but there's no Internet access out here. Effie said that half of the year-round residents at the lake rely on the library's computers for Web access.

"Where are we going?" Plum asks as we turn into the day care's driveway.

"I just need to stop by here really quick," I say.

"Can I stay in the car?"

I start to say yes, and then realize I don't want to leave her anywhere alone. Not at the pool, and certainly not out here near these woods.

"Why don't you come with me," I say.

We walk through the chain-link gate to the doorway, and I knock on the door. I can hear a loud TV blasting cartoons inside and the sounds of kids squealing. There is the distant sound of a dog barking, probably in the backyard. I don't remember there being a dog here before.

Lisa opens the door, looking frazzled. She's got a baby in her arms again, and there's a line of spit-up running down her T-shirt. A baby gate separating us looks like it's seen better days.

"Hi, Lisa? I'm Effie's friend? The bookmobile? Um, we were here the other day, handing out flyers about the little girl that went missing."

"The cops say it was a hoax," she says, her chin jutted out defiantly. Angrily.

"Well, that's not why I'm here," I say, feeling flustered.

"Then why *are* you here?" she asks. "I don't see no bookmobile."

"It's actually about one of your neighbors. The guy who lives in that house down the road, the one with all the trailers?"

She shrugs. "What about 'em?"

"I just thought you should know he's a registered sex offender. I don't know if you knew that already, but with the kids here . . ." I trail off.

Her expression is not what I expected. Not shock or dismay, but anger.

"This is my place of business," she says, hoisting the baby up higher onto her hip.

"I know," I say, nodding. "And I thought you'd appreciate knowing. Apparently, the state doesn't require any notification for the neighbors. . . ."

"Do you have any idea what would happen if these kids' parents found out?"

"What?" I say, baffled.

"They'd be *gone*. Every last one of 'em, and where would that leave me?"

I don't know what to say. I am stunned.

"And why should I believe you anyway? You come here making shit up about some little girl in the woods, and now you're telling me my own neighbor's some sort of pervert?"

"I'm sorry," I say.

The dog barks louder and louder.

"Let him in," Lisa hollers over her shoulder. I can see the silhouette of a boy behind her in the living room. I hear a sliding door open, and the sound of nails across the floor as the animal comes running through the house, barking, barking.

I start to back up.

"I'm sorry," I say again. "I just thought it was your right to know."

And then the dog is at the precarious baby gate that separates me from Lisa. It growls, its teeth bared. It's a large black dog, a square head, its ears hacked off.

Holy shit. It's the dog from the white truck.

"Plum, honey. Go get in the car. I'll be there in one second," I say, and she runs to the car in the driveway. I hear the door slam shut.

The dog is growling, pushing against the baby gate.

Lisa yanks the dog back by its collar with her free hand and starts to close the door. "Wait," I say. "Whose dog is that?"

She stops, just as the door is about to slam shut, but she doesn't answer me.

"It's just that I saw someone, the night I saw the girl. He was driving a white truck, and he had a dog. *That* dog. I remember the ears."

I can only see a sliver of her now. Somewhere in the depths of the house a baby cries.

"It's *my* dog," she says. "I don't know what you're talking about."

And then she is gone. The door slammed shut.

I go to my car and open the driver's side door. Plum is already reading a book she's pulled from her backpack, eating an apple slice from a plastic ziplock bag.

"That was a mean dog," she says, without looking up from her book.

I nod. "I know. I'm sorry if you were scared."

"I wasn't scared," she says. "I wonder what happened to its ear. It looks like somebody cut it off with scissors. No wonder it's mean."

I nod again.

I am reeling as I back out of the long driveway. A half dozen little faces are pressed against the house's windows, peering out at me.

Plum shoves her book back into her backpack and sits staring out the window.

"You okay?" I ask.

She nods.

I shouldn't have dragged her along on this little visit. But then again, I hadn't exactly expected it to go like this either.

"I miss Zu-Zu," she says softly.

"Oh, sweetie," I say, partly relieved that her sudden sullenness has nothing to do with whatever it is that just happened at that house. But mostly I am concerned. Her eyes are full of tears.

"I bet you do," I say. "Maybe when we get back to the camp we can write her a letter. Put together a care package for her?"

"What's a care package?" she asks, interest piqued.

"It's like a box filled with things that she loves. Treats. Books or cookies. Something to make her happy if she's feeling homesick."

"I got homesick once," she says, nodding knowingly. "At my friend Maddy's house. Daddy had to come get me in the middle of the night."

I nod.

"What if Zu-Zu gets homesick in the middle of the night? Would my daddy go and get her?"

"I'm sure he would," I say. "But if we send her a care package, maybe it will keep her from getting homesick."

And thinking about care packages makes me think about art camp. About the smell of the musty cabin, the lumpy mattress. About the girl I was back then. A girl who could find poetry in chickens. A girl who wanted nothing more than to make beautiful things with words. I feel suddenly, strangely homesick for that girl with all her beautiful longing and hope.

Plum looks out the window again, studies the green that whirs past us as we drive the last stretch around the lake before we see their house through the trees.

"I didn't think I would miss her. Because she's actually not very nice, but I do. I even miss her yelling at me."

I smile and we pull into the driveway.

The clouds I saw at the pool earlier are filling the sky now. We eat dinner outside, but the air feels ominous, thick. Effie builds a fire in the stone fire pit, and we make s'mores. Effie's all turn out golden and perfect. I burn almost every single one.

When Plum goes in to bed, Effie and I sit by the fire and I tell her about what happened with Lisa. First, about her strange reaction about Lincoln Sharp.

"Isn't it weird that she'd be more concerned with losing business than with the safety of the kids?" I ask.

Effie shakes her head. "Jesus."

"Do you know her well?" I ask. "Lisa?"

"No, not at all. Just from my bookmobile route," she says.

"Have you ever seen a dog there before?"

"No," she says, shaking her head. "Not that I can remember. Why?"

And so then I tell her about the dog.

"Why would she lie about it being hers?" she asks. "It doesn't make any sense. Are you sure it's the same dog as in the truck?"

"Yes. I remember because its ears were messed up. Like somebody tried to cut them off with scissors."

"I have never understood why people do that," Effie says.

"What's that?"

"Cutting their ears. It seems so cruel."

I think of Plum's similar reaction. It's so funny to see how traits — both physical and personality — are passed down from parent to child. Physically, Plum is the perfect amalgam of Devin and Effie. But her personality is all Effie. Sweetness and compassion, a raw vulnerability, that reveals itself tender, like a bruise.

"Oh my God, I totally forgot to tell you about Ryan, the lawyer. Remember that art camp I went to in high school? He went there too."

"Seriously?" she says.

"I *know*. I don't remember him, but he remembers me."

"That's nuts," she says.

"I always forget how small this town is."

"So he says you can't go to the cops about this guy. What are you supposed to do now?"

"I don't know. My plan had been to get Strickland to dig a little deeper. To at least go check this guy's place out. But Ryan said that I shouldn't give the cops any more ammunition. They're trying to make the case that I'm a liar, that this whole thing is some sort of elaborate scheme to get attention. I guess he thinks this is just going to exacerbate the problem. But meanwhile, there's a freaking pedophile living down the road, next to a day care for Christ's sake, and nobody seems to give a shit."

Effie sighs, rubs her temples with her fingers.

"Never mind that there is a little girl somewhere out there. While we're here playing point-the-finger, she's probably cold and hungry and scared." What I don't say is that all of this is assuming she's still alive.

We both look at the fire, watch as a spark alights on a sliver of wood. Listen to the crackle and hiss as it catches, as it sparks and ignites. As it combusts and burns.

We sit by the fire until it is not much more than a pile of blackened remains and glowing embers. I can see Effie is exhausted, but I also know she'd stay out here with me all night if I needed her to.

"You should go to bed," I say.

"You okay?" she asks.

I nod, and she stretches and yawns before standing up. She comes over to me and hugs me. She smells like burned marshmallows, and I can see a little bit of white sticky fluff in her hair.

"You're wearing some of Plum's s'more," I say.

"Ugh," she says. "I'm going to go take a shower."

"I'll be in in just a little bit," I say.

After she goes inside, I use a stick and break up the remaining embers, push them around until they turn to ash. I finish the bottle of wine. When the fire is nearly out, I make my way across the dewy grass and into the camp.

I know I need to check in with Jake. It's Monday; the auction was today. Despite everything, he's going to want to share the news. But now that the auction is likely over, or at least the bids are all in, I wonder what excuses he'll come up with to stay in New York. I know that he won't come back with Devin on Wednesday. I almost don't want to hear his lame attempts to justify his absence. I'm already angry as I dial his cell number.

Effie is in the shower; I can hear the groaning pipes in the walls.

I sit in the kitchen nook, doodling on the

notepad Effie keeps near the phone. The phone doesn't even ring but rather goes straight to voice mail, and this pisses me off. It's nearly midnight. He'll tell me tomorrow that he was out celebrating. That the entire office went down the street for drinks. And I won't have to ask if she was there. Because I will hear it in every single one of his sighs. In between his words.

"Hey, it's me. Just calling to check in to see how the auction went. You're probably out celebrating. Give me a call tomorrow," I say. And then I hang up.

Effie comes out of the shower with her hair turbaned in a towel. She smells like soap. She looks at me expectantly. "Did you get a hold of Jake?"

I roll my eyes. "No."

Effie says, "Try not to worry. I'll help you figure out what to do tomorrow."

I think she's talking about Jake. As if there can be a solution to this problem. As though any of this is fixable. Or worth fixing even.

She goes to the sink and gets a glass of water.

"There's got to be a way to get someone to look into this Sharp guy. Maybe I can call it in for you? Like an anonymous tip?"

I shrug. "I just need to sleep on it, I think."

The first time I hold her, I am alone.

The woman at the orphanage said that I was allowed to come twice a week until the paperwork came through. That I could not leave the building with her, but that I could see her. Speak to her.

My stomach is in knots as I follow the tiny woman through the orphanage, to the courtyard where she is sitting, playing with the stacking toys. The rainbow-colored plastic rings of my own childhood.

"Esperanza," I say. I have been practicing her name. Like a prayer. Like a poem.

The children are held only twice a day; when she hears me say her name she holds out her arms. And so I go to her, not waiting for permission from the woman who has finally allowed me entrance here.

And then her fragile legs wrap tightly around my waist, and I breathe the scent of her hair. Her tangled hair. Her cheek is feverish against the bare skin of my chest. Her heart thumps against my own.

I bring her gifts. The soft stuffed dog, which she calls Amada, *pan dulce, champurrada,* embroidered dresses. But mostly I hold her. For each hour I am allowed inside these walls, I cling to her. Study her tiny fingernails, the lines that traverse her small pink palms. I memorize the shape of her nose, her eyes. I commit to memory the exact hue of her skin. *Mine,* I think, as she plays with my hair and curls into me. *Mine.*

It is impossible to leave her. Tears sting my eyes as her cries follow me down the long dark hallway and back out into the heat and sunlight.

At night I describe her to you, as if the simple act of saying her name, of explaining the smell of her skin (like a sweet spice with no name, like citrus) can make her real to you.

"When are you coming?" I ask. I have been here for five weeks. Any day now, she will be able to come home with us. "Her hands . . ." I start, but realize that words sometimes fail. There are no words to describe what it feels like when her hand curls around my own.

"This is really happening?" you ask.

"Yes," I say, certain of this, perhaps for the very first time. "Please. Come as soon as you can. I need you. She needs you."

I wake in the middle of the night, breathless, at the sound. An explosion. The sky detonating outside the cabin. It feels like someone has shaken me awake, but I am alone, twisted up in the cool sheets. I look at the window, and rain beats against the glass like pellets. I'd forgotten about the thunderstorms here, the electric buzz of the air. The violent utterances from the sky. In the city, storms are merely inconveniences. Never like this. Never *consuming* like this.

Thunder cracks again, and even though I know it is the storm this time, rather than a bomb, I still startle at the sound.

Normally, I have to drag myself from sleep, especially after a bottle of wine. But I am wide awake, my entire body electrified. A flash of lightning fills the cottage and I see myself, my legs, my arms, illuminated.

I feel an uneasiness, something I can't quite pinpoint. Because while my body is wide awake, my brain still feels muddy. Thick. It's almost as if I've forgotten something. It feels like a tickle at the back of my throat. An itch. And then, as my hazy thoughts begin to clear, clouds parting, lightning flashes again.

The little girl.

Oh my God. She is outside, alone, in this storm. I feel like I might cry. My throat constricts, my chest compresses. Thunder rumbles ominously, a warning. A threat.

By the time the lightning flashes again, I have crawled out of bed and am getting dressed. In the dark, I dig through my open suitcase for a pair of jeans and a sweatshirt. I slip on socks and my sneakers. I am not sure where I will go, what I will do. I only know that I can't stay here in this safe little cottage, protected from the assault going on outside, while she's out there alone. I feel the same nagging anger at Jake, at Andrews and Strickland, at all the people who have given up. At myself, even, for letting them.

I push against the door, but it resists. The wind and rain seem to want to keep me inside. When I am finally able to get the door open, the moment I step onto the little wooden porch, I am drenched. *Water,* the psychic said.

I'll need a flashlight, I think. And so I run

up the pathway toward the camp, slipping on the slick grass, feeling my knee buckle then quickly righting myself. But the door is locked. Effie locked it behind me when I left last night. We never worried about locking the doors before, but now even she doesn't feel safe here.

I run back to the guest cottage, duck inside, and fumble around my purse, looking for my keys, which have a penlight as a keychain. I pull my sweatshirt hood over my head and go back outside to my car, unlocking it with the key rather than using the remote to keep it from sounding its alarm. But as the engine clicks on, the radio blares, and I move to turn it off. I turn on the heater, feel the warm air blow from the vents across my goose-pimpled skin. I check the glove box for a flashlight, but there's nothing inside save the car's registration, a couple of CDs, a charger that plugs into the lighter.

I back out of the driveway slowly, and then I am on the road. I drive south around the lake, but I can't see the water. I can only see the rain that is coming down in hard sheets now against my windshield, all of the windows. It's like I'm in a car wash. I click the wipers to the fastest setting, but their sweeping arcs are futile against the watery assault.

I don't know where I am going; I only know I can't stay inside that safe cocoon of a cottage while that little girl is out here. How could I have not considered the rain? The weather? This is New England in the summer. It is hospitable to no one, never mind someone exposed to the elements.

I feel overwhelmed by the sense that I have failed her: that the pathetic search, the ambivalent police, are my fault. I imagine if it had been anyone else who had found her, if it had been Devin or Jake for Christ's sake, people would still be looking. Searching. The search wouldn't end until she was found. Until she was safe. But I am unreliable. Untrustworthy. Unhinged.

There are no other cars on the road, but I still drive slowly, cautiously. Part of me hopes that she will just appear again. That she will emerge from the woods into the low beam of my headlights. And this time I won't be distracted. This time I will go to her, grab hold of her; this time I won't let her go.

But the road in front of me is empty. My headlights illuminate nothing but rain and dirt, trees. She isn't going to simply materialize. The idea that she will come back is magical thinking. I know this. It's the fingers crossed, breath held inside a tunnel. Another foolish wish on a star.

A couple of miles down the road, I pull over and turn off the engine. Without my headlights, it is dark. I really wish I had a real flashlight. It's stupid to be out here like this. When I get out, I feel like I have been swallowed by the night. Like a blind person, I try to navigate the road using my other senses, but the rain distorts things. Confuses things. I find the edge of the road and walk. I walk for at least a half a mile, searching. I study the edge of the road, looking for the mailbox. Looking for the driveway that leads to that man's house.

Everyone else has given up on her. But I have not. I will not. Not until I find her.

I should be afraid, but instead I feel only determination as I walk up the dark gravel driveway. Sharp's porch light is on, an eerie beacon, but the truck is not there, which, I hope, means he's not home. I feel emboldened by his absence. And it isn't until I get to the collection of trailers that my pounding heart catches up with me.

It is still pouring rain. My clothes are soaked, heavy. I feel like I am carrying an extra fifty pounds. Stealth is nearly impossible, and so I am grateful for the storm. For the cacophony of rain. Of thunder. I'd forgotten how loud storms are. How deafening.

I walk slowly, carefully, through the labyrinth of metal outbuildings: this maze of rusted husks. There's a teardrop trailer, two horse trailers. Grass and weeds grow through them, nature trying to reclaim the metal. There's one of those campers that at-

253

tach to a pickup truck, but the hitch is sunk into the ground. This is like a graveyard. Like a strange garden.

In the distance I can see a single-wide trailer with plywood windows, and I start to feel sick. What am I doing here? Still, I move forward. The sky rumbles angrily. I step over broken bottles. Trash. This is a wasteland, a dump.

Suddenly, I trip and feel the familiar cold shock as my foot sinks into a large puddle of water. I gasp. As I pull my foot from the depths, I see a streak of lightning in the distance. It's like a flash has gone off, and my eyes water, blinking to adjust. It's not a puddle though. It's a *pool.* A plastic kiddie pool.

I think of the psychic again. *So much water.* Could this possibly be what she meant? And what the fuck? What is this guy doing with a kiddie pool? I feel sick to my stomach, but I rush forward, a renewed sense of urgency. I get to the boarded-up trailer, but the latch is padlocked.

This trailer, for some reason, has been liberated of its wheels, and so the bottom is flush with the ground. I wonder why on earth someone would have taken the wheels off of a trailer. But then again, why someone would have a compound of rusted-out trailers in their yard is also a mystery.

Another crack of thunder, and the entire world shudders. And then, beyond the sound of the rain, I hear an engine. A truck. With a bad muffler. And the light is coming from not one but two sets of headlights. I go behind the trailer, I hold still, hold my breath, try to make myself disappear.

I hear car doors slamming, and then the sound of voices. Of two men talking. My ears strain, but it is impossible to decipher their voices in the rain.

I drop to the ground, to my hands and knees. As I start to crawl, I feel a sharp pain. I wince and try not to cry out. I lift my knee up and grope to see what I've knelt on. It feels like glass, but it's just something plastic. I pick it up and peer at it in the dark. I can't tell what it is though, and I'm too afraid to turn on the penlight, so I shove whatever it is in the pocket of my sweatshirt.

I peer out around the edge of the building. Sharp's pickup is parked in the driveway, and there's another vehicle behind it. The two men's silhouettes move like beasts in the night, unloading something from the back of the second vehicle. Another truck, filled with landscaping equipment. Garbage bags. In the weak porch light, I can see.

Massachusetts plates.

I am low-crawling quickly along the ground like a soldier at boot camp. I have to get the hell out of here.

The entire world smells of rain and mud. There are leaves all over my body, mud in my eyes, in my hair. If I could burrow into the ground, under the ground, like a gopher, I would. I am moving faster than I would have ever thought possible.

I don't stand up though, until I have made it to the road and am sure they haven't seen me. Only then do I stand upright and run. I run until my lungs are on fire, and I find my car where I left it. I am breathless. My heart feels as though it is beating outside of my body.

I turn to the lake and it seems like something alive, its surface battered by the rain that continues to fall.

I've left the car unlocked, and so I climb in, aware that I am going to ruin the upholstery with the mud and rain I am wearing like a second skin. I need to get out of here. I don't want them to see my car with its New York plates, if they haven't already.

I reach into my sweatshirt pocket for my keys and my hand touches something plastic. I pull it out, but it's still too dark to see. I am worried about turning on the overhead light, so I quickly turn the car on and hold it up to the faint glow of the dash.

It's a plastic barrette, an orange bunny barrette. The kind Effie used to put in Plum's hair.

I am overwhelmed with a sense of déjà vu. Like trying to remember a dream. The barrette. Oh my god . . . it's the little girl's barrette.

Pink tutu, ladybug rain boots. Curly hair. And I remember now this barrette hanging precariously from one of her curls. I recall that fleeting impulse to reach over and snap it shut, the same odd instinct to fix the reporter's earring, which had lost its back. That familiar urge, that compulsion to take care, to fuss and right and steady and fix: an urge I had felt a thousand times with Zu-Zu, with Plum, with Jake even. A mother's fingers rubbing away a smudge, smoothing a cowlick, clearing the yellowy wax from an ear. Though more often than not, it has been an impulse to ignore. An electrical current connecting to nothing. A broken synapse.

I remember the overwhelming feeling of tenderness toward the girl though, exacerbated by that barrette come loose in her curls, *this* barrette.

But I didn't tell anyone. I completely

failed to mention the orange plastic barrette that clung by its sharp teeth to one curly lock. I didn't tell Sergeant Strickland, the reporter, even Effie, who made up the flyers with my description. It was the one detail I forgot.

As I drive back to the camp, the realization of everything I have just seen and heard, of what I just found, collects and accumulates like a gathering storm. Lincoln Sharp, the man with the truck. The dog at Lisa's, her lies. The barrette. *The barrette.* So much hinges on this little piece of orange plastic, but I fucked it up.

I pound my palms against the steering wheel until they feel bruised and tender to the touch. What am I supposed to do now? How can I still save her?

Oddly, my first thought is to tell Jake. Though that impulse, like the other, is based on habit. On a body's involuntary reflex. But that current too has been broken. Failed. Shorted out. It connects to nothing anymore.

Effie. I need to talk to Effie.

I am filthy, covered in mud and leaves. I check my reflection in the rearview mirror. I am unrecognizable: a monster that has crawled from the murky depths of somewhere. It is 4:45 A.M.; no one is awake. Only the faintest bit of light suggests that morning will come. I make my way to the guest cottage. I am exhausted, but I can't climb into those clean sheets in these clothes, so I strip them off and fall asleep nude on top of the coverlet.

I wake when the sun begins to burn my cheek. I can barely roll over, my back aches from crawling along the ground last night. I need to get into the shower before Plum wakes up. I put on my robe and knock quietly at the door to camp. Effie gets up early; I know she will be in the kitchen making coffee.

When she sees me, her mouth opens into a startled O.

I don't know how to explain anything that happened last night without sounding like a lunatic, and so I simply hold out my hand. I have been clutching it in my fist the whole night, even as I slept. When I open my palm, the skin is red and pocked from the sharp plastic tines.

"What is that?" she asks.

My throat is thick, and I shake my head. Tears coming so quickly now, there is nothing I can do to stop them.

"It's hers," I say. "It was in her hair. It

must have fallen out."

Effie picks it up, takes it from my palm, and studies it like a foreign object, an artifact from another time and place.

"You didn't mention it," she says, her eyes seeking something in mine. "You didn't say anything about a barrette."

"I forgot," I say, choking on the words. On my failure. I don't know how to explain that moment, that my hand longed to reach and touch her tangled hair, to snap it shut.

And now I worry that she too won't believe me. That maybe I *am* crazy. If I had really seen this barrette, why did I fail to catalog it with all the other details? How could I have forgotten when I remembered everything else?

No.

I *saw* her. She's real. This is the proof of her existence, not of my insanity.

A sob escapes from my throat, and Effie pulls me close.

"Where?" she says. "Where did you go?"

I shake my head.

"Where did you find it?" she asks again, this time in the same tone of voice I have heard her use with the girls when they aren't being forthcoming. "Tess, you have to tell me where you found it."

"At Sharp's," I say.

I feel her entire body tense. "You went to *his* house? In the middle of the night? What if he had a gun?"

I realize then how truly insane this sounds. I don't know how to explain that it was the rain, the storm that propelled me out of my bed and into my car. That I couldn't stand the thought of her outside alone as the sky made its assault on the earth. I don't know how to justify this odd trespassing. The only thing I have to offer is this little orange barrette.

I take a hot shower, watch the night swirl down the drain in muddy rivulets. I pluck out leaves that accumulate in the rubber drain catch and toss them in the trash. It takes three shampoos and rinses before the water from my hair runs clear.

When I come out of the shower, Effie has made breakfast and hands me a cup of coffee. I sit down in the kitchen nook, and she sits across from me. Plum is still asleep. She will likely sleep another hour or two before she stumbles down the stairs, bleary-eyed and hungry.

And over coffee and thick slabs of hot coffee cake, I tell Effie everything that happened. But this time I am careful not to forget a single detail. The trailer, the child's swimming pool. Sharp, the truck with the Massachusetts plates. I even tell her about what the psychic had said: *Water, sharp.* I struggle to remember the other things she said, that I dismissed. She said she saw red, felt there was something underground?

"We have to tell the police," she says. "They can't ignore this."

"I was trespassing," I say. I think of the hardware store signs, the neon orange missives nailed to Sharp's trees. BEWARE OF DOG. NO TRESPASSING. "If they find out I did this, the police will have everything they need to make a case against me."

"But you have *evidence,*" she says. "You have proof now. If not that he has her, that she's been on his property." She gestures to the barrette, which sits on the table between us.

"But they don't *know* about the barrette," I say. "I never told them. I forgot."

"What about DNA?" she asks. There must be something on there. Her hair?

"But according to them, there's no missing child," I argue. "Nothing to compare the DNA to. She does not *exist.*"

Effie sighs, crosses her arms, and holds her shoulders. "I think you should tell Ryan. There's got to be some sort of — what do you call it? Like client confidentiality?"

"Attorney-client privilege," I offer. I have been here before. I know about secrets between lawyers and their clients. "But won't he drop me? Normal people don't do things like this."

Effie smiles and reaches across the table for my hand. "You're not normal people."

And I know she doesn't mean it as an insult. That she may be the only person in the world who, despite everything, still believes me.

"Okay," I say. "I'll call him later."

"Good," she says.

"But I have another call to make first."

Mary McCreary, *psychic detective,* pulls into the driveway in her beat-up red Mustang just past eleven. All signs of last night's storm are gone. The sky is blue again, though spotted with clouds. Plum and Effie are making tie-dye T-shirts in the yard. Their creations hang from the long line stretched between trees: electric and bright. It's not even noon, but I'm drinking a beer, trying to stave off the anxiety, which gnaws at me like a small but determined chipmunk.

I wonder, as she gets out of the car and waddles into the yard toward me, if I have made a terrible mistake. This could be total hocus-pocus. I worry I am just reaching for anything to help me support my building case.

I stand up and walk to her, hand outstretched.

"Hello, hello again," she says. I notice this

time that she has tiny teeth and childlike hands.

"Can I get you a beer?" I ask.

She nods. "Yes, *please.*"

I don't tell her where I found the barrette. I don't want to influence her at all. I don't want to feed her the information; instead I'm hoping that she'll come up with it on her own. Proving, somehow, that this isn't all just wishful thinking but rather that she is able to somehow read these clues better than I can.

We sit together at the kitchen nook.

I put the barrette in her palm, and she eyes me suspiciously. I also don't tell her to whom it belongs, though I have a feeling this is obvious, or else I wouldn't have asked her to come all this way.

She curls her small fingers over the barrette; it disappears inside her fist. She closes her eyes and takes a deep breath.

I hold my own breath and wait.

For several moments there is nothing but the rattling sound in her chest.

And then her fingers uncurl and she drops the barrette as though it has burned her. I half expect for the pink flesh of her palms to bear the branding of the little bunny.

"What?" I say. "What is it?"

"Sharp," she says.

"I know, I know," I say, impatient for something she hasn't already offered. For something new. "Lincoln Sharp. What else?"

She shakes her head. "No, *teeth*. Sharp teeth."

I study the barrette, those innocuous plastic tines. Tears sting my eyes. This was stupid. Maybe I *have* lost my mind.

"It's scary, scary. With sharp teeth," she says, her voice childlike. "She's afraid of the scary black dog."

My heart stops like a cork in my throat.

The dog.

"Where did she go?" I ask, and Mary seems disoriented. A sleepwalker suddenly lurching into consciousness. "Mary, where is she now?"

She shakes her head.

"Please, tell me where she is, where she ran? You said she saw a dog? When? Before or after I saw her?" I am so desperate for answers I almost forget who I am asking. She's a quack. I don't believe in any of this bullshit.

But still, she didn't know about the dog. She didn't know about Sharp either.

"You said something about something being underground. Do you mean a grave? Please? You said there was red . . . is that blood?"

"I'm sorry," she says. "It doesn't work like that. They're just flashes. Just little bits and pieces that come. They're not in any sort of order."

"But what am I supposed to do now?" I ask. "What does it mean?"

"I don't know," she says.

When Mary leaves, I follow her red convertible around the lake toward town, but as I near Hudson's I realize that my tank is almost empty. And so I pull into the dirt lot, and she disappears down the road. She has a dentist appointment this afternoon back in Burlington. This was all she could offer today.

Before I get out of the car to fill the tank, I check my phone. There are no missed calls, but there is a text from Jake. CMB. His shorthand, his adolescent text speak, irritates me. He's forty-five years old. What's he so busy doing he can't spell out *call me back*? I still haven't spoken to him since he and Devin left on Sunday morning. I know I need to tell him about the police, but that is a conversation I'd rather not have. The longer I wait to return his call, the longer I can prolong the inevitable. And so instead of texting him back, I toss my phone in my purse. Out of sight, out of mind.

But that's not true; I am distracted. And so it takes a few minutes before I realize the gas pump isn't turning on. I already entered my PIN. I selected the grade. I lean over and fiddle with the handle; it's secure in the gas tank opening.

I grab my purse and head into the store.

When I get inside, I see it's the same boy who was working the night that I found the girl. He's Billy Moffett's son, Effie told me. And he does look a little bit like a younger version of Billy, the one we knew all those years ago. He's sitting behind the counter, picking at his cuticles with a pen cap.

"Excuse me," I say. "I can't get the gas to turn on."

He looks up. "Oh, hi."

"Hi. The gas isn't coming on."

"Did you fiddle with the nozzle?"

"Yeah."

"Did you select the grade?"

"Yes. I did everything. It's just not turning on."

He ducks behind the counter, I guess to whatever machine controls the tanks.

"Go try it again. If it don't work this time, just pull up to the next pump," he says.

"Thanks," I say.

"Wait," he says, a flash of recognition on

his face. He points his finger at me, bobbing it up and down. "You're that lady who found the little girl."

I sigh and nod.

"There's still a few folks showing up to search," he says. "Even though the cops said it was a hoax."

"Really?" I look toward the doorway to the back room. But it's dark back there. No signs of life.

"Yeah. Yesterday they came about noon. Maybe five or six of 'em that are still looking."

Something about this warms my heart, though I know it has nothing to do with me, and everything to do with the possibility that there is a child out there alone in the woods.

I'm sure the police have already spoken to him, but he seems friendly, and so I say, "Hey, I don't know if you remember that night I came in. You were working, I think. I bought a bottle of wine?"

"Yeah," he says. "You know, some people were saying you were drunk. That you were hallucinating or something." His skin colors red and he stares down at his bloody cuticles.

I smile to assure him I've heard this all before, that it doesn't bother me.

271

"Well," I say. "There was another guy in here. A guy filling up his white pickup truck. He had painter's overalls on? A big black dog in his truck. Flatlander," I add, trying to ally myself with him. "Massachusetts plates?"

"Yeah, I know him," he says.

I am taken aback. I *know* him. Not I *remember* him.

"Yeah? Does he own a camp on Gormlaith or something?"

"Maybe," he says, shrugging. "Comes up pretty much every weekend. Sometimes during the week too."

"Do you know his name?" he asks.

"Nah," he says. "He's not real talkative."

"Does he ever use a credit card? Maybe you would have a copy of one of his receipts?"

"Shit no," the boy says. "Excuse my French. He always pays cash. Has a huge roll of cash usually. Must be thousands a dollars he's carryin' around in his pocket."

"Really?" I say. "Does he maybe have a girlfriend up here?" I ask, thinking of Lisa. "Have you ever seen him with anybody else?"

He shakes his head. "Nope. Just comes in, fills up his tank, buys a twelve-pack and takes off. Ain't never said two words to me."

"So how long has he been coming around here?" I ask. Most people with summer camps on Gormlaith come and open them up after Memorial Day. Just at the end of mud season when the snow has finally mostly melted, and things are starting to bloom.

"About six months, nine months?" he says, shrugging.

"Wait. You mean in the winter too?" I ask, confused. Summer people don't come up here in the winter. Especially not to do landscaping. "You sure it's the same guy?"

"Yeah. Guy with the dog. Messed-up ears," he says. "I remember because it was like ten below windchill one day, and he had the poor dog chained in the back of his truck. No freaking ears. It musta been freezing. I'm an animal lover, and I remember it pissed me off. 'Scuse my French again."

"That's terrible," I say, nodding. My heart is pounding hard in my chest.

"I even wrote down his plate number, thought about reporting him to the authorities. That's animal cruelty, ain't it?"

"You wrote down his plate number?" I ask, stunned.

"Yeah, course I didn't wind up doin' nothin'. Felt weird with him being a regular customer and all. Seems like a nice enough

273

guy. And ever since then the dog's been in the cab of the truck with him anyway."

"Do you still have it?" I ask.

"The plate number?" he says.

I nod.

"What for?"

"The police never talked to you about this?" I ask. "A few days ago, when everybody was still looking for the girl?"

He shakes his head, shrugs his shoulders. "Nobody talked to me about nothing."

I feel my body tremble. They *never* believed me. Not even enough to ask this kid a simple question.

"I got it right here," he says, bending down under the counter. "I wrote it down in the same place where we keep a list of folks who bounced checks with us." He plucks out a sheet of paper littered with names, sets it down on the counter and turns it to face me. He taps at the paper. His cuticles are raw and scabby.

"Right there," he says. *Dog/MA pickup 993 MX1.*

I pull my phone out of my purse and enter the info into my notes app.

"Thank you," I say.

"Let me know if the gas still ain't coming out," he says as I rush out the door.

The streets are busy when I get into town. It's lunchtime, and so people are out on the sidewalks, headed to lunch at the Miss Quimby Diner, into the bank and post office to run errands. Quimby is a typical small town in that it has one main street, one place of commerce. Most businesses have been around since I was a kid, but a few others come and go, the storefront signs different each time we come to visit Effie and Devin. When we were kids we always used to dream about opening up a bookshop on this street, the kind of bookshop that has a big orange cat that sleeps in the window. But instead, Effie became a librarian, and I went to the city and became an editor. Funny how dreams change. How reality deviates from what it is that we truly want. I can't help but wonder what this means for Zu-Zu. For Plum. For me and for Jake now.

I make my way to the park, to Ryan's office, nervous about spilling everything. He's the only lawyer I've got, quite possibly the only lawyer (besides his partner) in town. I really can't risk losing him in case the cops actually follow through with the charges against me.

I climb the stairs, and this time the door to the offices is shut. I push it open gently, and poke my head into the lobby.

There's a woman sitting at the reception desk this time, and she looks somewhat familiar.

"Tess?" she says, standing up. "Oh my God, I heard you were in town!"

I feel my cheeks redden as I struggle to place her face. Jesus. Does everyone in town know who I am? Coming here has been like one endless reunion.

"You don't know who I am, do you?" she says.

I smile, hesitate, hope that it will come to me.

"It's okay, it's okay," she says, waving her hand in front of her face. "It's Beth. Beth Fowler."

The name rings a bell, but a bell that is so far away, I can barely hear the jingle.

"I was . . . um . . . *bigger* . . . in high school," she says, standing up from the reception desk now. She's an attractive woman, about my age. Athletic-looking. A blond bob and soft brown eyes. "I lost a hundred and fifteen pounds two years ago. Remember, we had Mr. Noonan for calculus senior year."

"Elizabeth Fowler," I say, nodding. "I remember you! Wow! That's amazing."

Elizabeth Fowler was in my calculus class, and I also remember she was on the track and field team: shot put and discus. She must have weighed two hundred and fifty pounds in high school. Yet, her face is exactly the same. It's as if this woman in front of me was hiding inside that girl all along.

"It's great to see you," I say.

And then we stand there, nodding. We really didn't know each other in high school. I'm pretty sure this is the longest conversation we've ever had.

"Are you on Facebook?" she asks.

"Oh, yeah," I say. "It's Tess Waters now. You should find me. Or I can find you?"

She nods. I nod.

"Um, is Ryan here? I called earlier but got his voice mail."

"Oh, he just went to grab lunch. He should be back any minute," she says. "Have a seat."

Ryan comes in just as I'm flipping open a tattered copy of *People* magazine. It's at least a year old.

He's got a greasy paper bag in his hands and a fountain soda. "Tess!" he says. "Shoot. I didn't think you'd get here so fast. Are you hungry? I would have picked something up for you too."

"I'm fine," I say. "Do you want to eat first? I can wait."

"No, come in. If you don't mind, I can eat while we chat."

"Sure," I say. "It was nice seeing you, Elizabeth."

"I actually go by Beth now." She smiles.

And I think about reinventing yourself. About how the past always lingers. You shed a hundred and fifteen pounds, change your name, but your eyes are the same. The self-conscious smile remains.

Ryan sits down and unwraps a big roast beef sandwich from a wax paper wrapper.

"So, have you heard anything more from Andrews?" he asks.

"No," I say, shaking my head. "Have you?"

"I called over after we spoke yesterday, told them that I would be representing you as your counsel. I let him know that any more communication with you needs to go

278

through me. Other than that, no."

He takes a big bite of his sandwich, and I figure now is as good a time as any to talk.

"Um," I start. "I came in because there's some new, um, information that I was thinking might help."

He chews slowly, cocks his head.

"So, last night I went by Sharp's house. . . ."

His eyes widen.

"Just to look around a little bit . . . to see if I could find anything."

He sets his sandwich down, chews and forces himself to swallow.

"You trespassed on his property?" he says.

"He's got all these trailers, like a whole collection of them. It freaked me out the first time I saw them, and now, knowing what I know, I just kept thinking about that woman. Jaycee Dugard? The one that man kept in his backyard. Or those girls in Cleveland? What if he has her? He's a registered sex offender. What if she's *there*?"

He is shaking his head slowly. "You know you really shouldn't be investigating on your own. Given the accusations, you might even want to stop joining the search party. . . ."

"Wait," I say. I need to at least get the story out. "There's one trailer that isn't on its wheels anymore. The windows are all boarded up. . . ."

"You went inside? Jesus Christ, Tess. That's breaking and entering."

"No," I say. "It was locked. And then he came home, and get *this,* he was with the guy in that pickup truck. The one from Massachusetts I saw that night."

He's not shaking his head anymore.

"Did he see you?" he asks.

"No. I left," I say.

"Do you have any idea how dangerous that was? How *illegal*?"

"Wait," I say, pleading with him to just hear me out. "I found something. Something important."

I reach into the small pocket of my jeans and pull out the barrette. My hand is trembling. I set it on the desk next to his sandwich.

"What is this?" he asks.

"It's hers," I say. "It was in her hair when I found her."

He picks it up, studies it. A dollar-store piece of plastic, the only evidence that this little girl is real.

"But here's the problem," I say. "I forgot to tell the cops about the barrette. I don't know why it slipped my mind. I was so focused on what she was wearing, I forgot all about it."

He sets the barrette back down on the desk and pushes it toward me. Returning it to me.

"You were trespassing. And you removed property from the premises."

I feel scolded. Like a child.

"She was *there*. Maybe still is," I say. "Should any of that matter if he did something to her? If he has her?"

He sits back in his chair and pushes his hands through his hair. "Well," he says. "There is some good news here."

"Yeah? How so?" I say.

"If a police officer were to have found the barrette through what amounts, essentially, to an illegal search of this guy Sharp's property, then it would be inadmissible."

I nod, waiting.

"*But,* you're a civilian. Not a cop. Usually, the exclusionary rule doesn't apply when a civilian conducts an illegal search. Unless you're working for the police, or as some sort of civilian police agent, the evidence won't be suppressed."

"What does that mean?"

"It means, you're one lucky chick."

"How so?"

"Well, first, that Sharp didn't come out and blow your head off. Which he would've had every right to do, by the way. You might

281

want to remember that the next time you think about snooping around. Second, I think this will force the cops to look into this guy."

"There's actually more," I say.

"Oh Christ," he says. "Do I even want to hear this?"

One thing I have learned over the years is that people respond to good news a lot better after getting bad news. Even I am this simple. This predictable.

"Yeah," I say, and smile. "I have the plate number for the white truck."

After dinner, Effie and Plum lie together on the daybed on the front porch, reading. I sit in a rocking chair and linger, avoiding the inevitable, enjoying the sound of Effie's voice as she reads to Plum, who is curled up next to her, her head in her lap. Effie told me that Zu-Zu stopped wanting to be read to when she was six, that she preferred to read to herself. But she suspects she'll be reading to Plum even through high school. Effie's voice is soothing, hypnotic even, and I find myself feeling drowsy. But I can't fall asleep. I need to call Jake again. I've avoided it long enough.

"I'm calling Jake," I whisper.

Effie nods.

Plum's eyes look heavy. She is fighting sleep.

I slip outside with the cordless phone Effie keeps upstairs and sit down at the picnic table, where I am still able to get a connection, before dialing Jake's cell number.

The phone rings once.

"Hey," he says, breathless. "Did you get my text? Why didn't you call this afternoon? I was worried about you."

I wince. I don't want him worrying about me. I don't want him feeling compassion or concern or tenderness toward me. It makes it too hard. It confuses me.

"How did the auction go?" I ask.

He pauses. "It was wild. We got offers from FSG, Knopf, Simon and Schuster, and Harper Collins."

"How much?" I ask. Because this is, ultimately, what matters. We can pretend otherwise, but the bottom line is always the bottom line in publishing, as it is in any other industry.

"All but one are offering six figures," he says.

"That's great," I say, trying to muster enthusiasm for Jake despite my feelings about Charlie. That smug asshole. "Who are you going to go with?"

"Wait. *Three* of them are offering six figures, but Judy at Knopf is offering one-point-five," he says. He is giddy, like a child. *"Million."*

"Holy shit," I say.

"Yeah," he says. "I *know.*"

284

This is Jake's first seven-figure deal. It could be a real game changer for the agency. These days a seven-figure advance is practically unheard of.

"How is Charlie handling it?"

"Well, he's Charlie," he says.

"What does that mean?"

"It means he doesn't want to give up world rights."

I picture him, the petulant little shit. The newest fist-pounding, feet-stomping Veruca Salt of the publishing world.

"How long do you have?"

"Until Friday," he says. "I'm trying to keep them from figuring out that he's putting up a fuss. But I feel like I'm dealing with a child."

I could have told him this would happen six months ago. Meanwhile, most of Jake's other clients are pulling in twenty-thousand-dollar advances, keeping their day jobs, and hoping for their big break. I have a half dozen writer friends who write brilliantly, beautifully, who have no retirement savings, no way to pay for their kids to go to college. This is a cruel, cruel industry. The spoils seem always to go to the spoiled.

"I'm sure he'll come around," I say, though I have no idea if this is true. And, though I should, I really don't care.

"How are things there?" he asks.

So much has happened in the two days since he left, I'm not even sure where to begin. Once, a long time ago, I would have gone into excruciating detail about the conversation, the accusations Andrews made. I would have told him about my midnight trek onto Sharp's property. I would have confided in him how scared I am. For the little girl. For myself. And he would have helped me work through it all. He would have helped me come up with a concrete plan, a step-by-step solution that would get me from point A to point B. Once, he wouldn't have even left me here to deal with this shit on my own in the first place.

But nothing is the same anymore. I am Alice on the other side of the looking glass, where things are both the same and completely different than they should be. Where the words are jumbled, and I can barely remember the way things are supposed to be anymore.

"Okay," I say. "The police called off the search. But people are still looking. Really holding out hope."

Hope. The word stings us both. I can feel his chest heave on the other end of the line. It's a sword, that word. A dagger.

Silence. And then finally, "Anything new at all? Has anyone else come forward? That guy with the truck?"

"Not yet," I say. "But there are a couple of leads."

"Like what?" he asks, and now it just feels like he's challenging me. Questioning me.

"Well, I found out some stuff about one of the neighbors. He's a registered sex offender." I figure this is the most compelling and concrete and convincing thing I've got.

He pauses.

"Tess, I read online that the police are calling it a hoax."

I feel my whole body grow hot, my nerve endings raw. I look toward the porch, where I can see Plum and Effie curled up together still, the orange glow of the light turning them into shadows.

"Do you think about her?" I ask.

On the lake, a loon calls out to another in that familiar mournful keen. But its cry goes unanswered.

Jake is quiet.

Once, he would have known right away what I was talking about. But now, I suspect his mind goes first to the woman he's sleeping with. To *Jess*. That Esperanza, like the little girl, has disappeared into the dark woods of his imagination.

"No," he says, a deep sigh that sounds both exasperated and exhausted. "Not anymore."

I squeeze my eyes shut, feel tears. When I open them, the lake and trees blur together in front of me.

"She would be ten," I say. "Like Plum."

The solitary loon cries again. Unanswered.

"She *is* ten," he says. "She's not dead."

I shake my head. It is impossible for me to imagine her still alive. Still on this earth. The day that we flew away from Guatemala, I had to pretend that she was dead, or I would never have been able to leave.

"I feel like you will never let this go," he says. "Never let her go. And I am so tired of competing with a ghost. I can't win."

I hold the phone away from my ear because his words hurt.

I want to tell him that *I* am tired of competing with all the others. With his clients. With his colleagues. With Jess and all the possible others. I am tired of competing with his papers and his laptop and his cell phone. Because that is a competition I can never, ever win.

"When are you going to come back?" he says. "So we can deal with this? Figure this out?"

I study my hands in the dark. The long

fingers. The nails bitten to the quick. I feel strangely unattached from myself. Both inhabiting my body and outside of it.

I turn to the window and watch as Effie leans over Plum, tucking her into the daybed, where she has fallen asleep. The simple gesture, the way she leans over and kisses her, is almost unbearable.

"Not until I find her."

When your taxi pulls up I watch you from the balcony. I peer down at the street as you pay the driver and gather your small suitcase from the trunk. You look up, as if you sense me watching you, and I wave. But I know that all you see above you is the purple canopy of jacaranda blossoms.

After nearly six weeks, we are like strangers. I have forgotten the details of your face. As we lie in the bed, and you fall asleep, I trace my finger along the scar that runs from your nose to your lip. You have shaved, and the scar is exposed, the raised welt and sleep making you somehow vulnerable.

We sleep through the morning, and wake in the midst of making love, our bodies reaching for each other, clinging to the familiarity of each other's flesh. Above us, the ceiling fan rocks as it stirs the thick, hot air. I think of other hotels, other countries, other cities. How is it that I love you more when we are away from home? When the world around us is unfamiliar? Something about traveling has always awoken me, made me hungrier for you. I have always felt closer to you the farther away we are from everyone else. But there is something else this time. Something beyond the strange smells and sounds, this thick fragrant air. Something beyond the normal sense of being together, alone, allied, among strangers. There is an urgency to this. Because soon, we will not be alone again. I think I am terrified of what we are about to become.

For six days, we live at this precipice. Waiting.

I am raw, tender, bruised by the time the call comes. My lips are swollen, and it stings when I pee. I order cranberry juice in the cafe, blushing when the waitress gives me a knowing glance. She thinks we are newlyweds, that we are just beginning this life together. And I think that she is both wrong and right.

"You must come right away," our lawyer says.

We are slick with sweat, my skin tight with dried saliva, my cheeks stinging from the scruff of your unshaven cheeks. The sheets are stiff, filthy. I worry I have forgotten to eat as I stand up and see stars, the world vignetting.

"She says we need to come right away."

You have not met Esperanza yet. You have not held her in your arms, smelled the tangerine scent of her skin. You do not know the sound of her raspy voice or the way her heartbeat feels under the pads of your fingers. She is still only a dream, a promise, a wish.

"This is real?" you say.

I nod and tears run hot down my cheeks.

On Wednesday morning, I call Ryan's office three times before I finally get through. I had asked him if I could go with him to talk to Andrews, to show him the plate number, the barrette, but he insisted that the information would be better coming from him.

When he finally answers the phone, he sounds like he's been running. His voice is muffled.

"I'm sorry. Did I get you at a bad time?" I ask.

"No, no . . . I rode my bike to work. Hold on, I just need to dry off." I hear rustling sounds. Imagine him wiping sweat off his forehead.

"You can call me back," I offer. "But call on the landline number I gave you. I'm at the lake."

"No," he says. "It's fine. I was just going to call you."

I grab a bagel from the cupboard and

search the drawer for a serrated knife. There is one bagel left from the ones we brought Zu-Zu, and I forgot to get them pre-sliced.

"So how did it go?" I ask. "With the police?"

"It went okay. I have a buddy at the PD. I asked him to run the plate number. I also asked him to look into this Sharp guy, told him that he appears to be a registered sex offender."

"He *is* a registered sex offender," I say. "Did you give him the barrette?"

I had been reluctant to leave it with him. It seemed like the only true thing I had connecting me to her. Relinquishing it felt dangerous.

"No," he says. "Not yet."

"But that proves she was there. It's *hers*," I say.

"I think it would be best if we keep that information to ourselves. For now anyway."

I can't find a serrated knife, so I grab a butcher knife and start to cut the bagel. It has gotten stale, hard in the last six days.

"Listen," he says. His breath is even now. Calm. "We need to let them think they're the ones building this case. I work with cops a lot. The last thing they want is to feel like some civilian is overriding them, doing their job. . . ."

"Well, if they actually *did* their job, then maybe I wouldn't have to," I say. And then the knife slips, cutting into the thin skin between my thumb and index finger. I wince and grab at a paper towel from the rack. It is soaked with blood within seconds.

"Tess, I know. I'm on your side. But just trust me on this. Let Andrews feel like he's the one putting these pieces together. Do you want to find her, or do you want to be the hero?"

My throat swells. I can feel my heart beating in the wound in my hand.

"I want to find her. I want *them* to find her."

"Then trust me," he says. "Lay low. Be patient."

I nod. He believes me.

"You should probably get stitches," Effie says, cradling my hand in hers. The slice is clean, deep. It won't stop bleeding.

I shake my head. "I'll be fine. I'll just get some of that liquid Band-Aid stuff," I say.

"Can I see, can I see?" Plum asks. She is the child of the iron stomach, the nerves of steel. I have watched her dissect bugs, pull a splinter out of her own heel. She recently had to have two adult teeth removed to make space, and Effie said she did it with

Novocain alone. I am humbled by her fortitude, by her grit.

Plum bends over and examines my hand, assessing the damage.

"I had worse," she says, finally, with a shrug. "Remember when I rode my bike into that barbed wire fence?" she asks Effie, as if it's possible to forget something like that.

"Look," she says, turning her shoulder to me. There is a raised pink welt like a seam in her skin.

"It's fine," I say, when Effie shakes her head again. "I'll just catch a ride with you into town when you go to the library. You can drop me off at the Rite Aid. I'd like to go with you on your route today too, if that's okay."

"Yeah?" she says.

"I want to see if that dog is still at Lisa's house."

"Actually, Lisa's not on my Wednesday route. I'm not scheduled to go back there until Friday," she says. "Besides, what good will that do?"

I shrug. I don't know how to tell her how restless I am. Now that Ryan has forbidden me from doing any more investigating on my own, now that the information I *have* managed to gather is out of my hands, I don't feel relief, but powerlessness. It's the same feeling I get the moment I buckle myself into a seat on an airplane.

Flying never used to scare me. I never thought much about it at all. I used to travel quite a bit for work, and Jake and I always prided ourselves on being adventurous travelers. In just one year, we went to Cambodia, Greece, and Brazil. But something happened after Guatemala. I could no longer get onto a plane without feeling a flush of terror and regret. Relinquishing control, trusting, had brought me nothing but heartache.

Yesterday, when I handed everything over to Ryan, I had felt the same way. I'd even thought, for a moment, that I would just leave his office and march down the street to the police station myself. But somehow, he'd managed to convince me that there was too much at stake. That if I refused to surrender this, if I refused to trust him, then it would all be for naught. And that it might ruin any remaining chance we had of the search being resumed.

I wander around Rite Aid searching for the first aid aisle. It is too bright in here, too cold. The Muzak on the overhead speakers plays some pop song from when Effie and I were in high school, and I get that sensation again that I am being somehow transported to a place where things are both recognizable but, at the same time, twisted. I could be in the cold, brightly lit bathroom at the high school, the tinny sound of the music coming from the school dance in the cafeteria. I could be slumped over in the bathroom stall, thinking I might never come out again. The pulsing of my heart in my ears is the same. Or I could be in the small bar where I'd stumbled that afternoon eight years ago, the one with the tiled floor and the barstools painted in candy colors. Music coming from a transistor radio on the countertop. The ceiling fan overhead whirring uselessly, endlessly. All of it dizzying. All of it unbearable.

I need to leave the store, but I have gotten myself turned around in this labyrinth of sundries and don't remember which way the exit is. I start to feel queasy as I try to retrace my steps. And then when I turn the corner, I see a woman pushing a cart.

She's an older woman, maybe in her sixties, and she is hunched over the little basket where you keep your purse. I can see that there is a baby in the cart, and she is cooing to it gently. But as I get closer, I can see that it's not a baby at all. It's a *doll.* Just a filthy, rubber baby doll.

"Mama's just got to pick up a few things, sweetheart," the woman says. And I feel that swooning feeling again. I dodge her cart and weave down the aisle away from her. I can't seem to walk straight; I feel almost drunk.

And then I am overwhelmed with a need to sit down. But where? I follow the overhead signs to the pharmacy and see the blood pressure machine. I sit down in its plastic seat, which cradles me in an unyielding embrace.

"Ma'am," someone, a girl in a blue apron, says. "Are you okay?"

I focus on her voice, which sounds like it is at the end of a tunnel.

I speak, try to pretend that this isn't happening again. My own voice sounds like it is under water. "I'm looking for liquid Band-Aids?" I say.

"Um, maybe you should go to a doctor?" the girl says.

I don't understand at first, and then look down at my bandaged hand and see that it is soaked with blood. It is startling. Shocking. No wonder I was feeling faint. But that isn't the reason, not the real reason. Still, I nod.

Effie drives me to the urgent care clinic, and by the time we get there, the lightheadedness has turned to nausea. She has me hold my hand above my heart to keep it from bleeding so badly, but the new bandage we put on in the parking lot of the Rite Aid is already completely soaked.

The nurse practitioner on duty takes one look at my hand and scolds me.

"And why exactly didn't you come straight to us?" she asks.

Her breath smells of coffee. That and the antiseptic smell of the clinic do not help the feeling that I am on the verge of vomiting. I try not to look at my hand as she sews it up. When she is finished, she gives me a tube of antibiotic cream and tells me how to care for it.

"Now I'm going to need you to come back in to get these removed in about a week. And if you see anything unusual, redness, swelling, discharge, or if you start to run a fever, I need you to call us right away. You think you can do that?"

I nod obediently. Chastised.

Effie and Plum are sitting in the waiting room when I come out, sheepish and embarrassed, a fresh bandage covering my wound.

"Can I see the stitches?" Plum says.

I ride in the bookmobile with Effie as she drives her Wednesday route. This route takes us deeper into the woods this time, beyond the picturesque Lake Gormlaith into the dark forest near the pond whose bottom is made of sawdust. We made the mistake of swimming there once when we were kids. Both of us got ear infections and were sneezing sawdust for weeks.

"Do you still go to the swimming hole?" I ask.

There is a beautiful spot not too far from here where Effie and I used to go to swim. It was so private, so remote, we didn't even bother with clothes. And best of all, there were long flat slabs of rock that sucked up the warmth of the sun. We'd lie on those rocks for entire days sharing secrets.

The last time we went there together was when I came to visit her when she came home after three years in Seattle. It was the summer after her ex-boyfriend, Max, over-dosed. The summer she met Devin.

"God, I haven't been there in years," she says.

"We should go," I say. "When you finish your route."

"That would be nice."

"What's a swimming hole?" Plum asks. She sounds leery.

I smile at her. "Do you believe in fairies?" I ask.

She scrunches up her nose. "Maddy says they're not real."

"But what do *you* think?" I ask.

I think of Star, the fairy who left them gumdrops. How she always seemed to visit when I did. I kept every letter Zu-Zu and Plum ever wrote to Star. Someday I plan to make a little book for them of all those notes.

She shrugs.

"Well, I know for a fact that there are fairy houses at the swimming hole. Your mom and I used to find them all the time." Her eyes widen, though I know she's trying to remain pragmatic about this. This is *ten:* when there is still the remote possibility of fairies.

"Can we go, Mama?" Plum asks, and Effie turns to her and smiles.

"Sure," she says. "I've got three more stops. We can go after that."

Traversing a creek is a narrow wooden bridge, which is barely wide enough for a small car, never mind the bookmobile, so we park and go the rest of the way on foot.

It is hot today, and I am grateful for the shade as we duck into the woods. The path here is not as well-worn as when Effie and I used to come here, and I wonder for a

302

minute if we're in the right place.

Effie leads, Plum trails behind, and I follow.

"Is that it?" Plum asks, pointing down toward the enclosed body of water, circled by a wall of rock. There is a small waterfall that feeds it.

"That's it," Effie says.

We all scramble through the thick foliage, enormous ferns tickling our arms and legs.

We get to the water and Plum says sadly, "I don't have my swimsuit."

"That's the best thing about this place," Effie offers. "You don't need a suit. It's private."

Plum looks skeptical. When she was a baby, she never wore clothes. She was a notorious nudist. It wasn't until she was about six or seven that she suddenly got modest. I remember Effie saying how sad it made her, how it signaled the end of something for her when Plum felt compelled to cover up.

"You can swim in your panties," she says. "Here. I'll do it too."

Plum looks back in the direction we came from.

"We're all alone," I nod, reassuring her that no one has followed us here.

She cautiously peels off her T-shirt and

slips out of her shorts. She's ten, but she still has the wonderful round belly of a little girl, a belly made for making raspberries, ticklish, evoking the best belly laughs in the whole world.

Effie strips down to her bra and panties too and reaches for Plum's hand. Together they slip into the glistening water.

"Can you come in?" Plum asks.

I hold up my bandaged hand and shake my head. "I'm going to look for fairy houses," I say. "I'll holler if I find one."

I walk around the perimeter of the pool, pretending to search under the brush and leaves. I study the trunks of trees, searching for evidence. And I think of how Effie and I used to do the same, even after we were too old to believe. Here, in this magical place, what we knew to be true didn't seem to matter. It was what we believed, what we dreamed, what we *wanted* that counted.

I remember being Plum's age, and searching just like this. I remember feeling a longing and yearning so deep it seemed like I could drown in it. I remember the urgency, like holding on to my childhood depended on it. That if we couldn't find some sort of proof fairies still existed, then we would lose something. That everything in the world hinged on this. I remember wishing, and studying the architecture of twigs, the placement of pebbles. Dreaming mossy roofs and knothole windows. And how Effie shared this same need. We weren't ready to be grown yet. And here was the last place where we were allowed to believe in magic.

I listen to the musical sound of Plum's laughter, the sound of her splashing in the water, and that same sense of urgency returns. I need to give her this. I'm not ready for her to stop believing yet. And so while she plays, I gather sticks and stones, soft patches of moss. I quickly assemble a primitive structure. In my pocket, I find a string, out of which I fashion a tiny swing for the fairy's front yard. I make a walkway of stones and a roof of dried leaves.

I come out of the woods just as Effie and Plum are climbing out of the water. Plum's arms are crossed and she's shivering, her teeth chattering.

"Lie down here," Effie says, motioning to a long flat rock, which is bathed in sunlight. Plum obeys, and Effie lies down next to her.

I watch them lying together, and my heart swells and aches. I watch their fingers intertwine, the woven pattern of Plum's brown skin and Effie's paler flesh. Effie turns her head and kisses Plum on the temple. I wait until Plum sits up, too hot now in the sun, her skin already dry.

"I found something!" I say.

"A fairy house?" Plum says, scrambling to her feet.

I wink at Effie.

"Come see," I say, and Plum scurries over to me.

"Where, where?" she asks, and I lead her by the hand to the place where the fairies live.

She marvels at the tiny swing, the little chairs I made from a couple of toadstools.

"Can we leave them a note?" she asks.

I reach into my pocket. "Shoot," I say. "I don't have any paper."

She frowns. "How will they know we were here?" she asks.

"Oh, wait," I say, smiling as I discover the two little Reese's Cups I had intended to give the girls the other night. I pull them out of my pocket and hand them to her.

She gingerly sets them in front of the house.

"Can we come back tomorrow and see if they got them?" she asks.

"Absolutely," I say.

At the library, while Effie catches up on scheduling her route and stocks the book-mobile with some new releases, I sit in a child-size chair at the long computer counter in the makeshift children's room they made in the annex because of the flooding, and go online.

"How to find someone who is lost in the woods"

Expert trackers say that when people get lost in the woods, they leave a couple thousand clues behind for every single mile they travel, though most are imperceptible to the eye: a snapped branch, a leaf imprinted with their sole, a crushed bit of moss. That searchers, if they are trained, can spot these clues. I think of our bumbling group in the woods. About our collective blindness.

People think you need to know all sorts of things about a missing person's personality, about their history, to figure out how to find them, to figure out the way they will behave if they are alone and lost in the woods. But one psychologist suggests that the key to finding someone in the woods is simply knowing one thing: their age. Most people lost in the woods are found within a one-to-two-mile radius from where they became lost. For children, this mileage is reduced to a range of two-thirds to one-and-two-thirds of a mile. Older children, between seven and twelve, tend to run, their legs informed by the impulse to flee, whereas smaller children, between three and six, simply burrow in somewhere.

If she is lost, not taken, that means that she is still close. That I could, if I was careful, find those clues. Find her.

I read the stories, one after another, of children found in the woods: nestled into caves and hollows. Found sleeping under piles of brush, inside formations of rock.

Adult humans can go weeks, even months, without food, but only three days without water. For a toddler, this is reduced to one week without food. And, depending on the conditions, dehydration could set in after only hours. I think of the rain the other night, of that vast lake across the road from where she disappeared. Pray that her instinct would be to drink if she found a puddle, a creek. And I even wonder, for a moment, if she'd be better off if she'd been stolen instead of lost, if she *had* been taken by someone; then at least maybe she'd still be alive. And then I think about what else this would mean, and it's too difficult to imagine.

When we get back to the camp after returning the bookmobile to the library, there are three messages on Effie's machine. The first is from Devin. He says he's decided to stay a few more days. The curator he's dealing with at Gagosian is out of town until Friday. Devin's family is all in Queens. He'll stay there, catch up with his nieces and nephews, and drive back home on Saturday.

The second message is from Jake asking if I've already paid the water bill. I am the one who manages our money: balances the checking account, makes sure the bills get paid on time. I worry about all the things that might get neglected without me there to take care, and part of me hopes he is lost without me.

When the third message starts to play, I pray that it's Ryan. That he'll have some news from the police department. But it's not. It's Effie's friend Mena, Sam Mason's wife.

"Hi, Effie! Just wanted to let you know we're flying into Burlington on a red-eye Thursday night. We'll be at the cottage sometime Friday. Can't wait to see you guys! Of course, we won't have the house set up yet, but if we can use your kitchen, I'll cook. Maybe Saturday night? Give me a call if you want. Otherwise, I'll call when we get there."

Sam Mason. The author that Jake is dying to meet. If he had any idea we'd be having dinner with Sam and Mena Mason on Saturday, I bet he'd forget all about Charlie's tantrums, all about Jess, and fly right up here. The possibility of this pisses me off, the *truth* of this.

"Would you mind?" Effie asks. "I haven't seen them since last summer. But if you'd rather not have company . . ."

"No, not at all. Of course. Please, don't put anything on hold for me."

"She's an amazing cook," she says. "Unbelievable."

"Tell her to make that soup I like! The lemon kind," Plum says. "And baklava."

Plum comes over to me in the kitchen nook and settles into my lap. She's too big for this, her legs long and skinny like a spider's. I lean down and sniff her hair. It smells like trees.

"End of new messages," the robotic voice announces.

I'm not sure what I expected. I have no idea how long it takes to track down a license plate number. Or what will happen after they do. I wonder if I'll hear anything at all, or if I'll just have to keep biding my time. Ryan had said we needed to let the police feel like they're putting these puzzle pieces together. But we are still holding on to the most important one: the barrette.

I can't help but feel like this is a big mistake. This is not a game.

"You should change your bandage," Effie says, motioning to my hand.

Even though I didn't go swimming, the bandage still looks dirty from our trek through the forest. I think of all of the cautions they offered at the clinic. I gather the stuff we picked up at the drugstore. I'd sat in the car this time, while Effie went in. No need to almost pass out at the Rite Aid again.

In the bathroom, I unwrap the gauze from my hand, toss it in the trash can, and study the wound, which doesn't even look real. My flesh is pale, and the black stitches that are holding my skin together seem almost primitive, barbaric. I use the special soap the nurse gave me, and the sting of it brings tears to my eyes. "Motherfucker," I mutter under my breath and grit my teeth. I apply the antibiotic cream next and then try to rewrap the wound. It's impossible to do with one hand. I grab the gauze and go out to the kitchen.

"Can you help?" I ask Effie.

"Sure," she says, setting down the knife she's using to cut an apple for Plum.

The phone rings, and I drop the gauze as I'm handing it to her. I am so accustomed

311

to muted cell phone rings or vibrations, the loud, jangling sound of the landline startles me, reminding me again just how on edge I am.

Effie picks up and cradles the receiver between her chin and shoulder as she opens the fridge door. "Hello?"

I watch, not wanting to give away how anxious I am. How disappointed I'll be if it's not Ryan calling with some news.

"Yes, she is. Hold on," she says, and nods at me. She mouths, "Ryan."

I take the phone with my good hand. Plum gets up from the kitchen nook, and I touch the top of her head as she squeezes past me through the doorway.

"Did they find out who the truck belongs to?" I ask, trying not to sound too eager, too demanding.

Ryan pauses on the other end of the line. I close my eyes, take a deep breath, and wait.

"The owner of the truck is a guy named Vince Alfieri. He's from Holyoke, Mass."

"The *college*?" I ask. I'd known some girls when I lived in Boston who'd gone to Mount Holyoke. Athletic, smart girls with big white teeth. *Moneyed.* When I think of Mount Holyoke, I think ivy-strangled bricks, sprawling grassy quads. Clean notebooks and golden retrievers. Polo shirts and leather deck shoes and tanned ankles. Lacrosse sticks and tiny pearl necklaces on pastel sweaters. Jake grew up in South Hadley; we'd gone to the Mount Holyoke campus a few times when we were visiting his parents.

"No. Holyoke the city. Industrial sort of place. Depressed economy. Lots of drugs there in the last few years. Drug-related crime."

"Oh," I say, all those visions of collegiate affluence slipping away. "Does he own property up here? At Gormlaith? Has anybody talked to him?"

"Not yet," he says. "But listen, here's the interesting thing. I had my friend dig a little into that guy Sharp's background too. To try to get some more information about who he is, what the lewd-and-lascivious conviction was for."

I can feel my heart beating in my hand.

"And?" I say, both wanting and not wanting to know.

"Well, he spent three years in jail for exposing himself to a neighbor."

"How old?" I ask, as if this can somehow keep her safe. If his previous victim was twelve or thirteen, then maybe that would somehow protect her. This little three-year-old girl.

"Five," he says.

"Oh God," I say, my hand flying to my mouth. I have to sit down.

"But that's not all," he says. I'm not sure I want to hear more. That I can handle hearing any more.

"That wasn't his most recent visit to prison," Ryan says.

I shake my head. What else could this monster have done? Images flood my mind, and I shake my head as if I can jar them loose. Blur the focus.

"He was actually in for trafficking," he says.

"Human trafficking?" I ask, horrified, thinking of a *60 Minutes* episode I saw recently about children being kidnapped from the streets in third world countries and thrown into the sex trade. Little girls.

"No, no," he says. "*Drug* trafficking. He just got out a couple years ago after a five-year stint at Norfolk."

"What's Norfolk?"

"State prison," he says. "In *Massachusetts.* It appears our friend Sharp's last known residence was in Springfield, Mass."

"Springfield?" I repeat.

"Just about ten minutes down I-91 from Holyoke. He discharged parole six months ago. After that he was clear to leave the state."

I struggle to make sense of what any of this means. Sharp is a convicted sex offender and drug trafficker. He's from Springfield, Massachusetts, but he's been living out here in the backwoods of Vermont for the last couple of years or so. The guy in the truck is also from Massachusetts. Could they be related? Just friends? Partners in crime, maybe? But what sort of crime? And what does Lisa have to do with any of this? I can't help but think of that house full of children. And those thoughts are more horrifying than I can handle.

"Does this Alfieri guy have any sort of record?" I ask, almost not wanting to know.

"Not as far as I can tell. Of course, if he's using an alias or something, then there might be more to the story. But on the surface, he seems clean."

"What do we do now?" I ask.

"Well, my friend at the PD passed this info along to Strickland."

I sigh, rub my temples. My head is starting to pound. "But he didn't believe me either; he thinks I'm some stupid drunk who hallucinated the whole thing. Or made it up for attention. He's just as bad as Andrews."

"Maybe so, but I know Strickland. I know how he operates. And the way Andrews threw him under the bus over the search, I suspect he's pretty eager now to save face. If he can somehow prove you were telling the truth, then he can save his own ass."

"So what does this have to do with her?" I ask. "With the girl?"

"To be honest, not a whole lot," he says. "But I have a feeling the police are going to become a lot more interested in finding her now."

I am seething. All of this has become an elaborate battle of the egos, and what's at stake is a child's life. I can't wait for this cockfight to play itself out.

With Jake gone, I wake up with the first hints of light in the sky. At home, I usually linger as long as possible before rising. Many mornings Jake is long gone before I get up.

"Don't you hate waking up after the day's already started?" Jake usually asks, like it's a race. As though by the time I roll out of bed I'm already lagging behind everyone else, as if I'll never be able to catch my stride.

I know he thinks I have just never transcended my adolescent tendencies to sleep as long as possible before being forced to get up and start my day. Even back when I was working, when the world demanded my presence, I was late to the game.

My intentions are always to wake early the optimism of my alarm clock–settir never wavering. But inevitably, predictab its sounding is followed by at least a dozen swipes at the snooze button before I am finally, reluctantly, pulled into consciousness.

Jake, on the other hand, rises early and takes a short run in the park, then comes home to shower and have breakfast before heading in to work. All the while I remain dreaming.

He is a creature of habit: after his run — coffee, a hard-boiled egg, a slice of toast with butter. Every day, no deviation. I, on the other hand, eat something different every morning: oatmeal, donuts from the bakery down the street, omelets made with an unpredictable assortment of vegetables and cheese and meats. I am impulsive in this, as in most other things as well. I grow bored easily, with food as with everything else. Mangoes, special sausages from the farmer's market, weird smelly cheeses. Whenever we took trips I always wanted to try the most exotic dishes; I'm the kind of person who tells the waiter to surprise me. Jake says he loved me at first because I made him feel adventurous. That if not for me, he'd never stray from his routine.

I used to imagine when we finally had a baby, that Jake would be better prepared. was already accustomed to staying up and rising early. His life was already measured into increments, each hour predictable and safe. Children love routines; this is what I read on the Web sites I searched. Jake would be that steady force, and I would adjust.

My own mother was like a scrap of paper in the breeze — her every moment dictated by the wind, by whim. As a child, I longed for the routine I saw in my friends' homes. At Effie's house, they had Taco Tuesdays. Pizza and a family movie on Friday nights. Saturdays, her father took her and her sister on outings (to museums and on hikes, kayaking on lakes, or exploring historic landmarks), but they were always home in time for supper, which Effie's mother ensured was waiting for them on the table. I used to think this would be the kind of family I would make. And that someone like Jake could make that happen.

But after Guatemala, any semblance of order I'd managed to establish, any routine, quickly devolved. I returned to the comfort of my own chaos, and Jake remained steady. Predictable.

How did I not notice? How did I miss the cues, the clues that something in Jake's routine had changed? I feel stupid and so, so sad.

■ ■ ■ ■

Like Jake, Effie wakes up early. By the time I get dressed and make my way from the guest cottage to the camp, I can see the light on in the kitchen window. Hear the sounds of the public radio station, smell the freshly brewed coffee.

"Knock, knock," I say.

"Good morning," she says, smiling, and gives me a hug. "How did you sleep?"

I shrug. I have been dreaming of the woods. I spend all night wandering, looking for her. By the time I wake up, my legs are exhausted. I must sleep with my entire body clenched tightly like a fist.

Surprisingly, Plum is up as well. She is sitting in the kitchen nook, writing. She is wearing soft pajamas; her hair is a puffy halo around her head.

I sit down next to her and snuggle into her.

"What's this?" I ask, looking over her shoulder.

"It's a letter for the fairy," she says.

"Oh, cool," I say.

I hope you liked the candy we left for you.

320

Maybe you can leave something for me, so I know you are real. Also, are you Star?

Love, PLUM

Effie is making a giant salad, chopping veggies and hard-boiling eggs. They rattle around in the boiling water on the stove. The kitchen is steamy. She is becoming more and more like her grandmother, Gussy, I think. Up early, already thinking about lunch. About dinner even. When we were kids I would never have imagined her so domesticated. We were little feral creatures when we were children. But I guess this is what motherhood demands.

"Hey, can I borrow your bike?" I ask her.

"Sure, it's in the shed. You going on a ride?"

"Yeah. I feel like I need to get out, get some exercise. All I've done since I got here is eat." The words feel hollow, and I wonder if she knows I'm lying.

"Plum might want to go with you," she says, and my heart sinks.

Plum looks up at me hopefully.

"I was thinking about going all the way into town. I don't think she can go that far yet, can she?"

"Oh, no. She just tootles around here."

"I can ride all the way. I'm really good at bike riding," Plum argues.

"You know what," I say, nudging Plum's shoulder. "How about tomorrow we take the bikes up to the swimming hole and leave this note for Star," I say.

She looks disappointed, but shrugs. "Okay."

"Will you be back for lunch? I'm just making a big chef's salad," Effie says.

"I should be back in a couple of hours," I say. "I just need to clear my head."

"Let me help you get the bike out of the shed," Effie says, wiping her hands on her apron. "It's a total disaster in there."

We find the mint-colored beach cruiser in the back of the shed, covered with cobwebs. There is a ratty rattan wicker basket attached to the handlebars, a rusty bell. I untangle it from the girls' bikes and back it out of the shed. The chain has slipped off and I need to thread it back on. The seat is low; I am a good head taller than Effie, and so I dig around for a wrench to raise it.

I haven't ridden a bike in ages. Brooklyn is not conducive to bike riding, at least not bike riders like me. I'm a drifter. I get so caught up in the scenery around me that I tend to weave into the road. I went riding once and was nearly killed by a semi. And even if I'm not in danger myself, I'd likely pose a risk to some innocent pedestrians.

Effie and I lived on our bikes as kids. They were the vehicles to our freedom. From the time we were Plum's age, we were allowed to go as far as our bikes would take us. We never worried about helmets, about strangers, about anything but the burning of our calves as we pumped our legs to pedal up hills, and the beautiful release when we made it to the top, the wind in our hair as we coasted down the other side.

"You're not going back to his house, are you?" Effie asks. I can see the worry in her eyes. The cautious plea for assurance that I won't do anything stupid.

"No," I say, shaking my head. "I'm just going for a bike ride. Jesus."

She frowns. This is not how we treat each other. In the decades that we've been friends, I can count our arguments on one hand.

"But tomorrow, I do want to go to Lisa's. She's on your Friday route, right?"

And then the realization hits me, that it's been a full week. A week ago, Jake and I were on our way up from New York. A week ago the biggest concern I had was how to deal with that woman's texted flirtations with my husband. It seems laughable now that I could have been so caught up in something so trivial. Such futile frustrations and sorrows.

"Oh, shoot, I totally forgot to tell you yesterday," Effie starts. "When we were at the library and I was checking my route, the schedule? Lisa canceled tomorrow's visit. Left a message saying not to come this week, that the kids are still reading the books they got last week."

"Huh," I say. "That's weird."

She shrugs. "Nah. Not really. People do that sometimes."

"You don't think it has anything to do with me?"

"I don't *think* so," she says, as if this is the first time she has paused to consider it.

"She was pretty pissed off when I brought up Sharp living so close to her day care," I say. "She knows we're friends. And if that dog really belongs to that Alfieri guy, maybe she's hiding something?"

Effie shakes her head. "Nah, I think you're reading too much into it. It happens. People cancel visits. Change the dates. It's no big deal. But the main thing is that she's not on my route tomorrow like you'd hoped. That's all. I just wanted to let you know. That we can't just stop by there tomorrow." I feel like a scolded child.

"Okay," I say, irritated. "Got it."

"Do you have your phone?" she asks, and I can hear exactly what Zu-Zu and Plum must hear.

"Yes, *Mother,*" I say, teasing. But there is a bitterness beneath my joking. I can taste it in the back of my throat. I hold up my phone to show her and toss it and my wallet in the basket, kick up the rusty kickstand, and throw my leg over one side.

"If you make it to town, can you grab a loaf of French bread from the Shop 'n Save?" she asks, and I feel like she is challenging me. Calling my bluff.

"Sure," I say, and push off slowly.

As I pedal away from the camp, I see Plum in the window. I ding the little bell and wave. I think about going the other way around the lake, the long way, so as not to be tempted, to not even consider what I am considering. But my legs have a will of their own, and so I turn right, follow the road that will take me past the woods where I found her.

It's foggy this morning; I can only see a few feet in front of me, and the condensation gathers on my skin, clings to me. I feel like I'm riding my bike through a cloud. It's thick and obscures everything; I almost ride past the spot in the road, almost miss it. At first I blame the foggy haze, but then I see what's different.

The yellow police tape is gone.

Someone has removed the yards and yards of it. Unwound it from the tangle of trees. Every bit has been removed, the woods returned to normal. There is no evidence, no demarcations that this was the spot where a little girl wandered into my life and then vanished. There is no lingering monument to our encounter.

I have always hated roadside memorials: the white crosses or street signs littered with stuffed animals and candles. Cards and flowers. The well-intentioned gestures turning into grotesque monuments after the first rain. The matted fur of the toys, the soggy mess, and dying candles. Neglected, abandoned, and then all but forgotten.

But now, I wish there was *something*. Some acknowledgment that she was here. Some simple recognition. Without this, it's as if she truly never *did* exist. As though she is, as everyone claims (as everyone would prefer to believe), a figment of my imagination. A fabrication. A dream.

But even in this sea of mist, even without the police tape, something deep and intuitive nags at me. The way the early morning light filters through the trees here. The bend of the road. My body has memorized the spot. I am a walking monument, I think. A breathing sepulcher. I am a catacomb for this lost girl.

I slow the bike down here. My heart is beating hard from the ride so far. It throbs rhythmically in my wounded hand. I have been gripping the handlebars too tightly; the ache in my palm extends all the way to my knees. I must have been pedaling harder than I thought. The bike only has one speed, which would be fine on flat surfaces, but the terrain here is rarely horizontal. I am breathless.

I try to remember the exact place where

she stood that night, the exact spot where she slipped out of my fingers.

I know I should keep going. I should just keep riding the bike all the way into town, park it outside the Shop 'n Save, and choose the best loaf of French bread to have with lunch. I should buy some flowers for Effie as well, pick up some gumdrops to leave at the fairy house for Plum to find. I should load it all into my basket and make my way home, forget about her. Let her go.

But I can't make my legs move. I am frozen in this spot. And even as I know I shouldn't, am absolutely aware that this is dangerous, that I have promised both Effie and Ryan that I will leave all of this in the hands of the police, I get off my bicycle. I roll it to the edge of the woods, lift it up onto my shoulder, and hide it in a thicket of deciduous trees. Even though I hear their admonishments, their pleas, I can't keep myself from grabbing my phone and wallet from the basket, and following her, the ghost of her, back into the woods.

Mist shrouds everything. The forest is a different place depending on the time of day. The last time I was here with the search team, it had been high noon, the sun burning through the foliage overhead. The forest floor marbled in sunlight. But now, the sunlight struggles not only through the canopy of leaves but also through the thick mist that clings to the leaves like gauze. It is cool and damp and loud here. The birds' songs, the clucks and trills competing. An orchestra warming up, a cheeping cacophony.

I think about the information I read online, about what a child lost in the woods will do. About how older children will run, but how younger children will simply find a safe spot and burrow in. That most lost children are found within a mile radius of where they disappeared. But a radius emanating from where? What is the center of this imaginary circle? Is it the spot in the road where I found her? Where she stood in her tattered tutu and ladybug rain boots? Is it outside Sharp's trailer where I found her barrette? Is it somewhere else? How am I supposed to find her if I don't know where it started? What is the locus? Where do I even begin?

I also think about the clues, about the thousands of clues they say a missing person leaves behind. The fact that it only takes a trained eye, an attentive searcher, to locate them. I search for her in the trampled leaves, in the heady scent of the trees. *Where are you?* I whisper. *Where did you go? What clues did you leave for me?*

Here is what I know, I think, as I walk slowly across the pine-needle-littered ground:

I found a child, a wounded child, in the middle of the road. And then she disappeared. Helicopters with heat-seeking probes did not find her. Dogs did not find her. A legion of volunteers did not find her. But she exists. She must exist, because I found the barrette that was in her hair.

Sharp, a registered sex offender and convicted felon from out of state, is living out here in the woods too. And this guy, Alfieri, is connected to both Sharp (I know this because I saw it with my own eyes the night of the storm), but also possibly Lisa down the road. I know this because of that dog — the dog that (if I believe the psychic) at some point scared the little girl. I think of the terror in Mary's eyes as she described its sharp teeth.

I walk through the woods, purposeful now. I am trying to think like a little girl who is alone in the woods and scared. If a small child's tendency is to burrow in, to find a safe place to hide, then where would she go? I use the rising sun as my compass, heading south. I know I must be close to

Lisa's house now. Her house is closest to the spot where I found her. Which means that maybe Lisa's house is where she saw the dog? But Alfieri blew past me on the road that night, headed *north* toward the lake, with the dog in his truck. Unless he returned later, after I left, this doesn't make any sense. And where was he going? To Sharp's? And what does any of this have to do with the girl?

I try to create not only the geography of her path, the geometry, but a chronology.

The barrette was in her hair when I found her, which means she was on Sharp's property *after* I found her. This means, I suppose, his yard is the center of that circle. That her possible paths should radiate from that horrifying point. That if what I've read is true, then she should be within a mile or so from that spot. But if so, why hasn't anyone found her?

And it has been seven days. Does the circle's center change with each day? None of the Web sites talked about this: how many circles. How many trajectories. I think of the water rings on Ryan's desk, interlocking. Endless.

I walk faster, try to imagine a child's logic. What would Plum do? Would she run? Or would she look for a place to hide? As the mist clears, the color of the forest changes. It brightens, a Technicolor wonder of a thousand shades of green. I become hot, the hair on the back of my neck sticky as I hike through the thick trees.

And then, abruptly, I come to a clearing. And I see the backside of Lisa's house. The backyard littered with toys. Would the little girl have seen this that night? Would she have been drawn by the colorful ride-ons, by the plastic slide and seesaws? There is a small playhouse, and I wonder briefly, stupidly, if she might just be curled up inside.

But then I see something else too, something I hadn't noticed before. An outbuilding, a sort of dilapidated barn. It's set back from the house about a hundred feet, right where the woods meet her yard. I walk carefully, cautiously along the wooded border, obscured, I hope, by the trees that are dense here, close together.

It's 7:30, still somewhat early, but I would imagine that kids would be getting dropped off soon. Parents who have to be at work by eight o'clock. But her driveway is empty. Even the black Honda, the car that had been in the driveway when Effie and I came, is gone. I strain to hear beyond the warbling chorus of the birds, but I don't hear the sound of children either.

That's strange. I move closer toward the house, try to catch a glimpse of something, anything to suggest that Lisa is inside. That it's business as usual today. But then I am overwhelmed by the realization that the house is empty. The porch light is out. Not a single light is on inside the house. From where I am standing, I can see a white piece of paper taped to the door, fluttering a bit in the wind.

I come out of the woods cautiously and then run down the hill toward the house. I am breathless when I reach the front door.

"Family emergency. Closed until further notice. Sorry."

Effie had said that she'd canceled the bookmobile's visit, but hadn't she said something about the kids just not being done with their books? Where is she?

I turn back toward the woods and look to the barn again. I peer behind me to make sure I am alone, and then run along the path, the dew-drenched grass tickling my bare ankles. The door opens easily and I go into the cool barn. Sunlight streams through the wooden slats. The combination of darkness and blinding light is disorienting. I shield my eyes and peer up into the beams.

As my eyes adjust to the light, I can see a hayloft above, and my heart pings. I climb up the ladder, wondering if she would have been able to do this, if she was old enough to climb. I try to remember how old Effie and I were when we were first able to climb the ladder into her tree house.

And if she could climb, would she have been afraid? I remember walking behind Zu-Zu when she was only three, making sure she clung to each rung, watching to make sure that her foot didn't slip, sending her tumbling backwards into me.

I reach the top and hold my breath as I peek into the loft, terrified of what I might find.

But she's not there. Of course, she's not there.

What am I doing here? Have I lost my mind?

I sit down in the loft, dizzy, vertiginous, and peer down at the floor, which is striped with sunlight. And my heart flies to my throat.

I blink hard. But when I open my eyes again, the sight has not gone away.

I climb onto the ladder, and back down quickly until I am standing on the floor. And I kneel down onto the dirt-packed ground. I reach my good hand out and tenderly touch the ground, the dark stain. I brace myself, but it is dry. I move to the next spot, and test it as well. Whatever stained the floor has had time to harden. To *congeal.*

I scramble to my feet and back away, unable to turn away from the horrifying vision in front of me. When I push the doors open, the entire barn floods with light and confirms that what I am seeing is not a hallucination. Not an awful dream.

Blood. The stains are dried blood.

It's as though there has been a massacre here.

My ears buzz and fill as if I am sinking into the depths of the lake. My vision goes black, save for the stars. And I am drowning in the night sky, filled with constellations. All of the unanswered wishes. I need to get out of here. I need to leave.

Willing myself not to pass out, I run blindly toward the driveway, feel the gravel beneath my feet, running toward the road. But I am losing, sinking.

"Jesus Christ," a voice swims to me, where I float adrift in this black sea. Hands grab my shoulders before I collapse. "Waters? What the hell are you doing here?"

"You should sit down," he says, and I feel my legs folding beneath me, cool wet grass on my skin.

At first I don't recognize him. I struggle as the black sea parts, to make out who he is. Why he seems both so familiar and so strange all at once. Without his uniform on, he could be anyone.

And then it comes to me. *Strickland.*

"What are you doing here?" he asks again. He hovers over me, arms crossed.

"I . . ." I stutter.

"You know that's trespassing?" he says, motioning with his chin toward Lisa's house. "It's posted."

For the first time, I notice that there are NO TRESPASSING signs posted at the trees on either side of the driveway. Also, a BE-WARE OF DOG sign.

"She wasn't home," I say, and feel the sour taste of bile at the back of my throat. The burn. "I just wanted to talk to her."

He cocks his head, waiting for me to continue. And strangely, that dubious sneer I am accustomed to is absent.

"I was looking . . ." I start, but then the image of what I saw, or at least *think* I saw, the darkly stained floor, comes in a vivid flash. The blood. It all comes rushing back to me, and bile rises from the back of my throat and floods my mouth.

I swallow hard to push it back down, and tears sting my eyes.

"Looking for what?" he says. But it is not an admonishment. He is, surprisingly, not scolding me.

I struggle to sit up, pushing myself up with my hands, and I feel a shooting pain that extends from the cut in my hand up my arm. "Shit," I say, wincing.

He extends his hand to me, and I grab it with my good hand so he can pull me up.

"Listen," I say, brushing the wet grass and leaves off my shorts. "I know you have the information about Alfieri and Sharp. But she has something to do with this too. You have to trust me. I saw Alfieri's dog here. They all know each other."

He pushes his shoulders back and cracks his neck. I wait for him to deny everything. To chastise me.

I study his face, which looks more boyish than it did before. The absent uniform has stripped away that smug assuredness. Removed an entire decade from his face.

"I know Lieutenant Andrews wants this to all go away. Wants *me* to go away," I start. I remember what Ryan told me about evidence coming from a civilian, that even if it's acquired illegally, it's still admissible. "But I know what I saw that night. And if I were you, I'd get a warrant to search that barn *and* Sharp's property."

His eyes widen.

"You have to tell me what you found," he says.

I hesitate. I've been burned before. I think about Andrews threatening me with charges for making a false report. I don't want to give him anything that can further implicate me. That could get me in more trouble.

"Why should I trust you?" I say.

He takes a deep breath, shakes his head. He peers out at the lake, which is glimmering through the trees now. It is going to be a beautiful day.

"She's his girlfriend," he says, turning back toward me.

I am completely confused. I have no idea what he's talking about.

"Vince Alfieri. Lisa Connelly and he are a

couple."

"Okay," I nod. That makes sense. But I don't know what any of this has to do with my trusting him. Why his sharing this information should make me feel safe.

"And Sharp?" he says. "He came up here when he got out of prison because his sister lives here."

"So?" I say.

"Lisa is Sharp's sister," he says.

I think about the way she responded when I told her that there was a registered sex offender living near her. The odd way she reacted. It makes sense now. And then I think about that curly-headed baby on her hip.

"How could she let him near here?" I ask, feeling sick again. Unless there's something darker, more terrible going on. "And what does Alfieri have to do with anything?"

I rub my temples. "So, the three of them know each other. Lisa probably met Alfieri through Sharp. Sharp and he were both in Massachusetts, right?"

He nods. "Yes," he says. "And we're beginning to think they might be in business together."

"Business?" I say.

He nods and runs his hand across his head, scratching. "I'm sorry. That's all I can say."

"Wait, why aren't you in uniform?" I ask. "What are *you* doing here? Where's your cruiser?"

He looks at me, and takes a deep breath. "Let's just say you're not the only one conducting an . . . independent . . . investigation."

"What?" And then it dawns on me. "Andrews doesn't know you're here?"

He shakes his head once to confirm.

"Now, please. Just tell me what you saw."

I can't ride the bike into town; my legs are shaking, my whole body quaking. And so I ride back to camp, quietly put the bike in the shed. I am not ready to talk to Effie about this, and thankfully, it looks like she and Plum have taken a walk or something, and so I quickly get in my car and take off.

At the Shop 'n Save, I loosen a cart from the tangled mess in the entrance and walk, dazed, through the electronic doors. It's cold in here, freezing cold. I shiver in my thin cotton T-shirt and shorts. Goose bumps pimple my legs. I have to keep reciting the list like a mantra: French bread, flowers, gumdrops. I see Effie texted me earlier asking if I could pick up some eggs too, and I'm glad I have the car; they would never have survived the bike ride home.

I am still trying to process what I saw in the barn and everything that Strickland told me, to read between the lines to figure out what exactly he was still keeping to himself. From the little bit I could gather from Strickland, Andrews didn't want to hear anything more about Alfieri, had no interest in Sharp. After publicly denouncing me, shaming me, and denying the girl, he couldn't exactly turn around and reinstate the search. It would have made him seem wishy-washy, not exactly a trait that people want from someone hoping to make chief someday. So when Ryan's friend at the PD started digging stuff up on Sharp and Alfieri, he knew enough to go to Strickland first. And Strickland, who had initiated the search, wasting the taxpayers' money on helicopters and scuba divers, had probably also been scolded. I am beginning to wonder if Ryan is right, that maybe Strickland only hopes to use all of this to save face, to salvage his *own* reputation.

I go to the floral section and pick out a bunch of flowers from one of the buckets: daisies and snapdragons. Hot-pink carnations. It is an explosion of color. I impulsively put my face into the bouquet and inhale. But grocery store flowers never smell the way they look. The scent is artificial. Chemically enhanced. The water from the bucket drips down my arm, making me even colder.

In the candy aisle I grab a bag of gum-drops, think about how I can get out to the swimming hole and leave them at the fairy house for Plum. I look down at my hand, the gauze filthy again, with a little bit of blood seeping through. I go to the pharmacy aisle next and buy more gauze, more tape. I'll be lucky if this cut ever heals.

As I am making my way to the dairy aisle for Effie's eggs, I see Ruth, Mrs. Lund's friend from the search.

"Oh, hello," she says. "Tess Mahoney, right?"

"Waters," I correct her, a knee jerking reflexively. But *Waters,* the name I took all those years ago, belongs to Jake. What will happen to it if I leave him? Will I lose it? Be forced to give it back? And who will I be then? "Sorry. It's Tess Waters now. Hi."

"I didn't expect you'd still be in town," she says, clucking her tongue.

I shrug.

"I mean now that they're saying there wasn't a little girl and all," she persists. Her face, which had seemed kind and grand-motherly before, appears angry now. Bitter. Her lipsticked mouth is pinched. "You got a lot of people worked up over this, you know. This is a small community. Like family."

"I know that," I say. "Remember, I grew

up here."

She shakes her head. "Then, of course, you understand."

I feel like telling her everything. Telling her that there is a registered sex offender living right where I found the girl. I want to tell her what I saw in that barn. I want to stand up and tell this whole goddamned town that the only reason why the investigation has been ditched is because of that asshole lieutenant's pride.

Instead, I push my cart past her, saying "Excuse me" as the edge of the cart catches on her purse.

I am seething as I push the cart through the dairy aisle to get the eggs. When my phone dings, I am tempted to hurl it into the freezer with the frozen pizzas and leave it there.

A text message.

bad news call me asap

Jake.

Christ. I try to think about what it could be. Maybe the publishers pulled their offers while they waited for Charlie to decide. Maybe they all realized what an asshat he is and opted out. Maybe it has something to do with her, *Jess*. I don't want to deal with any of this. None of it matters. All of it is so inconsequential. So trivial and inane.

I cradle the cell phone between my shoulder and my ear as I grab a carton of eggs from the cooler. Out of habit, I flip the cardboard lid to check for any broken ones. They are all intact.

"Hey," I say when Jake answers.

He sounds so far away. I put the eggs in the cart and use my hand to hold the phone properly.

"What's up?"

There is nothing but silence, and I pull the phone away from my ear and study the screen to make sure we're still connected.

"Jake?"

"It's my mom," he says, and he sounds strange. Like a boy.

"Your *mom*?"

There is nothing on the other end of the line. And then I can hear a stifled sob. "I'm at home," he says.

"At the house?"

"In South Hadley," he says. His parents' house in western Mass.

"Jake?"

"She had an aneurysm," he says. "She was doing the dishes. And she just fell over. Dad found her."

"Is she . . . okay?" I ask, feeling hot despite

the cold freezer aisle.

"She's in the ICU," he says. "It doesn't look good, Tessie. I really need you to come down here."

"When are you coming back?" Plum asks, standing at the open window of the driver's side of the car.

"I'm not sure, honey," I say, and reach out to touch her hair. It's in two braids today, ending with two small puffs. "I promise I'll be back as soon as I can."

"Pinkie swear," she challenges, pushing her tiny little pinkie finger toward me. We hook them, and then she backs away from the car, starts cartwheeling across the lawn. Without Devin here to mow it, and with the major rain we got last week, it is overgrown already. A thick, plush carpet of bluegrass and clover.

Effie comes out of the camp holding a small, insulated lunch box; the screen door slams behind her.

"I made you a turkey sandwich. There's iced tea in there and a couple of brownies too. Zu-Zu's famous triple-chocolate fudge.

Do you need anything else?"

I take the bag from her and shake my head. "You didn't need to do this. I could have just swung by Hudson's and grabbed something on my way."

She bends down and leans into the window.

"Do you know how to get there from here?" she asks.

I nod. Jake and I have visited his folks on our way home from Vermont many times. It's on the way. Just three hours, a straight shot down I-91.

"Do you think she's going to be okay?" Effie asks.

"I don't know. Jake didn't have a lot of information. I think it happened last night. He drove up from New York and just got there this morning."

"Call me when you get there?" she says.

I nod.

"What are you going to do about . . ." she starts, and then sighs. "This?"

I shake my head. I haven't told her about what I saw in that barn, or that I saw Strickland out of uniform. I promised him I wouldn't say a word. We have an agreement now. Strickland, suddenly my secret ally.

"Ryan and the police have my phone number. I'm hoping this stuff with Shirley isn't as bad as it seems, and I can come back up here in a day or two."

A day or two. It's already been a week. I can't let myself think about how futile this is all beginning to seem. How the chances of it ending well seem to be growing smaller and smaller. The possibilities of what has happened to her growing fewer and fewer.

"I love you," she says. "Give Jake a hug from me." I can see that it pains her to say this, to offer this affection. Effie is fiercely loyal. I know there's a small part of her that thinks I shouldn't go down there at all. That what he's done (what he's *doing*) is unforgivable. But she also knows how much I love Shirley.

Leaving here always hurts. I have to remind myself as I round the lake that I am coming back. But still, as I drive by the spot (restored now to its pristine, unadulterated state), I can't help but feel like I am betraying her. Leaving her behind. I also wonder, as the dirt road crushes under my tires and the wind blows through my open window, if Jake would do the same for me. Would he drop everything? Would he forget everything he was doing to go to me if I needed him?

As I drive, my mind drifts, and I realize I am going 80, 85, 90 miles per hour. It's easy on these desolate roads to forget. For your foot to grow heavy as your mind wanders.

Jake said that she's at Baystate Medical Center in Springfield. I've never been there. And it seems crazy to me, as I pass the exit for Holyoke, the city, not the college, that before this week I'd never given Holyoke, Massachusetts, a single thought. And now, here I was. This is where Sharp was living before he came to Gormlaith. And Alfieri was from Springfield, where I am headed. I try to focus on the reason for this trip. To forget about what I am leaving behind.

I text Jake as soon as I park at the hospital, and he gives me directions to the ICU.

I stop by the gift shop and pick up a bouquet of flowers, noting how much more expensive they are than the bunch I picked up for Effie just this morning. This morning feels so long ago, and now Gormlaith feels distant as well.

Jake greets me in the ICU waiting room. I am overwhelmed by something when I see him, though I can't pinpoint exactly what it is. My impulse is to hug him, to hold him. Like Effie, I am inclined to suspend all grievances, to let go, this emergency some-how negating what he has done.

I once worked with a woman at Norton who was a horrid person. Everyone hated her. But when she got throat cancer, it was as though she'd received some sort of pass. Her bitchiness, her cattiness, her back-stabbing and abrasiveness were somehow forgiven. Cancer exonerated her from all her bad behavior. I felt guilty for getting irritated with her, though her worst qualities were amplified by her illness.

Still, when he moves toward me, I don't turn away. Instead, I hug him, smell the familiar scent of his shampoo. And I soften.

"Where's your dad?" I ask.

"I sent him home to sleep," he says. "He's been up all night."

"So what happened?" I ask, and we sit down together in the uninviting plastic chairs in the waiting area. They are linked together, immoveable.

He recites what it is that the doctors have told him. A massive cerebral aneurysm burst in her brain. It's a miracle that she survived at all. Had she been alone in the house, had Dick not come into the kitchen the moment that he did, I'd have been coming down here for a funeral.

"Can I see her?" I ask.

"I think so," he says, and asks the nurse at the desk if we can go in.

I have loved Jake's mother since the moment I met her. His father, a professor at

Amherst, has always intimidated me. But Shirley is like a warm breeze. She is all air and sunshine. I have known this woman for almost twenty years. When I met her, she was younger than I am now.

Seeing her like this makes me ache. And then everything disappears. My anger at Jake, everything that has been happening at the lake. This woman has been a mother to me when I had none. How could I have been so selfish to even consider for a moment not coming here to see her?

She is sleeping, medicated. And it strikes me that hospitals have a tendency to strip you of everything that makes you human. Hair, skin, bones; the skeletal essence is all that remains in a hospital bed. There is no room in a hospital for the dirty jokes she loves and her full-body laughter. For the curlers she sometimes wears in her red hair halfway through the day before she remembers them. The hospital is inhospitable to a wink before the shot of Irish whiskey, which she drinks from an airplane bottle she keeps stashed in her bra.

"Ma," Jake says, reaching for her hand. And it is only paper-thin flesh, spotted with freckles, the architecture no different than any other hand. Though this is the hand that held mine when we got back from Guatemala. The hand that stroked my hair until I fell asleep. The hand that knitted the tiny blanket and sweaters and then later packed them all away in boxes stored on high shelves in our closet.

I sit down in a chair next to the bed, terrified of accidentally disrupting the equipment that surrounds her: the whirring, humming, dripping machines that are keeping that blood clot from doing any more damage than it's already done.

I reach for her hand, and am startled by how cold it is.

Jake is in the doorway; he seems to be waiting for me to tell him what to do.

"Can you get me a coffee?" I ask, and he seems grateful for a project. For a mission.

I hold on to Shirley's hand as gently as I can and am aware of the softly beating pulse just beneath her skin. I study her face, which, without her careful makeup, seems paler, older. I have never watched her sleep before. I have only seen her as she usually is, a whirling body full of life and energy. Dancing in the kitchen to the imaginary songs that played inside her head. Digging in the soil of her garden.

"Hi, Shirley," I say, and my throat swells.

Jake had explained that the ruptured aneurysm caused a bleed in her brain, effectively causing a stroke. That one moment she was fine, washing dishes, listening to the radio, and the next moment her body conspired against her. An explosion, a detonation in her brain. It was a live grenade she didn't know was there, and it went off. She's lucky to be alive, though it's impossible to know yet the extent of the damage. If she makes it through the next twenty-four to forty-eight hours, she will then be transported to Boston to see neurology specialists. Because even if there is no significant damage done to her brain already, there is still a chance, an even greater chance, of this happening again. Her body could be riddled with these horrific landmines. It is all delicate, fragile, now. Dangerous.

When Jake's dad returns to the hospital, he looks a hundred years old. I mistake him for an elderly patient as he shuffles, head down, shoulders hunched, toward us.

"Tessie," he says. "Thank you for coming down."

His usually gruff voice, his caustic demeanor, is gone. It's as if he himself were a walking aneurysm: puffed up, dangerous, always on the verge of bursting. But now, he is deflated. Bled out.

He holds on to my hands and studies my

face as though he's forgotten who I am. And for just a moment, I feel a pity so deep it nearly swallows me. But it's not pity at all. It's a sort of odd longing. Out of place. Confused.

In two years, Dick and Shirley will celebrate their fiftieth wedding anniversary. They met when Shirley was a student of Dick's during his first year of teaching at college. It was a forbidden love affair, kept secret until she graduated. And even then, her father apparently came after Dick with a shotgun (literally, Shirley was from the Appalachian wilds of West Virginia, where shotgun weddings got their name) when Shirley announced that she was pregnant. They lost that first child, who was born with a hole in his heart, but went on to raise three boys (Jake being the youngest). They moved around a lot when the boys were little until Dick got his tenured position at Amherst and then they settled here. Forty-eight years. A million meals, a million conversations, a million head colds and family vacations and miles spent together in the car. A million dreams fulfilled or deferred. And yet, every time they were together, Dick looked at her like she was still that nineteen-year-old coed. It embarrassed Jake how his father mooned over his mother;

when they held hands or Dick nuzzled into Shirley's neck while she was trying to do something else, Jake would roll his eyes. Mortified like a twelve-year-old who has just caught his parents making out.

But it was deeper than affection, deeper than the raw energy that seemed to pulse between them. There was a tenderness between them that I have never felt with Jake. Not once. And somehow, somewhere along the line, I must have gotten the wrong idea that he would one day look at me the way his father looks at his mother. Is it possible that I was that stupid? That I believed this was some sort of genetic inheritance held in a trust to be released, disbursed at a later date?

"Dad, we're going to get some dinner. Can we bring you anything?"

Dick shakes his head and shrugs his shoulders. "I'm okay. I can get something in the cafeteria."

"Well, call me if you change your mind," Jake says. "We'll be back in a couple of hours. Text me if Mom wakes up."

Dick nods and looks at us, as though he is looking for something he's lost. But it's not here. And I think maybe it never was.

We find a little pizza shop in a brick building near the hospital; next door is an Irish pub and grill.

"Pizza?" Jake asks.

I shake my head. "How about a drink instead? Looks like they've got burgers too."

We go inside and take a seat at the long wooden bar. There's a Sox game on and a half dozen men in Sox caps grumbling. None of them acknowledge us.

I am grateful to be sitting side-by-side rather than across from each other. It's easier this way to avoid looking at him.

"What happened?" he asks, motioning to my hand.

"Bagel injury," I say. "So, what did Charlie decide?"

Charlie and he are supposed to make a decision by tomorrow. Part of me wonders if Jake will be conducting business from the hospital waiting room, from the parking lot. It must have killed him to have to leave New York in the middle of the biggest deal of his career.

He shakes his head. "I don't know. I'm not really thinking about that right now," he says, hurt. "How are things going up at the lake? Anything more with the girl?"

There is so much he doesn't know. It feels like our lives have divided; after that night, mine continued on without him. (And his without me as well.) I wonder if this is what it feels like to split up. Just the decision and then the parting. And then I think that maybe it started a long time ago. A weak seam, the fabric slowly separating until one day you notice the rip. And it's too late to repair. The damage too complete.

"The police have some leads. They're looking for the guy in the truck," I say. "They traced his plates. He's actually from here. Springfield."

"A tourist?" he says.

And I realize, the threads are gone. Nothing is holding this together. *Us* together.

People who've been together as long as we have usually have children. And even when their marriages fall apart, they stay. For the kids. But I wonder if that's just an excuse. Because without children, I am still struggling to find reasons not to leave. It's harder though, the reasons less compelling.

"When do you think you'll leave?" he asks, and I don't know whether he's talking about Gormlaith or something else.

I turn to him, sigh, and shrug. I shake my head, and he looks at me sadly. He knows. He understands. These nuances, these gestures are unmistakable after all this time. A language that has grown over the last two decades.

"Do you love her?" I ask.

"Tessie," he says, shaking his head.

"Do you love *me*?" I ask. This question is harder.

He frowns. Sighs. "We want different things," he says. "We have always wanted different things."

"What does that mean?" I ask.

He looks sad. Like a boy.

"I was never enough for you," he says.

"Of course you were," I argue. "That's ridiculous. I'm not the one who found someone else. Who *fell in love* with someone else."

"Yes," he says, smiling sadly. "You *did.*"

And I feel the tear, the rip down the center of me. The frayed edges.

The bartender watches us from the far end of the bar. I am crying now. Jake reaches over and grabs my hand, studies it like he's seeing it for the first time. Like it's something that belongs to him but that he's forgotten.

"You want something that doesn't exist," he says. "That will never exist. No matter what I do, I can't ever, ever give it to you. And I'm tired, Tess. I am so tired of failing." His voice catches. And when I look up at him his eyes are full too.

"I'm sorry," I say, shaking my head. And I

mean it. I am so full with remorse. With sorrow. Because I *knew* this. Felt his resistance and ambivalence. Yet I truly believed that it was something to be overcome. Something that he would simply get over. That once she was in his arms, in our lives, that all that reluctance would slip away. All along I knew this, yet I persisted. Insisted.

"Me too," Jake says.

Someone opens the door, and the bar is filled momentarily with sunlight. It burns my eyes.

"I'm not coming home," I say, and I don't know whether it's an assertion or a question until he nods. Agrees. No protestations. No pleading.

And just like that, it's over. But instead of feeling angry or defeated, instead of clinging or raging, I feel only the tremendous release of finally, finally letting go. Of letting *him* go.

"Excuse me," I say, leaning across the bar. "Can I get a couple of shots of Jameson?"

The bartender delivers the shots, and I push one in front of Jake, trying to lighten this moment. Treat this grim occasion as a cause for celebration. To offer him something to do with his hands. But he shakes his head.

"Come on," I try, but already feel his

silent disapproval, disappointment.

"I'm going back to the hospital," he says, and then pauses. "Please, Tess. Don't do this again." He motions to the shot glasses.

And I feel ashamed, stupid. I consider nodding, leaving the shot glasses on the bar, and going with him. But that doesn't seem like the right thing to do either.

"I'll meet you back at the house later," I say. "I'll get a cab."

"Okay," he says, standing up. He plucks a twenty-dollar bill from his pocket and sets it on the counter. "Thank you," he says softly and kisses the top of my head.

And this, more than anything, hurts. As though my leaving him is a gift. Something he has been too afraid to ask for that has suddenly been presented to him, wrapped in a beautiful bow. My entire body aches.

After the door closes behind him, I drink both shots and study the Sox game on the TV. I leave the bar six beers and another shot later. When I stand up, the entire world seems to have tilted a bit. The bartender holds me up, righting me against the earth, which seems determined to spill me off its edges, and helps me into the waiting cab.

The cab drops me off at his parents' house. Jake and his dad aren't home yet. I let myself in with the key Shirley keeps under a flowerpot and stumble upstairs to the attic guest room where we stay when we are visiting. It is raining, and I fall asleep to the sound of the rain pattering against the roof.

A tangle of sheets, of legs. Our bodies knotted together in an intricate web. I remember the dewy filaments of us. The way we stretched and expanded. It felt both tenuous and, miraculously, invulnerable.

I loved you. Once.

It feels impossible to say this now without feeling both angry and sad. As though the truth of this has somehow been negated, as the years have been obliterated, by your simple, willful, careless act. And this infuriates me. Enrages me. How could you take this absolute, this historical truth (I loved you once) and make me wonder at its veracity? How can you call into question the one certainty I have left?

Do you remember our first apartment? The rust-ringed drain, the sticky floors? The pervasive *drip, drip* of the bathroom faucet, and the light? God, the light that fell through the one smoky stained glass window, that illuminated the ratty mattress we salvaged from the downstairs neighbor in a kaleidoscope of colors. I felt like a cat, curled into that spot of colored sunshine each morning. It was in this warm spot of light that I became privy to your secrets. The mundane details of your life, the habits somehow exotic to me. Even the way you rose out of bed so different from my own. The alarm startled you, but rather than slamming your hand against the snooze button, as I did, you shot up, your back erect. Like a soldier. Every movement had a purpose. There was an efficiency to you that thrilled me. A purposefulness. You'd sit on the edge of the bed, crack your back, first twisting to the right and then to the left. Then your neck. Crack, crack. I studied the architecture of your spine.

You showered and shaved. You unfolded the ironing board and ironed your clothes. I remember the hiss of steam, the delicious scent of starch. You were the one who made the coffee, prepared breakfast. I can still remember the sound of the blade on the wooden cutting board, the smell of strawberries. And while you readied yourself for the world, I would stay in that warm spot on the bed. Until the sun shifted, until the last possible moment. Only then would I rise. Grab the mug you'd set out for me on the counter, sit down at the small table where you'd have left me the paper.

You used to pack me a lunch. Do you remember that? I remember wrapping my robe around me and watching you from behind the newspaper, which I never really read, as you spread peanut butter on one slice of bread, jelly on the other. As you carefully sealed a plastic Baggie with crackers and cheese, apple slices, inside. I remember thinking, in those moments when you didn't know I was watching, that someday you'd make a wonderful father.

Maybe it was then that I realized what I wanted. When it came to me, as surprising as a summer storm. When I understood what was missing. The one thing that would complete this portrait we'd begun to paint. A child. Maybe, a little girl.

Of course I didn't say anything then, not when everything was so new and fresh and fragile. But I knew. Though I also knew that I would need to be patient. That neither of us was ready yet. We needed stability in our careers. We needed to get married. We needed to buy a house. We needed to make money, save money. We were still so young.

But I loved you. The proof of this is in my silence. In my patience. In the moment when you gently extricated yourself from the web we'd spun, and I lay alone in a spot of sunlight content to wait. I thought then that we had all the time in the world. What I didn't know then, couldn't know then, was that love makes fools of us all.

Early in the morning, I tiptoe past Jake asleep on the couch. I leave a note asking him to call me, to keep me posted about his mom. To give her my love. On my way out the door, I look at Dick's empty loafers sitting next to Shirley's moccasins and feel a sadness so profound, it nearly brings me to my knees.

It's really over, I think. Just like that. That aneurysm, that swollen pulsing thing, has burst. And now there is just the slow, awful bleed.

I grab a coffee and a sweet cake donut from the Dunkin' Donuts on my way out of town. And as I drive back to the lake, it's surprisingly not Jake that I'm thinking about. It's not even Shirley on my mind. Instead, I keep checking my rearview mirror. Looking for that white truck. I wonder if Alfieri will be making a weekend visit to the lake. It's Friday.

I drive straight back to Effie's, but she and Plum are not there. Just like at Dick and Shirley's, I know where to find the hidden key, but again I feel like a thief, like a trespasser, as I let myself into the empty camp.

The kitchen still carries the smells of morning: bacon, coffee, the sweet scent of soap and shampoo wafting from the bathroom. I can see that Effie has made a pile of ingredients on the counter (a shiny purple eggplant, three lemons, white pepper and cinnamon); I almost forgot that her friends Sam and Mena are coming tomorrow. I also forgot to tell Jake that I am finally going to get to meet Sam Mason.

This, I think, is grief: every little thing a reminder. I wonder how long it will take before I stop thinking about him. I smoked in college. When I finally quit, it took several months before I stopped thinking about it every day. And it wasn't until the thoughts were gone that I realized I finally had it beat. But I'd only smoked for a few years. Jake and I have been together nearly twenty years now. The world has become a minefield of memories; I must be careful where I step.

Effie has left a note on the kitchen table.

Bookmobile this morning. If you get home by noon, meet us in town at the Miss Quimby Diner for lunch? My treat XOXO.

I am not sure what, if anything, I can do until I hear back from Strickland, and so I decide to go ahead and meet them in town. Maybe I can stop by and check in with Ryan.

The problem is that Strickland was not on duty when he found me outside the barn. He wasn't supposed to be there either. And so in order to get a warrant, he'd have to come up with a pretty compelling explanation for why he and I were both trespassing on Lisa's property at the same time. He asked me to give him a day to figure out the best way to proceed.

Part of me is grateful for the delay. Flashes of what I saw, or at least *think* I saw, in that barn are haunting me. If it was blood, then what happened in there? And where the hell did Lisa go? If she left, I wonder if Sharp has left too. And if they are gone, if they have the little girl, then what will happen to her?

It is hot and humid. The air is filled with electricity. There's another storm coming, according to the weather reports. The sky feels swollen, ominous. It's not raining yet, but I suspect it will be soon.

It's only 11:30 when I get to the diner. I know how busy it gets at lunchtime though, so I secure a booth for us, tell the waitress that I'm meeting two other people, order an iced tea. Pretend to study the menu. I don't need to though; I know it by heart.

I am hungover still from the whiskey. It hasn't hit me until now. I am so grateful when the waitress brings over a large carafe of ice water with lemon slices suspended inside. I gulp down three glasses, feel the ice water cut through the nausea.

When Lieutenant Andrews walks into the diner, a shiver runs through my body, but I don't know whether it's from the ice water or something else. Thankfully, he doesn't see me. He's busy slapping some other local on the back, chatting up a storm like he's running for mayor or something. I half expect him to pick up the baby that's sitting in a high chair at the next booth over and take a selfie.

Finally, he sits down at the counter and picks up a newspaper someone has left behind. He shakes it out and starts to read, engrossed in the sports page, barely looking up when my waitress pours him a cup of coffee.

I stare out the window, study the sky, wonder if I have an umbrella in my car. And then all of a sudden, my heart stops.

The white truck. It's parked across the street in front of the feed store. The dog's head is sticking out of the passenger window. I struggle to see if anyone is sitting in the driver's seat.

I reach into my purse and grab my wallet, pull out a five-dollar bill and leave it on the table.

I glance at my watch. 11:45. I need to get out of here without Andrews seeing me and before Effie and Plum show up, before Alfieri takes off again. I run down the wooden steps and into the dirt lot where my car is parked. I hear the rumble of thunder in the distance and feel a couple drops of cold rain on my bare arms. I duck into my car, watch and wait.

A couple of minutes later, the rain starts to come down hard, obscuring my view of the feed store parking lot across the street. I turn the key and start the windshield wipers. And then he emerges with a large bag of dog food, which he heaves into the back of his truck. As before, the back of the truck is still filled with landscaping gear. A lawn mower, a rake, a shovel, a half-dozen full lawn bags. It makes no sense. If he's just arriving in Quimby, why would he already have bags full of clippings?

He climbs into the driver's seat, and I slowly pull out of my parking spot. He backs the truck up, his tires spitting gravel in its wake, and I pull out after him.

I try to keep my distance as we drive through town. We pass the library just as Effie and Plum emerge from the heavy front doors. My heart thuds, hoping they don't see me. Hoping they don't try to stop me. But they don't know I am back from Massachusetts yet, only that I would be back sometime today. Plum is carrying a bright purple umbrella, and she's wearing matching rain boots. I am reminded again that the little girl is out there in only a tutu and a pair of rain boots, with a storm coming. And I think of Lisa, the ladybug rain boots inside her door. What the hell does she have to do with this? Where has she gone? And if she is gone, then why is Alfieri back here?

We come to the fork in the road that will take us on the route toward the lake. He idles at the stop sign, and then turns right. The way to the lake is to the left.

For a moment, I think about turning toward the lake. Forgetting about it. Going back to the camp. I consider just climbing into the bed in the guest cottage and sleeping off this hangover. Listening to the sound of the rain on the roof — now that I am sober, let all of this sink in. *I have left my husband.* I almost laugh at how peculiar that sounds. How strange and sad.

But my hands seem to have a will of their own, and I hear the tick-ticking of the signal before I realize that I have flicked the signal upward. Right. And then I am trailing behind him. Following him who knows where.

There are no other cars on the road, and it strikes me that all he has to do is look in the rearview mirror and see me and my New York plates to recognize me from that night. He had studied me at Hudson's. And if he watched the local news or listened to the radio at all last weekend, he would have heard about me.

When Effie and I were teenagers, we used to ride our bikes out this way. There used to be a drive-in restaurant where we could buy maple creemees, greasy french fries. Other than that it's all fields and farmland. Rolling hills spotted with ranch houses. The occasional dilapidated barn. If you keep going, you'll arrive at the road that will take you to the ski area. In high school we partied at the chairlift shack on Franklin Mountain.

The rain is coming down hard now, and the scenery is remembered rather than seen; my actual view is limited to the two half circles cleared by my windshield wipers, which are struggling to keep up with the rain.

Suddenly, the truck disappears, and I realize he has turned onto a dirt road. I worry at first that it's a driveway, but then see it's marked: BLACK FLY BOULEVARD. Vermonters and their wry sense of humor.

I slow down and give him time to think that I have passed before signaling right (for whom, I have no idea) and then turning down the road. It's insane. I know this. But I have come this far. There's no turning back now. And there literally is *no turning back*. The road is a rutted, dirt road, enclosed in a tunnel of foliage, barely wide enough for one car. If I wanted to leave, I'd probably have to throw the car in reverse and back up.

I drive slowly, second-guessing this decision even as I proceed.

The rain is rendering the road into a sea of mud. The leaves on the trees hang heavy, some of the branches low enough to scrape the hood of my car. I feel like I am being swallowed.

It dawns on me that there is the very

distinct possibility that I will get stuck out here. This car is designed for city streets, for highways. What the fuck was I thinking? I reach over to my purse, which is sitting on the passenger seat. I grab my phone and turn it on. No signal. Of course not.

I keep driving slowly. The one thing that you can count on here is that all of these roads are connected, arterial. Labyrinthine but always leading somewhere. If you just keep driving, you'll inevitably come to a road that is familiar. I remember bringing Jake here once when we started dating and getting lost. I'd been cavalier while he seemed slightly panicked. For an hour we bumped around on back roads, and then just as he was about to kill me for getting us lost, the road opened up and we were on pavement. On a main road that I knew would lead us, eventually, back to Quimby.

But my insouciance is gone now, as the road becomes less *road* and more of a muddy, overgrown path through the woods. I am scared. It's not safe to go any farther; if I do, I'll definitely get stuck. If I'm not already. I am almost too afraid to try to back up.

I sit still and try to think about what my options are. I can stay here until Alfieri comes back. I can try to back up the quarter mile I've already driven. Or I can get out of the car and try to walk where I had hoped to drive. To see where Alfieri has gone.

I pop open the glove box in the futile hope that there is an umbrella in there. But I am pretty sure I remember seeing it on our kitchen table on the way out of our house when we left last week.

Shit.

The rain is still pounding down, and the moment I step out of the car I am drenched. It is loud, the rain beating on the leaves like a billion tiny drums. But beyond that is another sound, though it takes me several moments to place it.

Dogs. It's the sound of dogs barking. And not just one or two dogs, but a *lot* of dogs. Snarling, yelping, growling. I move cautiously up the road, just a few steps. There is a driveway. And through the wet tangle of leaves, I can see the white truck parked in front of a trailer: a trailer surrounded by an elaborate system of pens. Dozens of dogs pacing inside these metal cages, all of them with the same clipped ears as Alfieri's dog. Bloody, scarred faces. The air smells metallic, the stench of feces and blood and dog piss nauseating. The sound horrifying.

I am running as fast as I can back to my car. And once inside, I turn the key, mutter a little prayer and then throw it into reverse. Remarkably, I have not sunk into the mud, and I am able to get traction. I turn to look over my shoulder as I back out, out, out, glancing ahead only once or twice to make sure he isn't coming for me. When I am finally on the main road again, I take off as fast as I can, not looking behind me once until I get into town. And then I pull up into the driveway of Ryan's office building on the park and realize I've been holding my breath.

Beth, his secretary, is standing at the copier. Her hand clutches her chest, and I catch my reflection in the mirror hanging in the waiting room. I am soaked, my hair plastered to my head. Leaves clinging to it. I brush them off.

"Tess?" she says. "What happened to you?"

"Is Ryan here?" I ask. "I need to speak with him. It's an emergency."

"Hold on one second," she says, and moves to the phone, but I am already headed down the hallway and throwing open his door.

"Slow down," Ryan says when I try to explain what I saw in the barn, and about Alfieri being back in town. About following him. "You went onto private property, trespassed, *again?*"

I nod. "I guess, technically, but that woman, Lisa, wasn't home. There was a sign about a family emergency."

"Do you realize that either one of them would have been fully within their rights to *shoot* you?"

I sit down. Will my heart to stop racing, my legs to stop shaking.

"You could have been killed. This is crazy," he says.

"Somebody has to do something," I say. "Why won't anyone do anything?"

"Listen," he says. "This is something the police should be handling. It's time for you to stop playing detective. You're going to get hurt. And none of this is helping her."

I feel like he's kicked me in the chest. All of the air has gotten knocked out of me.

"Give me the barrette, please," I say.

"Tess . . ."

"I need it back," I say, holding out my hand.

He opens his drawer, without taking his eyes off of me, and pulls it out. He places it in my outstretched palm.

"What aren't you telling me?" he says softly.

"I've told you everything," I say. "Everything."

"I mean about Guatemala. About what happened after?" he pauses, and then reaches for my hand.

"What does that have to do with this?" I say. Why is he trying so hard to make this about that? It's not the same. She's not the same girl. None of this is the same.

In the dream, I run from the orphanage with her in my arms. Her breath is hot in my ear, her heart pounding against my chest, her small arms strung tightly around my neck. She is pulling my hair, the gentle sting at my scalp of a single strand creating a solitary and focused spot of pain.

I feel the street beneath my feet, the pounding of my sandals against the pavement. I do not look back as they call after me.

The streets in my dream are both similar to and different from the ones I wandered all those weeks as I waited. The air is thick and hot and mephitic, the stink of garbage strong. I bury my face in her hair so that I do not have to breathe this smell of rancid meat and rotting fruit, this fetid air that fills my lungs.

A man sits in a doorway, his shirt baring a bulbous growth, which he rubs gently with his hand as he clucks his tongue. And I run, and run.

I peer up when I hear a woman's laughter, and see clothes strung on a line on a crumbling turquoise balcony. The embroidered blouses hanging there mock me: the tiny flowers conjured from thread. It only takes one tug, one pull for the thread to begin to unravel.

And so now I duck down the alleyways I once avoided.

Mama, mama, mama, she whispers in my ear, her tiny fists clutching at my hair.

And it is this solitary and certain tug that I still feel when I wake to the bright lights of the hospital.

I leave Ryan's with no more of a sense of what to do next than I had when I got there. I need to talk to Strickland. He is the only one who can actually, *will* actually, do something. I have to trust him; right now, I have no other choice.

I sit in my car in the parking lot and dig through my purse for the card he gave me that night, then dial his number.

"This is Strickland," he says, probably mystified by the 718 area code.

"Hi, it's Tess Waters," I say.

"Waters," he says.

"I need to talk to you," I say.

He coughs.

"I have something to show you," I add.

"My shift ends at five. Meet me at Mc-Donald's," he says, and then hangs up the phone.

5:00 is still two hours from now. I debate whether I should go back to Effie's house or if I should stay in town. If I go back to the camp, then I'd have to explain to Effie why I'm leaving again. She doesn't know about Strickland. She doesn't know anything about what I saw in the barn, or when I followed Alfieri.

And so, I decide instead to just drive around to kill time.

I grew up in Quimby in the seventies and eighties. Not much has changed since then besides what fills the storefronts. It is a time capsule, this town, a place that holds my memories. Every time I come home, I feel like I've just dragged a box out of storage filled with mementos. I am both nostalgic and saddened by this place.

Here is the corner where I smoked my first cigarette. Here is the river where Michael Knapp kissed me. Here is my elementary school, my high school. Here is the house where I grew up.

I park across the street from the little brick split-level house near the high school. It looks pretty much the same as it did when I was little. The tree out front that I used to climb, whose branches and leaves served as my own private hideaway, is gone now, which makes the house seem exposed. Vulnerable somehow. I think about the way the house looked to me the first time I came home from college in Boston. How its simplicity and modesty had embarrassed me. I am ashamed now of that shame.

This is the house where I was a child. The bay window where we always put our Christmas tree. The porch where Effie and I used to camp out in sleeping bags on hot summer nights. The small window upstairs to my room where I slept and played and cried. This is the house where my mother died.

The front door opens and a woman comes out. She is thin, pale, wearing only a dingy tank top and a pair of cutoff shorts. Her face is long, drawn, and her hair stringy. I think she is younger than she looks. She is followed by a guy who is similarly thin, sickly thin. They sit together on the front steps and she leans against him, her head resting on his shoulder. I feel embarrassed, an odd voyeur.

I start to turn the key in the ignition; it's 4:45, if I leave now I will get to McDonald's to meet Strickland right on time.

A car pulls into the driveway next to the house, and the guy on the porch stands up, ambles down the steps. His faded jeans cling to his narrow, bony hips. He is like the Scarecrow in *The Wizard of Oz,* nothing but sticks beneath his clothes. He walks over to the open driver's side window, pulls some loose bills out of his back pocket, and bends down to the driver. When he stands upright again, he's holding a ziplock bag. As the car backs out of the driveway, he glances across the street, notices me, and shoves the bag in his back pocket.

I turn the key.

On the porch, the man opens up the screen door and ducks inside. The woman stands up to follow him. Her legs are pale, and the backs of her knees are mottled with bruises, scabs.

Track marks.

I squeeze my eyes shut trying to unsee this, as though I can restore the image of my house, the yard where I learned to walk, the walls that held my whole childhood inside. But it is spoiled. Tainted. I remember finding the syringe in the woods. What has happened to this place?

Strickland is sitting in a booth near the back of the restaurant by the bathrooms. I sit across from him, and he nods in acknowledgment. He has a tray in front of him with a burger, french fries, a soda.

"I didn't know what you liked. If you're a vegetarian or whatever."

I shake my head. "I'm not hungry."

He takes a tentative drink of his soda but says nothing.

"Alfieri is back," I say. "I saw his truck in town today, and I followed him out past the old drive-in. Somebody out there is keeping dogs. Pit bulls, I think. I don't know what this has to do with anything, but I thought you should know."

One of his eyebrows rises, though almost imperceptibly. "Do you know the address?"

"Listen," I say. "I know you are hoping to get something on this guy. And I hope you do. I really do. But I'm having a hard time understanding how this is helping her."

"Who?" he says.

Seriously?

"The little girl," I say in disbelief. "That child. Christ, why did I even come here?" I start to stand up.

"Wait," he says, reaching out for my arm.

"What?" I ask. "What the fuck is this? I thought you were going to help me."

"It's drugs," he says.

"What?" and I think about the couple I just saw sitting on the porch of my childhood home.

"I've been tracking Alfieri. He makes a weekly run from Holyoke up here and back. Sharp and he are in cahoots, and Lisa figures in somehow too."

"What about her barn, what I saw?"

"Dog-fighting," he says.

"What?"

"Gambling. The pit bulls you saw? The blood stains, they're not human. They're from the dogs."

I shake my head. But the momentary relief I feel gives way to disgust. Terrific. These freaking low-life drug dealers are fighting dogs too. And all of this next to a day care center, down the road from my best friend and her daughters. But none of this has anything to do with the little girl who stumbled out of the woods and into my life a week ago. None of this will save her. None of this matters at all.

And I realize that he doesn't care about finding her. He only wants to make some big bust and save face after the disaster last week.

"You don't think she's real, do you?" I ask. "You think I'm crazy too."

I think about Ryan, the way he looked at me, the pity in his eyes. *What happened after Guatemala?*

Strickland sets down the burger, and wipes his hands on a napkin. "Miss Waters," he starts.

I reach for my purse, and for a moment he looks scared. Like I might just pull a gun

387

out of it and shoot him. And for the briefest moment, I have a fantasy of doing the same.

"What is this?" he says.

We both stare at the orange bunny barrette, sitting next to a limp french fry.

"It belongs to her. I found it on Sharp's property. If you don't fucking go there and find her, I will."

The rain stops as I drive back to the camp, the sun emerging triumphant and hot from behind the receding clouds. When I walk into the kitchen, Effie is on the phone with Devin.

"I'm so proud of you," she says into the phone. "This is amazing."

A little pang, a sharp sting. I haven't told her yet about Jake. About what happened between us at that Irish bar. I haven't told her that everything has fallen apart.

"It's really happening," she says when she hangs up. *"Gagosian."*

"That's amazing," I say. "Is he beside himself?"

"He can't believe it's real," she says. "This is so, so big."

"How is Zu-Zu doing?" I ask. And she reaches for her phone on the table. "She sent me these today." She smiles. It's a picture of her leaping in front of Rockefeller

Center. I hold the phone, peer at the screen, swipe my finger across, and look at the photos she has taken of her dorm room, of the dance studio, of her bloody toes. In the last picture, she is pressing foreheads with another girl whose hair is also tied back into a tight bun.

"She's already got a friend," Effie says. "It doesn't look like she's very homesick."

"I'm sure she misses you," I say.

"Oh my God," she says, shaking her head. "I am such an asshole. How is Shirley?"

I sigh. "They still don't know. There was a bleed in her brain, so she may have some permanent damage. They'll probably transfer her to Boston as soon as she's stable."

"Oh honey," she says, and reaches for my hand. Her hands are tiny, childlike in mine.

"It's okay. I think she's going to pull through. They say the first twenty-four to forty-eight hours is the most critical. Jake said he'd call tonight."

"Why are you back here already then?" she asks.

I take a deep breath. "I'm leaving Jake."

She squeezes my hand and I look up at her. Her sweet face that I know better than my own.

"Are you sure? It's not just . . . everything that's happened?"

390

I shake my head. "No," I say. "It was time. It was time a long time ago."

"I'm so sad," she says, her voice cracking.

And this, more than anything, brings it all home. And I am angry at Jake for ruining everything. Angry at him for letting me go. For not wanting me, for not wanting *us,* as much as he wanted everything else. I have eight years of anger stored up, eight years of disappointment and frustration and regret.

Tears run hot from my eyes. Then I realize I am falling apart in Effie's kitchen. I wipe at my eyes with the back of my wrist.

"Where's Plum?" I ask, worried she's just witnessed this.

"She rode her bike over to a friend's," she says.

"Are you kidding?" I ask. "With everything that's going on?"

Effie waves her hand in front of her face, dismissing my concerns. "She's fine. It's just up the road."

"Are you sure?" I say.

"She's *fine,*" Effie says. "She'll be home by suppertime."

I know I should tell her about all the new stuff that's come up, the fact that in addition to a pedophile, she has drug dealers, animal abusers, God knows who else living down the road from her. That people are dealing drugs in broad daylight in town. But I have promised to keep my mouth shut. Until the police make their move. Plum is just up the road at her friend's. She's *fine*.

"I think I need to take a nap," I say, exhaustion overwhelming me.

"Go," she says, and leans in to hug me. "I'm sorry about Shirley. And about Jake. Get some sleep and we'll talk about it later."

In the guest cottage, I toss and turn. There is a small fan, which drones on and on, uselessly spinning the hot air around and around. I throw the sheets off, kick at them as if they are intentionally binding me. I slip in and out of sleep for hours before my body and mind finally relent.

I wake up to a banging at the door. I am disoriented. Confused. At first I think I am in that hotel room. My body aches in that same desperate, impossible way. As the dream dissipates, I think I am in the guest room at Jake's parents' house. When the banging comes again, I realize I am here. Through the window, the sky has the golden cast of late afternoon: those golden hours before twilight.

"*Tess,*" Effie says. Her voice is panicked. And I think, *Oh my God. Shirley has passed away.* While I was sleeping, Jake's mother died. My heart thumps hard in my chest as I struggle to extricate myself from the twisted sheets.

I stumble out of bed. My hand, which I have slept on, is tingling, asleep, but underneath the pins and needles is the prevailing steady pain of the wound. Still confused, I look at my knuckles, expecting to see them bloodied and swollen.

I unlock the door, ready myself.

Effie's eyes are puffy, red. Her hair is disheveled; she is hugging herself.

"What's the matter?" I ask.

"It's Plum," Effie says. "I can't find her."

It feels like my entire body is made of pins and needles now.

"I thought she went to her friend's house," I say.

"I called over there when she didn't come home, but they said she left over an hour ago."

I try not to panic, to be logical.

"Did you go down to the boat access area?" I ask. As though Effie hasn't searched everywhere already, as though this wouldn't be the *first* place she looked. Effie was there the night Devin's sister, not much younger than Plum, drowned.

"She would never have gone anywhere near the water by herself," she says, shaking her head, wringing her hands. "She knows better."

"The tree house?" I try.

Effie shakes her head again. "She's gone," she says.

"You need to call the police," I say.

I wait at the house as Effie drives around

394

the lake, banging on all the doors, asking if anyone has seen Plum. She's called Devin and he is driving up from New York. I couldn't listen to their conversation. It was too familiar, history repeating itself.

I pace back and forth in the kitchen. Outside the sun is still bright. It is 6:00. There are two hours of daylight left.

It's Lieutenant Andrews who pulls up this time, and my heart sinks.

He saunters out of his car, shutting the door and pushing out his chest as I rush outside to meet him.

"Well, well, if it isn't Tess Waters," he says. "How's this for déjà vu?"

"My friend's daughter is missing," I say, determined not to let him get to me. "She rode her bike to a friend's house and she left to come home over an hour ago. But she never came home. You need to look for her."

"Seems to me, there's a story that goes like this," he says, sneering. His voice is mocking, singsongy. "Something about a little boy crying wolf. You know that one, right? The boy hollers and hollers, about the big bad wolf that's come to eat the sheep, gets the whole village riled up. But there's no wolf."

I take a deep breath, try to stay calm.

395

"But you forget, Lieutenant. In the story the wolf *does* come to the village. That's how the story ends," I say, furious. "The wolf actually comes."

"Touché," he says. Except the way he says it rhymes with douche.

I hate him. But I need to keep calm, to play this game if I want him to help me.

"She's ten, she's has dark curly hair, green eyes. Here is her school picture." Earlier I sat down and clipped apart the professional photos that Effie brought to me in a sheet, the images repeating again and again on the page.

He looks at the photo, and I hope that it will be enough to move him. This beautiful child enough to break through that stone wall.

"This Devin Jackson's kid?" he asks. Devin is one of only a couple black men in this town. Their kids are likely the only mixed kids.

I nod, irritated.

"He donated some of his art for the last Policeman's Ball. Not my taste, but it brought in a lot of money at the auction."

I don't know if this means he's going to help me or not.

He crosses his arms, studying me.

"You know, if you're fucking with me, with

this town, again, that's all the DA will need to proceed with the charges against you."

I nod and nod. "I don't care about the charges. I just want to find her."

This time, there are no helicopters, but there are dogs. By the time they arrive, it is 7:00 P.M. Daylight still, but only an hour left.

Effie is still driving around, handing out the photos to everyone, searching the edge of the road for her bicycle. It is bright purple with streamers. It would be hard to miss. I stay at the camp in case she comes home, to keep Devin updated. He calls the landline every fifteen minutes checking in. And though I should expect him, each time the phone rings, my entire body goes limp.

I try to think about what I can do to help. But there is nothing. And then I think of Mary, the psychic. This house is full of Plum's things. Effie gave the police one of the shirts from her hamper to give the dogs her scent. Maybe if I gave her one of Plum's stuffed animals, one of her hair ribbons, she'd be able to find her.

I try to remember where I put her business card. I search my wallet, but it's not there. I check my pockets. Nothing. And then I remember tucking it into the visor of the car.

I go outside to my car. When I open the door, I am greeted by that familiar sour smell of the wine. I wonder how much longer it will linger. If it will always smell like that night.

I sit down in the passenger seat and flip the visor down. The card is there. I pluck it from the little pocket and start to get out of the car, and then I see the grocery bag sitting on the floor. When I got the call from Jake about his mom I must have forgotten it here. I reach down and pick it up, realize there are a dozen eggs inside. I reach into the bag to pull them out, figure they should go outside in the plastic bin. And I realize there's something else in there as well.

Gumdrops.

The gumdrops I bought to put in the fairy house by the swimming hole. I promised Plum that I would take her back there to leave the note for Star, to see if she'd come and taken the Reese's Cups we left. She wouldn't go swimming alone, but she might go looking for fairies.

I go to the shed where I left Effie's bike, climb on, and pedal away from the camp as fast as I can, my legs burning as I go. All around me, in the woods along the road, I hear the sounds of the dogs. The policemen tromping through the brush.

Please, please, please, I think as I pedal up the incline.

The road is rutted from the last rain. I have to ride in the center of the road to avoid the gully-like tracks left behind. I think, ridiculously, about bowling with Jake back when we first started dating. We were drunk. I was practically seeing double, as I threw the balls down the lane, each of them winding up in the gutter. I was so wasted I walked out of the bowling alley with the rented shoes still on my feet. Didn't realize it until the next morning when I found them at the foot of Jake's bed.

Something about this memory fills me with a deep sort of shame. A familiar shame.

As my legs burn and I pedal and pedal furiously against the incline, I feel like I am in a dream where I am moving my legs as hard as I can but not making any progress. I get to the spot before the little wooden bridge, and set my bike down. I search the edge of the woods for Plum's purple bike, seeing nothing. *Please, please, please.*

But her bike is not here. I feel in my pocket for the psychic's card and think I should have called her. She could be on her way here already.

I head into the woods anyway. I am not entirely sure why, but I push my way

399

through the overgrown path. I can hear the trickling of water, the swimming hole is close. The golden light from the sinking sun gilds every leaf.

I can see the swimming hole from the overlook, and I scramble down on my butt, hollering, "Plum? Plum!"

I try to remember where I built the fairy house for her. How far away from the water it was.

"Plum!" I scream as I jump from one flat rock to the next.

And then I see.

The I HEART NY T-shirt. Two puffs of curly hair.

"Tessie?" Plum says, standing up. She's crying, one of the ribbons she wears in her hair come loose.

I run to her, the branches scraping my bare legs.

She falls into my arms, and I hold on to her. As though she too might just slip back into the woods if I let go.

I hold on to her shoulders and say, "Plum, your mom is so worried about you. Why didn't you come home? Where is your bike?"

"I got a flat tire," she says. "But I was worried somebody might steal it, so I hid it in the woods by the lake."

"Why didn't you come to the camp? I

would have brought you here."

"You promised we'd come here today, but then you left."

My throat constricts.

"You told me she was real. But look," she says, pointing at the fairy house. It's amazing that it survived the last rain. The two chocolates we left there earlier are still there. The fairy didn't come and take them. I didn't come and take them. If I had been here, if I had been thinking, I would have exchanged the gumdrops for the chocolate. I would have made sure she had everything she needed to hold on to this dream. I've ruined everything.

Never mind what could have happened to her out here. Never mind the wolf that lives in these woods.

"I bet she couldn't come because of the rain," I say weakly.

She scowls.

"Fairy wings aren't strong enough to fly in the rain. Didn't you know?" I am almost pleading with her.

But it's too late.

This is *ten:* she knows there is no such thing as fairies. She knows they are not real.

She sits on the seat of my bike, and I pedal standing up. When we get back to the camp, the sun is dipping into the lake. No one is there. I need to call Effie, but her cell doesn't work here. Nobody's cell phone works here.

I dial Devin's number on the landline.

"I found her," I say when he picks up. "She's okay."

"Oh my God," he says, and it sounds like someone has just sucked all of the breath out of him. "Where *was* she?"

"She was looking for fairies," I say. "It's my fault."

"No," he says. "No. Is she okay? Can you put her on?"

"Plum," I say. She's trying to pour herself a glass of lemonade, but the pitcher is too heavy. "Talk to your daddy, honey."

I take the pitcher from her and hand her the phone. She takes it and walks into the other room. I pour the lemonade into the plastic tumbler, the one with the picture of Elsa from *Frozen* on it. I bring it to her in the living room, where she is talking to Devin about her turtle.

"Mommy says we're going to get a bigger terrarium for Harold. And maybe we can get another turtle? So that he can have a friend. I think he's lonely. He looks kind of lonely."

When she hangs up, I think about putting

her in the car with me and driving until I find Effie. But Effie could be anywhere.

And so instead I pick up the phone and call the police station. My heart in my throat, I tell the woman who answers that the little girl reported missing earlier this afternoon has been found. I ask if she can please radio Andrews. Let everyone know to stop searching.

Effie arrives first, followed by Andrews's cruiser.

The sun has slipped away now; it is evening. Exhausted, Plum has fallen asleep on the daybed on the porch. Effie runs past me through the camp to her, curls up next to her. I can see her body heaving, the sobs wracking her entire body.

I go outside, feeling like an interloper, and stand next to the cruiser.

"So I understand you found the little one," he says.

I nod.

"Huh," he grunts. "Funny, how you seemed to know right where to go."

"She was looking for fairies," I say as if this explains anything.

"In that story," he says. "The one about the boy? There's a message, right? A moral?"

"It's Aesop," I say. "Of course there's a moral."

"What is it again?" he mocks. "Oh, yeah, nobody believes a liar . . ." He points his finger at me, tsk-tsking. "Not even when they're telling the truth."

After he is gone, I stand outside, not wanting to go back into the camp. Not wanting to interrupt the reunion between Effie and Plum. I don't belong to this family. I am nobody's mother. And soon, I will be nobody's wife either.

What I want is a drink. Just a big tumbler full of wine. I want to forget the panic that has dissipated now into a terrible, lingering hum, which trills in my limbs. And nagging at me is the one feeling I can't seem to shake. No matter how hard I try. When I am finally able to put my finger on what I am feeling, I am ashamed. Even horrified.

I'm *jealous*.

I am jealous that Effie got Plum back. It's ridiculous. Insane. Of course, I wanted to find her. For her to be safe. It's not that. But what about me? What about all those things that I have lost, those irretrievable things? It seems that everything *I* lose remains lost. For years now, I have had to resign myself to forfeiture. I am always, always relinquishing things. Whether stupidly squandered or foolishly misplaced, whether abandoned or stolen, so much of what I have loved and wanted has been consigned to oblivion.

I go back into the camp and find the dusty bottle of whiskey I spotted next to the dish soap and bleach in the bottom cabinet below the sink. I grab one of the metallic tumblers from the cupboard, a wave of nostalgia flooding me. I remember Effie and me bringing these same cups filled with Diet Cokes and stolen vodka out to the front yard one summer, getting drunk and falling asleep in the sun, the sunburns so terrible that we couldn't sleep on our backs for a week. I always chose the green one, Effie the blue.

I pour the cup halfway with whiskey then top it with ice and lemonade.

I just want to stop feeling this way. I want to stop thinking about all those lost things. I want to be able to let go. I want to loosen my grip, to stop fighting. It has all been so futile. I have wasted years of my life hanging on to a dream, chasing something so ethereal, impalpable. I've been clinging to ghosts. I think about Plum and the fairy, her realization, the sad resignation. She's ten years old, and she already knows better, has learned the lesson that it has taken me a lifetime to learn.

I go outside to one of the Adirondack chairs and sit facing the water. The lake is still tonight, the moon's reflection aglow on the surface.

As I drink, I feel the ache in my shoulders subsiding, the muscles in my legs and arms and back relaxing. This is better than a chiropractor, I think. Better than yoga. When Devin arrives home, it's almost midnight. Effie has put Plum to bed, and I can hear the soft sounds of their voices, see their silhouettes, their bodies clinging to each other in this terrible relief. And I drink.

Effie comes outside not long after, bringing me a blanket, which normally lies draped over the arm of her couch.

"You okay?" she asks.

I nod. I know that if I try to talk, to explain what is going on inside my head, I'll ruin everything. To begrudge her this, to admit to the wickedness that lives inside of me, would be irresponsible. Cruel. She is my best friend. She is the one person in the world I trust. I may be angry, and I may be drunk, but I am not stupid.

"I'm fine," I say. "I'm so sorry. About the

fairy house. About everything. I'm so glad she's home."

She nods and sits down in the empty chair next to me.

"You could stay here," she says. "With us."

I am confused.

"I mean, instead of going back to New York."

Tears fill my eyes. Even my home is not my home anymore. I try not to think about what will happen to the brownstone now. I squeeze my eyes shut, and see the antique tub with its perpetually drippy faucet, the ceilings laced with cobwebs I could never reach, the smudgy windows and chipped paint on the crown molding. I think about the first night we spent in the house, back before we even owned a couch. When we sat on pillows on the floor, too afraid to start a fire in the fireplace, we'd lit a bunch of tea lights. We did love each other once.

I think about the extra room, the way I'd stood at the hardware store around the corner looking at the paint-chip display, the spectrum of possibilities. I'd gone back three or four times before settling on the lilac color, the one that I thought might remind her of jacarandas.

I remember the smell of the paint as I rolled it onto those old walls, covering the water stains and cracks in the ancient plaster. The heft and heave of the window I opened to get some fresh air and how the sounds of the city flooded the room. I recall the toddler bed I special ordered and the antique dresser I found at the flea market and rolled on a dolly fifteen blocks home. I remember the framed illustrations from the children's books I found in the used bookstore around the corner, how I'd cut the pages out with a razor blade before placing them behind glass. I think of the paper cranes I folded: a thousand of them, which I hung from the ceiling, each one tethered by an invisible string, creating the illusion of flight. And I remember the blanket Shirley knitted for me arriving in the mail, the soft white cabled blanket she must have worked on for months, folded and tethered with a pale purple ribbon.

"Did I make a mistake?" I ask, and I am not even sure which mistake I am referring to. There have been so, so many.

Effie reaches for my hand.

"No," she says, shaking her head.

Effie leaves me and goes to bed, and I drink. I drink until the ground feels uneven beneath me. Until my limbs, my entire body, feel separate from myself. I struggle out of

409

the Adirondack chair and make my way across the grass, the blanket wrapped around me. I stumble down the path to the cottage and after fumbling to get the door open, to get my clothes off, I collapse into the bed, kicking the heavy covers off of me. The smell of Effie's laundry detergent suggests she's washed the linens recently, most likely while I was with Jake and his mom. Shirley. My heart aches. I stare up at the tongue-in-groove cedar ceiling and begin to spin. I fight off the urge to vomit, simply because I'm not sure I can get out of the bed again. I fight the waves of nausea, press my hand flat against the wall to anchor myself on this rocky sea. And then, thankfully, finally I pass out.

I dream of Guatemala. I dream the smell of jacaranda, the nauseating sweetness of mangoes, of the violent beauty of dragon fruit. I dream her flesh in my arms. I dream of dogs ripping and tearing each other apart, an arena of hurt. Of the needles, of the couple on the porch, smiling with teeth like dogs. Of Plum, of panic. Lieutenant Andrews standing over me, *I'm going to need you to calm down now, ma'am,* he says. Threatens. *Just calm down.*

"*Ten calma.* Please," the lawyer says.

"Don't tell me to calm down. Where is she?" My throat is raw. My whole body raw.

We sit across the desk from her in her small office, and I can feel your grip on my arm tighten, to keep me from leaping over the desk and tearing her eyes out. To keep me from killing her.

"This morning, there was a raid. At the orphanage. The children have been seized."

"Seized?" I picture the armed guards, the ones who stand in the doorways of the shops and banks in the city. Their smug grins as I hurried past.

"Some of the children were there illegally," she says. "Stolen. From their mothers. It's a serious problem here. The kidnapping, the black market . . ."

"Mothers? We were told she was an orphan. Her mother is dead."

She shakes her head, closes her eyes.

"They can't do this. We have papers," I say. "We paid the agency . . ."

"Thirty thousand dollars," you say, nodding, and this makes me hate you.

"The papers have been signed," I say. "You told us everything would be finalized."

"I'm trying to reach the agency," she says. "No one answers."

"Call them again," I say. "Find out when we can get our daughter back."

"It is terrible," she says. "I am so sorry. There is nothing I can do."

"No," I say, shaking my head. "This must be a mistake."

And I stand up, make my way to the door. "I'm going to the orphanage," I say to you.

You look like you have just woken from a dream. Disoriented. Dazed. You shake your head. "No. Let's go back to the hotel," you say. "I'll call Oliver. We need an American attorney. Someone to contact the agency directly."

"No," I say. "I'm going to find her."

I don't know if you are following me. I can't hear anything but my own breath. By the time I finally get to the orphanage, my body is slick with sweat. I lick my lips and they are salty, but I don't know if it is sweat or tears or both.

I ring the buzzer and then bang on the closed door until my knuckles are bloody, until

412

a small crowd has gathered. And when my arms no longer work, and my legs will no longer hold me up, I sit on the ground, look up at the bare branches of the jacaranda tree. The ground beneath me is plastered with their wilting petals.

"Please, get up. We need to call Oliver. Call home," you say.

But I can't get up.

"Get up," you yell, and I don't recognize you anymore.

But my body complies. I feel it moving, sense the pavement under my feet. But I feel as though I am watching this from far away. From above.

In the hotel, I climb into the bed and stare at the ceiling fan rocking and spinning its useless circles. I listen to you on the phone, trying to make sense of this. To get answers to the questions. But no one can explain who took her. And when you call the agency, the phone connects to nothing. The numbers like the wrong combination to a lock.

For three days, I cannot get out of bed. For three days I do not bathe or eat. I can barely sleep, and when I do, I dream of stillborn babies. That I am in the hospital being told that I have given birth to a dead child. But

Esperanza is not dead.
   She is just gone.

I wake up later — minutes? hours? — consumed with anxiety. This is when the self-loathing sets in. After the giddy thrill is gone, after the release, after the alcohol has run its course through my body, metabolized, turned into sugar. It is with this jolt that I have awoken nearly every night for years now. Every fear, every regret, every sorrow amplified in this miserable hour of the night. In this terrible abyss. At home, I used to press my hand against Jake's back, count his heartbeats in order to distract myself. To keep from reciting the litany of failures and fears.

But Jake is not here. And I am afraid that if I search for my own heartbeat, that I will find nothing: the ticktock of this clock stopped. It is irrational, I know, but this is the mad hour, the manic hour. A time to endure, to survive. I feel like a warrior in a battle with myself, my brain and heart locked in conflict.

There is no logic to any of this. The thoughts that consume me are fragmented. I think of Plum, the fairy. I worry not about the danger she could have been in, all of the terrible things that could have happened to her, but about the gumdrops. How do I get the gumdrops there so that she will still believe? So that I can salvage that wonder, that magic, that I have somehow stolen by my own selfish concerns. And I wonder if this is why Jake is sleeping with another woman, because I am selfish. Because after a while I stopped caring about him, stopped giving to him, stopped feeling anything but disappointment. Every wish and want and demand I had of him left unanswered. *I'm so tired of failing,* he'd said. I try to imagine Jess, conjure her. I wonder if she will move into the house when I am gone. I try to picture her in that lilac room. Which inevitably transports me to Guatemala. And then there I am again, my brain circling endlessly to this vortex. Like water to a drain. No matter how far I stray, my mind is determined to return to that moment. That horrifying moment. That black hole, rabbit hole, inside which I find myself every single night. But even as I let it consume me, it becomes confused by a new pit, the widening aperture, the depths of which I cannot even fathom.

But when morning comes, as the darkness dissipates, so too does the madness. And I am gifted with a sort of amnesia. A forgetting. Until night falls again.

As the sky lightens with the first hints of dawn, I feel like shit. I feel dour: my mouth, my breath sour. I fumble around in the pocket of my jeans crumpled on the floor looking for some gum. A hard, stale stick of Juicy Fruit that floods my mouth with a terrible sweetness. I spit it out into my hand and chuck it into the wastebasket by the door.

I am parched, and my head is pounding. I don't want Plum to see me like this. I don't want anyone to see me like this. What I need to do is to get some fresh air, to run, to maybe even take a dip in the lake. A baptismal dunk in the cold water. I want water inside me, but I also want to be submerged.

And so I pull on my bathing suit, a pair of shorts, a T-shirt, and quietly make my way to the road, careful to steer clear of the camp.

The sky is opaque, the trees filmy with mist. It must have rained last night, though I don't recall hearing it. Everything is wet, and the dirt road is muddy. As I start to run, I have to dodge puddles and potholes. I leap across one particularly large puddle, and my head pounds when I land. If I run hard enough, I wonder if I can sweat the rest of the toxins out of my body.

I run on the left side of the road, so that any oncoming cars will see me, though it is early and the summer people have not yet begun to arrive in earnest. It is the last Saturday of June, though, and by next weekend, the camps around the lake will be full: the Fourth of July celebrations in full swing. But for now, I am completely alone.

While my brain is fuzzy, my head still thick with the hangover, my body seems to be revived. I am hardly even out of breath when I will myself to keep going as I pass Sharp's driveway and push farther, to the place where the road curves away from the water. Where I lost her. *I lost her.*

I consider running past, just continuing on. Past Lisa's driveway (I picture the note on the door, battered, tattered, and flapping in the breeze). I imagine the journey to Hudson's, where I can buy a huge bottle of Gatorade, sit outside at one of the picnic tables, and replace my electrolytes. Rehydrate. But my legs are slowing.

We may have gotten Plum back yesterday.

But that doesn't change a single thing about the fact that there *is* a wolf in these woods, and a little girl. I feel myself tumbling headlong into the rabbit hole, into that awful abyss.

I peer into the trees, into the thick green tangle. She is out there somewhere. I believe this. I have to believe this. But still, I feel the inklings, the awful tickle of doubt that scratches away at my certainty. I stop and bend over, breathless. I hold on to my knees and try to keep from passing out. My eyes fill with stars. *No,* I think. *Keep it together, Tess.*

I walk across the road to the edge of the woods, and look again. The rising sun burns through the trees, creating scattered beams of light. It is like a cathedral. Jake and I honeymooned in Italy, and we spent an afternoon at the Duomo di Milano. Of course, it was majestic, ostentatious, overwhelming. But more magical than any of the architectural feats were what the stained glass windows somehow did to simple sunlight. How nature and man seemed to merge in these colored beams. How light was transformed, imbued with grace. I remember thinking that this could be enough, for some, to prove the existence of

God. I remember being stunned into silence by it.

And like a penitent, I am drawn to the light again.

There is no path here. I am waist high in ferns and other foliage. I push through the brush, twigs scratching at the bare skin of my legs. I dodge the low-hanging branches, the rain that has gathered on the leaves spilling onto my skin, cooling it. These are the woods between Sharp's house and Lisa's house. If I am correct, she was here. After I saw her, she would have had to pass through this patch of woods to get to Sharp's trailer, where I found the barrette. I think about Alfieri driving past me that night. Maybe he was headed to Sharp's. If she stumbled onto Sharp's property, then maybe he found her? I think of the dog growling at me through the window, baring its teeth. *Sharp.*

I walk with purpose, though I have no idea where I am going, only what I am looking for. Others have searched here, *I* have searched here, but we must have missed something. Of the thousands of clues left behind, what did we not see?

A bird calls out loudly, startling me. I clutch my chest and then laugh. It's just a bird. *Jesus, get a grip.* But then I hear something else. At first it sounds like the low rumble of thunder. But the sky beyond the tops of the trees is bright. There are no storm clouds looming. The sound is incongruous with the sky.

I hear it again, and I stop, wonder if my ears are playing tricks on me. Birds call out, and I proceed. But then I hear it again; it sounds almost like snoring, a sort of gargling and croaking sound. And then I hear movement through the brush.

It's something growling.

My heart starts to pound hard in my chest. My legs opt for flight before my brain has time to react. But I don't run back to the road. I run deeper into the trees. The growling sound intensifying.

I run as fast as I can, stumbling over exposed tree roots and brush, slipping on the damp pine needles that carpet the forest floor. I run blindly, deeper into the woods, stupidly thinking I am somehow going to lose whatever it is that is tracking me if I disappear into the forest. Is this what was going through her mind when she fled from me? That she could lose me if she herself were to become lost?

Tears are streaming down my eyes now, but in the distance I see something, which makes my pace quicken. There's some sort of clearing, a place where the trees open up.

And in that clearing is a building.

It's red. Just a sliver of scarlet, like a shimmery red piece of glass in the light.

It's hard to see, between the fog and the trees. But there is a spot of color in the distance, and I know that if I can just get there I will be safe.

I can't hear the growling sound anymore, but I worry it is simply because my ears are occupied with the sound of my blood pulsing in them. I don't turn around. I don't stop. I just run and run until I reach the clearing and see now that it is a house. A dilapidated one-story house, a shotgun house. Red clapboards. Red roof. It is encircled by red quince bushes, red and pink columbine. An aneurysm of red. There is a grassy hill on the other side of the house, and sitting in the driveway is a broken-down red pickup truck.

So much red, Mary had said. Could this possibly be what she saw?

I turn around, peering into the woods behind me as if to confirm with the trees what it is that I'm seeing, and that's when I see the dog.

A brown pit bull, its shoulders hunched, teeth bared, stares at me with beady, hungry eyes.

And so I run to the porch to bang on the back door of this house, readying myself for the attack. Waiting for his teeth to sink into my bare calves, to tear apart my flesh while I pound at the door. I imagine the futile struggle, prepare myself for death by dog.

But miracle of miracles, the door is ajar. I push into the house and slam the door shut behind me. The dog is on the porch within seconds. I can hear its nails scraping against the wooden door, and I wonder if it is strong enough to get inside.

"Help!" I scream then, suddenly aware I have just entered someone's home. And I realize I might not be any safer in here.

Still, I lock the deadbolt, my hands trembling. My entire body convulsing with what could have happened outside. And what might happen next.

"Help!" I scream again, hoping for mercy.

But I am met with silence.

No one is home. I have come into the back of the house, a small, dark foyer. There is a doorway to my left, and in front of me is a kitchen. It is dark in here, dusty. Pink floral wallpaper curls like peeling sunburned skin from the walls.

It's then that my senses are able to refocus, and the smell hits me. It is something rotten. Meat, tinged with a sort of sickening sweetness. I feel my stomach roiling, and I turn to the door on my left and hope that it is a bathroom. I lift my T-shirt to cover my nose, but the stench is too potent. I push open the door to my left and see a toilet. Dirty, rust-ringed, but I am so grateful. I kneel onto the filthy linoleum and vomit.

My head is pounding now. The hangover winning.

I stand back up, flush the toilet, and peer into the cracked mirror over the sink. I turn on the rusty faucet, though it is missing its handle, and the water runs brown into the cracked porcelain sink.

I need to get the hell out of here, but I am trapped. I go back out into the hallway and peer out the window. The dog is poised on the porch, still barking and growling. I feel like I might be sick again.

I am afraid to find what is causing the smell. It is unlike anything I have ever smelled before. Like rancid meat. Like garbage left out in the sun.

What the hell am I supposed to do?

"Hello?" I cry out again as I make my way into the kitchen. Flies buzz over the sink, piled with dishes, and the trash can, which is overflowing. Maybe this is where the smell is coming from?

Every cupboard door is open, and there are open jars. A peanut butter jar scraped clean, an empty bag of sugar. Potato chip bags, the plastic innards of cereal boxes with only crumbs remaining. There is a can of something — soup? — with a knife sticking out of it, as though someone has stabbed it. Thick lines of ants crisscross the counter, swarm in shuddering huddles on the crumbs.

"Hello?" I try again, as if there's any chance that whoever lives here could some-how still be here, lurking in the shadows.

The kitchen opens up to a dining room, though there is no dining room table. The room is full of boxes and bins. Garbage bags filled with clothes, some opened, the sleeves of sweaters and shirts reaching out.

The next room in this long chain is what

appears to be a bedroom. There are two mattresses on the floor. One wall is painted a sort of Pepto-Bismol pink, and there is a purple Disney princess sleeping bag on one mattress. No sheets, caseless pillows, their ticking stained with yellow circles. There is a plastic Barbie castle in one corner. A box of condoms scattered on the floor. I can barely breathe.

I shield my eyes from the bright sunlight that pours through the bare windows in the last room, the living room. I step carefully across the threshold and gasp.

The woman sits prone on the chintz couch. Head thrown back as if in laughter. As though whatever happened to her occurred mid-conversation.

As my eyes adjust to the bright light, I can see that her skin is blistered. Bloated. Around her arm is a belt of urine-colored tubing. A needle stuck in her arm, poised like a dagger in this putrefying, petrified flesh.

I turn away, bile burning my throat, the stench burning my eyes. Weeping, I return to the bedroom. I want to throw open the windows, but the dog is circling outside. I sit down on the mattress, afraid I might pass out. I put my head between my knees and try to breathe deeply, but it feels like I am inhaling the gases, and I worry that the toxins will enter my lungs, permeate my bloodstream.

I look up again, see a dresser I hadn't noticed before. The drawers are pulled out, the contents erupting. On top of the dresser is a wooden box, a McDonald's bag, and a framed picture.

I stand up and reach for the picture, knowing before I even look what I will see.

A young woman, presumably the one in the other room, stands in front of this same red house. She has one hip jutted out, her face gaunt, defiant as though challenging whoever is taking the photo. She seems not to even notice the little girl perched on her hip. The child leans her head against the woman's chest, thumb stuck in her mouth. Her eyes are wide and her hair is curly. She's wearing a bright pink raincoat, the sky behind her ominous. And on her feet are a pair of ladybug rain boots.

I cover my face and run to the kitchen, to the counter where I saw the soup can. I can see now there is blood on the blade; she must have been trying to open the can with a knife. This would be how she got the cut in her hand. She was just trying to eat.

I feel a sob rising in my throat, but then this tremendous sorrow turns to rage.

This goddamned woman, this *mother,* shot up in her living room, overdosed, leaving her four-year-old child to fend for herself. I study the signs on the kitchen counter: the empty bread bag, peanut butter jar, torn Jell-O packets. On the stovetop is a pot with dry macaroni noodles burned to the bottom. I open the refrigerator and find an empty twelve-pack of Miller High Life, a bottle of Sriracha, a half gallon of sour milk. In the freezer, which is a cavern of ice, I see a few loose Otter Pops and a freezer-burned pound of ground beef.

How long was she here alone with her mother's body?

I see this house, this rotten stinking house now as she must have. I wonder if she ate that whole bag of sugar. The floor is gritty with it.

I imagine her trying to wake her mama up.

And I think then of the dog. That goddamned dog that Lisa or Sharp or Alfieri seems to have set free to roam these woods. The guardians of whatever illicit activities are going on here. I try to piece together what happened. How she found her way from this house to me in the road, and why on earth she would have fled from me. I could have taken care of her.

And now, I am terrified it is too late.

I still don't know her name. And so as I frantically make my way back through the house, checking each small room for some signs of life, I have nothing to call out to her. Stupidly, ridiculously, I scream, "Hello? Hello?"

I check the closets. I check behind the furniture, inside all of the kitchen cupboards. I check the bathroom again, throwing back the mildewed shower curtain liner that hangs from rusty rings.

She's not here.

And so I go back into the living room, try to avoid looking at the woman's body as I make my way to the front door, in case the dog is still waiting for me in the backyard. I figure if I can just get down the driveway to whatever road it connects to then I can flag someone down. It is morning now, and I pray there will be someone out on the road. A bicyclist even, another runner.

I start to open the door, growing dizzy as I realize I have been holding my breath. I sway a little, press my palm against the wall to steady myself, and then grab the doorknob.

But then I hear the sound of tires on gravel, and when I look out the window, I can see the white truck pulling up the drive.

I run to the back of the house, to the kitchen. I search the counter, and find a phone amid the clutter. I reach for the receiver, feel its cold heft in my hand. I press it against my ear and pray.

A dial tone. Oh my God. The phone *works*.

Fingers trembling, I dial 911 and when the operator comes on — "911, what's your emergency?" — I have no words for what has happened here. For what *might* happen here now.

I hear a truck door slam and then another, the heavy sound of two sets of boots as they climb the steps.

"*Hello? 911.*"

"I found . . ." I start as one of them tries the doorknob.

"It's locked," a man growls.

"No, it isn't."

"Where the hell's the key?"

"It's just stuck. I didn't lock it behind me."

"Excuse me, ma'am, you're going to need to speak up," the dispatcher says sharply.

Bang, bang, bang. Is he kicking the door?

I whisper into the phone as clearly as I can. "I found a dead body. It's been here a long time."

"A body? Where are you now, ma'am?"

Bang, bang, bang.

I see a piece of mail on the counter and grab it, and I sink down to the floor, trying to make myself small, press my back into the counter, and study the address on the envelope. *Karina Rogers.*

"505 Lost Pond Road," I read. "It's a red house."

"Okay, ma'am, we'll send someone right out."

"Wait," I say. "There's a man trying to break in."

"There's a man trying to break into the house?"

"Yes," I say. "Please, please send somebody quickly." I think about how long it took Strickland to arrive the night I found the little girl. How long will it take before he finds me in here?

"Can you get out of the house?" the dispatcher asks. "Is there a way for you to exit?"

I am too afraid to look out the back

window to see if the dog is still there, canine sentinel standing guard, though I think I can hear its wet breath still. The low, steady growl.

"No," I say, and shake my head. "Please send someone quickly."

The blows are harder, louder. I scurry on my butt backwards, hitting the handle of the fridge with my head. A sharp pain sears in my skull.

"Hello?" the woman's voice is tinny inside the receiver.

I try to think about where I can hide. The bathroom maybe. I crawl on my hands and knees as quietly as I can to get to the small back hallway. I think of the knife on the counter and wonder if I should go back and grab it.

And then the front door gives.

I hear them stumble into the living room, listen as Sharp reels.

"Holy *shit,*" he says. "What the fuck, Vince?"

I hear him staggering around the living room, imagine him yanking up his shirt to cover his mouth. The smell is so strong, but it is no longer making my eyes burn.

"I told you," Alfieri says.

"Motherfucker."

"Delivered to her just over a week ago.

Looks like she shot the whole fucking moth-erlode herself. Kid musta been on her own for a couple days before I found her."

Kid? My ears prick up, tears sting my eyes.

"Fuckin' brought her home that night and found this shit."

Alfieri found her?

I struggle to make sense of what they're saying.

So that night the little girl must have left this house, wandered down through the woods into the road where I found her. Then she got scared and ran back through woods to Sharp's property. Alfieri would have been pulling into Sharp's just after he blew past me on the road. He must have found her, recognized her, and decided to take her back home, here, to her junkie mom. I picture the barrette slipping from her tangled curl as he scooped her up. She would have seen his dog in the truck then, and it would have growled at her. Bared its teeth at her. Scared her. *Sharp.* I have to stifle a sob.

I hear them coming toward the kitchen.

I manage to get to the bathroom, and I crawl across the filthy floor on my hands and knees. My wounded hand throbs, and the gauze bandage is stained again. I try not to think about what sort of diseases I might pick up here. About all the terrible things that have happened in this house.

I push the door closed gently with my foot, and I startle when it latches shut. I pray they didn't hear the sound. Pray that it was imperceptible against all the noise they're making as they tear the house apart.

"Fucking junkies," Sharp says, slamming open cupboard doors.

"It's not here. I already looked," Alfieri says. "I told you. She blew it all herself."

"You think Lisa's gonna come back for the kid?" Sharp asks.

"Highly doubtful," Alfieri says. "She's bailed."

"What are we gonna do with her then? Can't keep her down there forever."

Oh my God, oh my God. They have her. My heart is pounding in my ears. I feel like I might pass out.

"Who fuckin' knows? Place has been crawling with cops; that's why I haven't come back here to deal with this. But it's just a matter of time before somebody comes up here and finds this shit, figures out it's her kid. That's all it'll take before they start searching again. And *that* is a shit storm I'd like to avoid."

My mind is reeling.

So after he found her, Alfieri decided to

bring the little girl here, back home to her mother, but found her overdosed. By the time he got back to Sharp's, there were cops everywhere searching for her. Dogs. Helicopters. And because they're drug dealers, they couldn't just go to the cops with her. So what *did* they do with her? Where are they keeping her? And what will they do with her now?

"Somebody finds the kid, dude, I'm going back to Norfolk," Sharp says. "We're gonna need to get rid of her."

Alfieri coughs and starts to gag. "Goddamn. This reeks. Let's just deal with one fucking disaster at a time."

And then there is an eerie quiet.

I think of the 911 dispatcher, wonder if she's still listening. Worry that she will say something, that he will hear her voice on the phone. Hope to God this is recording. That she's heard every word they've said.

I squeeze my eyes shut. I try not to breathe. Not to make a single sound. I try to make myself invisible. And I wait.

Then, I hear their footsteps receding. Back through the house: stomping across the kitchen linoleum, then on the wood floors of the bedroom, and finally back into the living room. They're in there for a long time. I press my hand against my chest, trying to keep my heart from leaping out of it.

What are they doing?

I hear the front door slam shut, let out a cry. It escapes from my lips, a sort of keening. When I try to stand, my legs are too weak. Trembling, as though the bones have turned to ash.

I can hear the truck as it backs out of the driveway, and I wonder where the hell the cops are. Jesus Christ, how long has it been?

I don't leave the bathroom until I am sure they're gone. Only then do I dare pull the door open and go back out into that house. I look around at the wreckage. It was already a disaster, but now it's completely trashed. Nothing has been left untouched. It is a miracle that he didn't find me.

I make my way through the bedroom. I stop and grab the photo on the dresser, peer at her face, those big eyes. I pull the back off the frame and slip the photo out from behind the glass. What have they done with her?

I need to be here when the cops arrive. To show them the picture. My God. I can do this, I think. Just make one foot step in front of the other.

But as I walk into the living room, I peer

into the bright light at the stained chintz couch and see.

She's gone.

I can't stay here.

The police are on their way, but instead of finding the body of that woman, that poor little girl's *mother,* they're going to find me, cowering in a bathroom of an empty house. I try not to think what will happen if it's Andrews who arrives.

The only thing I have, the only evidence that remains, is the photo of the little girl. The ladybug rain boots. God, *were* they the ones I found at Lisa's? Was I that close to her? Where is she now? I trace her sweet face with my fingers. It is hard to give this up, this one thing that proves I am not crazy, that she is real. But it is only a photo. She is still out there somewhere. *Down there,* Sharp said. Underground? Is this what Mary meant? Is she in someone's basement? *They have her.*

I go to the living room, where the coffee table is scattered with cotton balls and syringes. Burned spoons. All the detritus of this woman's sad life. I put the photo in the center, prop it up against a crumpled-up piece of tinfoil. Right there so that it will be the first thing they see when they come into the house.

The best thing for me to do would be to run out the front door, down the gravel drive to Lost Pond Road. I seem to remember taking that road once, a shortcut from the lake into town. But this is the way the police, the ambulances probably will be coming. It would be suicide.

I have no choice but to go back the way I came. Through the woods. I need to get to Sharp's house. Does his house have a basement?

I go to the fridge, open the freezer, and find the frozen pack of ground beef. The package is covered in crystalline white. I tear it open and hold the frozen chunk of meat in my hands.

When I hear the sirens, I hurry out the back door. The dog is waiting for me, and so I hurl the meat as far as I can. He picks up the scent and goes after it, and I run.

I run through the woods, my body somehow recollecting the trajectory that brought me here, and when I glance over my shoulder the red house becomes just a spot of blood in the distance. I can hear the sirens wailing.

The dog seems to have forgotten me, but I keep running. My legs burn. I fall down once and then again; I can feel the stitches in my hand ripping and wince at the pain, feel blood seeping warmly through the bandage. I worry that this, the scent of my blood, will attract the dog again. I run until I am standing in the thick tangle of trees behind Sharp's compound. And then I stop.

Alfieri's truck is in the driveway. Alfieri is not in the cab, but his dog is. His blocky head hangs out of the passenger's side. His nose twitches and he salivates. Karina Rogers's body is somewhere in the back of that truck. Like so many lawn clippings, I think. Though I have a feeling it's not lawn clippings or leaves in those bags.

I sit down on the cool ground and put my head in my hands. I feel sick. The adrenaline that got me here has now pooled in my stomach. I am nauseous. Woozy. What am I doing here? This is insane. I am in so far over my head. In this so deep. Anybody else would give up, leave it to the police. Anyone in their right mind.

But when I squeeze my eyes shut, I see her again. Standing in the middle of the road, her pale belly protruding over the waistband of that tattered tutu. I think about the room she and her junkie mother were sharing, cannot imagine the unthinkable things she must have seen. I am the only one who believes in her. The only one who cares about what happens to her. I have no choice.

Sharp's back door swings open, and the two men emerge together. No little girl. They both get in Alfieri's truck. Alfieri revs the engine and then throws it into reverse, and then they are gone.

I run to the clearing and down the sloping hill to his backyard. I look at the house, study its foundation. It's really just a mobile home on a slab foundation. No land-level windows. No basement. God, then where is she?

I weave through the rusted graveyard of broken-down cars and appliances and discarded furniture to the trailer where I found her barrette. The trailer that is not on wheels but flush with the ground. Is it possible they've been keeping her in here?

There had been a padlock on the door the other night. I go to the door and see that the lock is still there. I tug on it, praying that it might just come loose in my hands. But it is locked tightly.

I bang on the door. "Hello?!" I say. If she's

in there, would she hear me? I press my ear against the metal door. Nothing.

I look around, futilely searching for something to pick the lock with. And then I realize I can probably just break one of the windows. They're boarded up, but if I can pry off the plywood, it would be just glass separating me from whatever is inside.

I yank at the board, nearly ripping my fingernails off in the process. It won't give. I need something to leverage it. I look all around and then see a metal pipe lying in the dirt next to the trailer. I grab it and shimmy it under the wood. Once it's lodged underneath, I lean all of my weight on it, and it gives. The plywood comes off, and I can see the window. I reach down to the ground for a rock and use it to smash the glass as gently as I can, praying that if she's in there she won't get hurt. And then I hoist myself up, trying not to think about the pain in my hand. The glass that is cutting my arms and legs as I pull myself inside.

"Hello?"

Inside it is dark and smells of cigarette smoke and mold. I push through some spiderwebs, kicking trash out of my way, waiting for my eyes to adjust. I move from one end of the trailer to the next. It is empty.

I don't know what I expected. Did I think

she'd just be in here, hiding? Waiting for me?

I sit down on the floor and shake my head. Tears are running hot down my cheeks. And then, in the dusty beam of light coming through the broken window, I see something. *Of course, this is why the trailer's wheels are gone.*

A door. In the *floor.*

There is a handle, which I grab on to and lift.

It is still too dark in here to see much of anything. And so I reach for my key chain, remembering the penlight meant to illuminate your car door lock. The light it casts is no more than that of the glowing tip of a cigarette, and so when I look down, I peer into a dark abyss. It is nearly impossible to see how far down the hole goes. But in the weak light, I see that there is some sort of ladder down one side. Some sort of manhole.

Underground, the psychic had said. Jesus.

I am Alice, if she had a chance to look down the rabbit hole before she fell. If she'd had a choice.

I take a deep breath and decide.

I turn around and start to climb down the ladder. It is like lowering myself into the pond. The surface is warm, while the murky depths are cold. Goose bumps riddle my skin as I descend. I keep the penlight shining, but its beam is pathetic, small.

I climb down maybe five feet, when I suddenly hit bottom.

I strain to see. The little bit of light coming in from overhead barely illuminates the room where I now find myself standing. As my eyes finally adjust, I can see it's like some sort of root cellar. Or bunker. The walls are made of dirt. It's a room, maybe about six feet by six feet.

It smells like the earth.

The walls are lined with crates.

I turn around trying to orient myself. I am in a hole, underground, beneath the trailer on Sharp's property. I feel bile rising to my throat again and press my forehead against the cool dirt wall.

Mama.

I shake my head.

Mama.

No. I press my hands against my ears. Please don't let this happen again.

But the voice is not inside my head. It is not the voice that has haunted me, the specter, the dream.

I feel in the dark, trying to follow the sound. There is a doorway of sorts that leads to a smaller room. I duck my head and go inside.

"Baby?" I say. I still have no name for her.

My shins hit something. I reach down to feel. It's a mattress, I think. A single, bare mattress. And there is the shadow of a girl, knees curled to her chest. She is backed up into the corner, like a frightened animal.

I kneel down on the ground, hold my arms open. I peer into her large wet eyes.

"It's okay," I say. "I'm here. I came back for you."

And then her arms are around my neck. And her hair is in my face. And as I stand, her legs wrap around me. I feel the scratchiness of her skirt and a strange, familiar softness. I make my way up the ladder, still holding her, but it isn't until I emerge into the trailer that I realize:

She's wearing my sweater. The one I left at the side of the road.

I clear the window frame of glass, and carefully climb out and then help her climb out and back into my arms. And then I run. Through the maze of junk in Sharp's yard. Down the gravel drive to the road.

I will run until we are safe. I will run forever if I need to, this time.

Her bones are sharp. My breath hitches as

446

I look at her emaciated limbs, which bounce against my legs as I run. I hold her head against my chest, cover her ears so that she won't hear me cry.

By the time I reach the dirt road that will lead back to Gormlaith, I can barely breathe, but I don't stop running.

The birds are singing loudly in the trees around us. The sky is turquoise. Her hair is soft and smells like the earth. Her skin is hot.

When the car pulls up next to us, and the man rolls the window down, I start to run faster. *No, no, no,* I think.

"Wait," the man says. His voice calls after us. Gentle and kind. "Are you okay?"

I stop and turn to look at him. It's a burgundy VW. He leans out the open window, his face tight with concern. He seems strangely familiar. Like I should know him.

"I found her," I say. I have no other words that can explain this: the terror, the relief.

"Sam," the dark-haired woman in the passenger seat says. "We need to help them."

But even as he helps us into the backseat, wrapping us both in a soft blanket from the back, I hold on tight. She holds on tight. We do not let go.

We leave Guatemala City.

There is nothing the lawyer here can do. And nothing Oliver can do at home either. This has happened before, he says. We should be grateful, he says, that we hadn't gotten her home already. Children have been taken from their new parents' arms, returned. It's a corrupt system, he offers. Preying upon the hopeful, the desperate.

Back in New York, I cannot work. I cannot eat. And I cannot sleep.

Like any mother of a missing child, I call the media. Newspapers, radio, TV. I tell my story a thousand times to anyone who will listen, and even to those who won't. I think that maybe, somehow, this will help me get her back. I sit and sweat under bright lights, microphones affixed to my blouses. I tremble and recite the story as though it is a prayer, an incantation that will conjure her. That will return her to me.

There is an investigation into the agency, and we find that we are not the only ones. There are other couples who have been preyed upon. Who have, like us, lost hope. And sometimes, the children are not even real. They are fabrications. These phony agencies the thieves of dreams.

And to you, she *is* only a dream. *My* dream. You never even met her. You never held her in your arms. For you, she is nothing more than an idea. A story someone once told you.

But to me, she is flesh, not a wish. She is black hair that smells of tangerines. She is dark skin, wide eyes, a beating heart. She is real. She is real. She is my daughter. And she is gone.

When *Good Morning America*'s producers call and say they are doing a story on criminal adoption agencies, I am so happy I could cry. I agree to come to their studio. To tell my story. Our story. I imagine in the show's audience of millions there will be someone who can help. Who will hear my plea and help me bring her home.

But you have had enough. You want to let it go, to just let her go.

And so I go alone. And I sit in front of the camera by myself.

But this time, when I begin to recite my story, when I describe the way it felt to stand at the locked door of the orphanage after the raid, the floor falls out from beneath me. Because in the audience, in the very front row, there is a child. Dark hair. Brown skin.

Esperanza.

I stop speaking and point.

She looks at me, her eyes wide and familiar.

"That's her," I say, jerking my head back to the woman who is interviewing me. "How did she get here?"

I am thinking that this is one of those episodes where they reunite long lost friends, lovers. Mothers and their children. I look around in disbelief, in manic wonder, waiting for someone to bring her to me.

I am smiling. My heart beating so hard I am sure the microphone pinned inside my bra will pick it up.

"I know this must be very difficult for you," she says. "Go on."

"How did you find her?" I ask, tears of joy running down my face. I stand up and start to go to the audience. She is right there. I can almost touch her.

On the video, later, I don't recognize that woman. The one who is weeping, gleeful. Charging toward a stranger's child in the audience before the two security guards got ahold of me.

The video and my memory stop there. I

don't recall anything else except for waking up in the hospital. The hazy feeling that all of this had been a dream. And later, when you came to get me. How the only words you had for me were "It's over now."

"Can you believe this?" I say to Effie as we watch the press conference later that night in the hospital waiting room. They are keeping the girl for a couple of days until she is stabilized. Effie had wanted me to go back to the camp: to eat, to sleep. Promised we would return in the morning. But I refused to leave. I will not leave her again. And so Effie brought food, a pillow, and a blanket.

On the TV, Lieutenant Andrews stands in front of a podium, flanked on either side by the state police. He is smug as he speaks, as he acknowledges the heroic efforts of his fellow officers, as he somberly reveals *his* version of the story.

While I was inside that trailer, the cops, including Strickland, arrived at the empty red house. He found the photo I'd left for him, and because of the information I'd given him, they were able to track Alfieri and Sharp to the breeders' property on the other side of town. They had brought Karina Rogers's body there to dispose of it in the woods, or maybe even offer it up to those dogs. Sharp surrendered after a standoff that lasted over an hour. But Alfieri refused, and when he started to fire a gun through the windows of the house at the cops, they fired back. He died of a single gunshot wound to the head.

"Nearly three hundred bags of heroin were found hidden among leaves and grass clippings in lawn bags. A stash of illegal firearms and nearly seventy-five thousand dollars in cash were located on Lincoln Sharp's property. We believe that Alfieri was a major player in a heroin ring originating in Massachusetts."

The "suspect," Vincent Alfieri, had been running heroin up from Holyoke for over a year, distributing it to small-time dealers like Karina. He was also running a nice little dog-fighting endeavor, using Lisa's property, a day care, as a cover.

Lisa was smarter than either one of the men. She must have sensed that her world was about to implode, because her "family emergency" got her halfway to Florida before she was pulled over in South Carolina by cops who'd been tipped off by the Vermont State Police.

What Andrews does not address is that hole underground. The place where I found her, cowering like a frightened animal. The hole where Sharp and Alfieri kept their stash of firearms, their drugs. Sharp had stocked his little cave with water bottles and other supplies. I imagine he thought he might be able to hide out there if anything ever went down. She'd survived the week on water bottles and dry oatmeal packets. The doctors assured me that it didn't appear as though Sharp had harmed her. Not in the way that I was most terrified of, anyway. His preference, Strickland told me, was little boys.

"We understand a child was found on Lincoln Sharp's property?" a reporter chimes in, and my heart begins to pound. "Is she the same child reported missing last week?"

Andrews coughs. "I'm sorry," he says. "I can't speak to that right now. There is an ongoing investigation regarding the child found on Sharp's property. It is likely unrelated to what we still believe is a false report last week."

"Lieutenant," another reporter bellows. "Is it true this child was found near the house where her mother overdosed? That she was alone for nearly a week? Is this related to the shoot-out? To the heroin sei-zure?"

Andrews nods again, but I can see his neck straining against his shirt collar. "Again, I can't speak yet to this aspect of the case. Information is still coming in, and our officers are working round the clock."

"If this is the same child that was reported missing last week, do you think that you let the community down? That your depart-ment called off the search prematurely?"

Andrews reddens, and I feel a surge of relief, of something close to justice for her. The community will demand answers.

"It is still our belief that the initial report was erroneous," he says. "Thank you."

When we first arrived at the hospital, I ignored the reporters who were waiting.

The TV shows the exterior of the hospital and a split-screen shot of my face: my Facebook profile picture. It's a photo from a trip Jake and I took to Rome, but they have cropped him out. Something about this tears at my heart. We were standing in front of the Trevi Fountain. He had just plucked a 200-lira coin from his pocket and handed it to me. *Make a wish,* he'd said. We'd just started trying to have a baby, and so this is what I wished for. *Please,* I thought as I tossed the coin into the water.

"Tess Waters, the woman who called in the report of a child wandering along Lake Gormlaith Road last week, is also reportedly the person who found a child alone on Lincoln Sharp's property. It is unclear whether the child was being held captive by Sharp, a registered sex offender, or had simply wandered there after her mother's death. It is also unclear what any of this has to do with the standoff with Alfieri and Sharp this morning. For now, Miss Waters is refusing to speak to the media. We will keep following this story as it unfolds."

I am trembling as Effie clicks off the TV.

"It's not over," I say.

"Yes, it is. She's safe. You found her."

When Effie's cell phone rings, my entire body feels jarred, like I've been rear-ended.

Effie answers. "Yes," she says. "Hold on."

She comes to me with the phone. "It's Sergeant Strickland."

I take the phone, take a deep breath.

"Did you watch the press conference?" I ask.

"I did," he says, and pauses. Clears his throat. When he finally speaks again, his voice is soft. "And I just wanted to let you know I plan to make this right. For you. For her. Whatever I can do."

"The false report?" I ask.

456

"No charges will be filed. I promise."

Strickland was the first person I called after the Masons, who were on their way to Effie and Devin's, found us on the side of the road. He was at the house with an ambulance within fifteen minutes.

The sun was bright, and the grass seemed impossibly green as they lifted her tiny body onto the gurney.

"I'm sorry," Strickland had said, and I started to thank him, but then I realized he was talking to her. He bent over and touched her hair, gently, like someone's dad.

"I have a little girl too," he said, looking up at me. He shook his head, and I recognized that look. The regret, the shame.

When they started to lift her into the back of the ambulance, I said to the EMT, "I'm going with her," and searched Strickland's face for help when the EMT started to shake his head.

"She needs me," I said. She was holding on to my hand so tightly, refusing to let go.

And so Strickland nodded at me, at the EMT. "It's okay."

I followed her into the back of the ambulance, and sat next to her as we pulled out onto the dirt road. Her eyes were wide and scared.

"It's okay," I said, and I stroked her hair

with my free hand. And she reached out for it, gingerly touching the blood-soaked bandage. She gestured to her own cut too. As if this somehow connected us.

I leaned over her, felt her curls touch my face. I turned and inhaled the earthy scent of her. "What's your name?" I whispered in her ear.

And she whispered back like a secret.

"Starry."

Over the lake, the sky explodes into colored fragments like a kaleidoscope of lights. We hear the collective gasp of everyone who has gathered at the edges of the water to watch the display. The air is warm, the moon bright.

We are sitting on a blanket spread out on Devin and Effie's front lawn.

"Look, look!" Plum squeals. She races across the grass trailing a lit sparkler behind her. It sparks and crackles, leaving a contrail of smoke like a secret message written behind her.

It has been one week since I discovered Starry in that hole underground. I have still not stopped trembling, and I have been sleeping in the camp rather than the guest cottage, afraid of the consuming darkness of the woods. Each time a firecracker goes off, something inside me detonates as well. I wonder if I will always startle like this, shudder like this.

When I called Jake, he said he would come up. He could come get me. Bring me home. And for just a moment, I thought that maybe that was the answer. That all of this had been some sort of strange dream from which I might just wake up. But even as he gently asked, "Do you need me?" he felt so very far away. *He* was the dream. And this, here, was reality. Truth:

This little girl.

Star Rogers. Three and a half years old. Daughter of Karina Rogers. Father unknown.

She needs me. And I need her.

"Did I miss it?" Ryan asks after he parks in Effie and Devin's driveway and finds us on the grass.

"Nope. Just getting started," Devin says, standing up and shaking Ryan's hand.

Ryan puts his hand on my shoulder and I look up at him. He gestures to the empty spot on the quilt next to me.

"Mind if I sit here?" he asks.

I shake my head. "Please," I say.

Ryan has been helping me navigate what should now be familiar terrain. I have to trust him, he says, though trust is an elusive, slippery thing for me.

"How are you?" he asks.

I smile, nod. I don't tell him about the nightmares. About how afraid I am.

"I've arranged a visit," he says. "With the foster family."

My eyes widen.

"When?" I ask, my throat swollen. My eyes filling with tears.

"Sometime later this week."

"I can see her?"

He nods, smiles.

My whole body flushes with heat, with relief.

"Thank you," I say, and he squeezes my hand.

"Look at that one!" Plum says, pointing up as the sky explodes.

We all look up at the burst of purple above us. And I imagine that each spark of colored light in the sky is a single star in an impossible constellation. All those wishes. I am swollen with a hope so big it makes my chest feel tight.

Quimby, Vermont, August 2015

In the morning, by the time the late summer sunlight comes into the little kitchen, I have already been awake for a couple of hours. I like to watch the sun rise now, to be a witness to the world as it wakes.

I have furnished this tiny house near the elementary school in Quimby with the few things I took from our house in Brooklyn. The rest I have pieced together from the end-of-summer yard sales and from a couple of antique stores in town. I left most things in our house in Brooklyn for Jake.

Jake's mom is getting better. Stronger, though it's still unclear how much of the damage will linger. After she finally got out of the hospital, Jake was able to go back to New York, where, fortunately, the offers for Charlie's manuscript were still waiting for him. He even managed to talk Charlie into selling the world rights. I can't imagine he'll stay in the house in Brooklyn much longer. I am counting on my share of the sale of the brownstone to help start this new life here.

Today I am painting the second bedroom. The can of paint sits open on the drop cloth, its creamy blue catching the sunlight.

Outside the leaves are beginning to turn, just a few red maples asserting themselves, reminding us that summer will not last, though it will still be another month before autumn comes and with it the crisp air. For now, the mornings are cool, but the afternoons are warm.

There is so much to do. For the first time in years, I wake early each morning with a sense of purpose. With Ryan's help, I have submitted all the necessary paperwork, and I started the training yesterday. Tomorrow I will get to visit Starry at the foster home where she has been staying since I found her again. The foster mother is a woman who was two years behind me in school. I remember her as being funny and warm. She's fostered over a hundred children; Effie assures me that Starry is safe. I bring her gifts: stuffed animals and little dolls. Ribbons for her hair and a pair of rainbow-colored tights. She likes bright things. Things that sparkle. We play hide-and-seek in the wide backyard behind their house. I brought Plum with me one day, and she taught her how to do a cartwheel.

Every day is one day closer to things being finalized. And today is the home visit; the social worker is scheduled to come at noon.

If everything goes as it's supposed to, the whole process could be completed by the time school starts again and the playground next to our house is filled with the voices of children. Before the maple tree in the front yard turns crimson.

When she was released from the hospital, taken into the custody of DCF, I hadn't wanted to let her go. But I couldn't go with her. I had nowhere to go except to Effie's house.

Mena made dinner for us that night, and I forced myself to eat.

And afterward, Effie and I went outside, walked down to the dock, and sat with our feet dangling in the water.

"Are you sure this is what you want?" she asked after a while.

One loon called out, and another answered.

"It's the only thing I ever wanted."

Above us the sky was clear, the stars bright.

"Aren't you afraid?" she asked. "That it will happen again?"

"Yes," I said. "I'm terrified."

And it is possible. It is always possible that someone will come out of the woodwork and claim her as their own. Of course, her mother is gone now. And Karina's own mother is long gone as well; she died of liver failure when Karina was only six. She literally drank herself to death. I worry about this cruel inheritance, pray that it is not her legacy. I will do whatever it takes to keep her safe. And so I have stopped drinking. No meetings in musty church basements with bad coffee and stale donuts. No need. I just stopped. And the clarity of everything is both terrifying and beautiful.

There are no certainties; that is the only certainty. Ryan has assured me that we are doing everything correctly, that the process is long and slow, but that we are doing everything we are supposed to do to ensure that nothing goes wrong. He is patient and kind. He has walked me through every step, untangled every knot in the endless curl of red tape. And I just comply: with the psychological evaluations, the medical evaluations, the financial audits.

He comes over for dinner sometimes. The last time he came, he kissed me. It was the first time I'd been kissed by anyone other than Jake since I was twenty-three. I wonder if this is what appealed to Jake, the simple, marvelous wonder of it. Of a life you didn't expect, of a life that maybe you'd somehow been denied. And so in the moment when our lips met, I forgave Jake.

After the sun comes up and fills that little bedroom at the back of the house with light, I put on a pair of overalls and tie my hair back. I dip my paintbrush into the creamy light blue paint, press the bristles against the side of the can, and carefully lift the brush, cupping my hand underneath it as I make my way to the window. The stitches came out last week. The scar is raised, red and fresh still. But it is healed, the skin repaired. The doctor says the scar will fade. It was too late for stitches for Star, but because she's a child, the doctor says the years will render the scar invisible. It will be as though she was never damaged, never harmed. I need to believe this: to trust in the body's resilience, in the power of time to erase scars.

I swipe the brush down the side of the window, carefully angling it so as not to accidentally get paint on the woodwork, which I want to remain white. Through the window, I can see the front yard: the lilac bush that will bloom in the spring, and the sugar maple that my landlord promises will fill the yard with a sea of colored leaves for her to jump in. Devin has hung a wooden swing from the tall branches. Zu-Zu and Plum both came over to try it out. I watched them playing on the lawn, and for the first time, the sorrow I usually felt, that bruise-like longing, was gone.

My girls, I thought.

When I am done with all of the edges, I pour the paint into the tray and roll the sponge until it is saturated. It goes onto the wall like a dream, and within only an hour, the room is bright and filled with light.

When the social worker knocks on the door, I am calm, calm.

"Come in," I say.

And she smiles brightly. "What a lovely little home."

ACKNOWLEDGMENTS

First, with enormous love and gratitude to Tricia and Scott for opening your big, big hearts and for your trust. This story would not be the same without *your* story. Thanks to Neal Griffin for your insight and expertise: for making my cops say the right things and my bad guys sound real instead of like some 1920s zoot suit–wearing gangsters. To my early readers — Jillian Cantor and Amy Hatvany for your willingness to read sloppy drafts and offer your sage advice. To my editor, Peter Senftleben, and the rest of the Kensington team who continue to turn my stories into beautiful books. To my agent, Henry Dunow, for your bottomless well of encouragement and support. To my family for being crazy and funny and always the softest place to fall. Lastly, to Patrick, who has been my biggest fan for more than two decades, and to my girls, Mikaela and Esmée, the real Mermaids of Gormlaith.

■ ■ ■ ■

A READING GROUP GUIDE: WHERE I LOST HER

T. GREENWOOD

■ ■ ■ ■

The following discussion questions are included to enhance your group's reading of *Where I Lost Her.*

DISCUSSION QUESTIONS

1. From the moment Tess finds the little girl in the road, people doubt her. Do you? Is she an unreliable narrator? Why or why not?

2. Discuss how Tess and Jake differ in how they handle the loss of Esperanza.

3. Why do you think it is so important to Tess that she find the little girl? What do you think would have happened if she wasn't able to find her?

4. Effie has been Tess's best friend since childhood. Discuss the evolution of their friendship. Do you have a friend like Effie?

5. The Vermont setting is, on the surface, the same pristine and beautiful place Tess has always loved, but underlying this beauty is something more sinister. How is

this a metaphor for other areas of Tess's life? Are there any places that you have loved that have changed in this way?

6. Discuss the different mothers in this story: Effie, Tess, Karina Rogers.

7. Tess repeatedly puts herself at risk in her investigation; would you do the same? How would you have reacted if you had come across a child in the middle of the road in the middle of the night? Do you agree with all of the decisions Tess made trying to find the girl?

8. Tess wonders while searching for the girl, "I don't know which is worse: thinking that she is alone out here in the woods or that she isn't." Which do you think is worse? Why?

9. The psychic's advice resonates throughout the whole story. Tess is skeptical at first, but then later seeks her help. Do you believe in psychics?

10. Effie thinks she has lost Plum in this novel; do you think that this will affect the

way she parents her daughters in the future?

11. This book is about a lot of different losses: the loss of a child, the loss of a marriage, the loss of a dream. Discuss the losses you have experienced. How have they been tempered by the things you've recovered or found?

12. How do you think Tess's experiences with adoption and Esperanza affected her reaction regarding the little girl? Do you think she would have been so tireless if she hadn't gone through that ordeal?

13. Discuss the police response to Tess's claims. Do you think they gave up too easily, or that they already put in more effort than they should have?

14. Reread the portion of Yeats's "Stolen Child" at the beginning of *Where I Lost Her* and talk about how it relates to the story and themes of the novel.

15. Did you notice that the fairy Tess tells Plum and Zu-Zu lives in the forest is also named Star? Talk about the similarities

between the little girl and the fairytale Tess created.

16. At one point, Tess argues that she's not the one who fell in love with someone else, and Jake counters that she did. Do you think she's just as much to blame for their marriage problems as he is? Do you think she cheated on him, in a way? Or do you feel that Jake's infidelity is the cause of their ultimate split? Discuss the devolution of their marriage and how it pertains to Tess's search for the girl.

ABOUT THE AUTHOR

T. Greenwood is the author of nine critically acclaimed novels. She has received numerous grants for her writing, including a National Endowment for the Arts Literature Fellowship and a grant from the Maryland State Arts Council. She lives with her family in San Diego, California, where she teaches creative writing, studies photography, and continues to write. Her website is www.tgreenwood.com